What if somebody was watching one of them?

Unable to think of anything else to divert suspicion, Tessa rose on her toes and pressed close to Gabe.

"Tessa?" he whispered again, this time against her mouth.

"Human-shaped shadow across the way," she mumbled.

Instantly his arms pulled her tight. He turned, making their profiles more visible to the garden, and gave her a thorough kiss.

He touched her lips with the tip of his finger. "Sleep well."

His eyes glittered in the light spilling out of the living room and Tessa could have sworn it was from laughter. A minute later he released her and Tessa grabbed the door frame for support.

Gabe McKinley's social skills might be rusty, but he knew how to kiss in *no* uncertain terms.

Dear Reader,

I loved visiting the California Gold Country as a child. One of my earlier novels is set in this beautiful region, and I've always wanted to return to it as a location. So I created Poppy Gold Inns, a bed-and-breakfast complex in the historic district of a former gold-mining town called Glimmer Creek.

Undercover in Glimmer Creek grew out of this setting, and is about the manager of Poppy Gold, who has returned to her childhood home following her mother's untimely death. Tessa is strong, idealistic and devoted to the business that helps support her family and hometown. But what does an idealist do when she meets a cynical former navy SEAL who's trying to catch the culprit stealing corporate information from her clients?

Classic Movie Alert: It probably isn't old enough yet to qualify as a classic, but I enjoy the 2001 film *The Majestic*, about another cynical man who is transformed by love and the good-hearted people in a small town. Check it out!

I enjoy hearing from readers and can be contacted c/o Harlequin Books, 225 Duncan Mill Road, Don Mills, ON M3B 3K9, Canada.

Julianna Morris

JULIANNA MORRIS

Undercover in Glimmer Creek

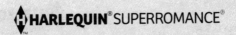

Recycling programs
for this product may
not exist in your area.

ISBN-13: 978-0-373-61009-9

Undercover in Glimmer Creek

Printed in U.S.A.

www.Harlequin.com

Julianna Morris grew up in a large, active family that was always competing, which included playing word games such as Perquackey and Scrabble. She also read voraciously, bringing stacks of books home every week from the library. Julianna hasn't lost her love for games or books and takes them with her even while exploring places such as Glacier National Park and the Blue Ridge Mountains. Of course, her computer is always packed as well, because inspiration is never far away in such beautiful locations.

Books by Julianna Morris

HARLEQUIN SUPERROMANCE

Honor Bound
The Ranch Solution

Those Hollister Boys

Winning Over Skylar
Challenging Matt
Jake's Biggest Risk

Other titles by this author available in ebook format.

To Eli, thank you for your service.

CHAPTER ONE

TESSA CONNOR KNELT on the hardwood floor and looked at the cat under the four-poster bed. "Please come out, Mr. Fezziwig."

Mr. Fezziwig yawned and continued bathing himself. He felt the room was his exclusive property and the people who rented the deluxe bed-and-breakfast suite were merely servants who catered to his whims.

"Believe it or not, the guests coming to stay tonight don't *like* cats," Tessa said. "I know you think there's something wrong with their opinion, but twenty-five years ago they honeymooned in this room, and they're sentimental about it."

The enormous brown tabby yawned.

"I understand how you feel, but you have to—"

"Tessa, I want you to meet the new maintenance employee," interrupted her father.

Tessa straightened and looked toward the door where her dad stood with a tall, unsmiling man.

"Hey, Pop." Tessa got to her feet and walked over to shake hands with the new guy. Lord, he had the most gorgeous gray eyes she'd ever seen…and the hardest to read. "You must be Gabe McKinley. Welcome to Poppy Gold Inns. My father is a terrific boss. You'll enjoy working with him."

"Thankfully, these days I mostly mulch flower-beds and jockey a lawn mower around," Liam Connor declared. "Tessa handles everything at Poppy Gold except maintenance."

They exchanged an affectionate look, yet a familiar stab of sorrow went through Tessa. She'd always expected to take over Poppy Gold when her parents retired, but then her mother had died a year and a half ago. She still remembered feeling as if the world had stopped turning, and it had been even worse for her father. For months he'd gone around in a shocked fog, barely eating or sleeping. When he'd decided running the business alone was too much for him, she'd resigned from her position in the contracts division at her grandfather's company in San Francisco to help out. Poppy Gold wasn't just a business to her—it was home.

"Your father has been showing me around," Gabe McKinley said. "You have quite a setup here, Ms. Connor."

"It's Tessa. We're informal at Poppy Gold. We… Oh, you finally came out," she exclaimed as a furry body butted her leg. She bent down and scooped Mr. Fezziwig into her arms. His purr boomed until he fixed his gaze on the new employee; the purring stopped as if turned by a switch, and his mouth opened into a long-drawn-out hiss.

Whoa.

Generally Mr. Fezziwig liked everyone, which made him ideal for the Victorian Cat Mansion, one of fifty-plus historic buildings that had been converted to a complex of bed-and-breakfast inns and visitor facilities. These days they hosted business retreats and special events along with tourists. The Victorian Cat was unique because of the amiable felines who lived there—repeat guests usually requested a specific cat for their visits, rather than a room.

"It may take me a while to become accustomed to calling my employers by their first names," Gabe said stiffly.

"Pop is your employer, not me," she clarified.

"Gabe is a veteran," her father interjected. "This is his first position since getting out of the navy."

"Thank you for your service." Though it was an automatic response, Tessa meant it sincerely. Pop and one of her maternal uncles had done a tour in the army, while another uncle had died flying a navy jet.

"Er...yeah." Gabe peered around the room. "I understand you have some sort of patchwork quilters group coming in a few days. And the day they leave, a number of executives are arriving for a retreat."

"That's right. Thomas International Products is one of our best business contracts, though it's a fairly small group this time." Tessa shifted the cat she held, uncomfortable for several reasons. For one thing, Mr. Fezziwig weighed a ton, and for another, there was something about Gabe McKinley that made her vaguely wary. Her father tried to hire veterans who were struggling to adjust to civilian life, but Gabe didn't seem the type to struggle with anything.

Appearances can be deceiving, she reminded herself. Yet it was difficult to picture him pruning trees and replacing sod torn up by energetic kids. He seemed more like someone accustomed to giving orders, instead of taking them.

"Could you finish the tour for Gabe?" her father asked. "I just got a call that an order needs to be picked up from the Sullivan Nursery down in Stockton."

"Sure, Pop. Are you taking the long truck?"

"No, the old one. It's large enough." He turned to Gabe. "Poppy Gold has a 1928 AA pickup. People have fun seeing it and think it's great that such an old truck is still being used. Tessa, can you also show Gabe our fleet of antique vehicles? I hadn't gotten that far with the tour."

"No problem. Call when you get back. If you

aren't busy tonight, come over and I'll fix you dinner." Tessa kissed his cheek.

When she was alone with Gabe McKinley, she gestured at Mr. Fezziwig. "Just let me deal with this fellow. I'll be right back."

Gabe must have missed the "I'll be right back" because he walked with her to the opposite end of the Victorian Cat. Since no guests had checked in for the day, she'd left the access open to her private, two-story apartment.

"So you live on-site," he commented.

"Yes, though Guest Registration handles check-ins." She put Mr. Fezziwig on a chair by the window and ran a finger down his neck. He was still looking at Gabe suspiciously, and Tessa understood exactly how he felt. Gabe had walked right in, past a sign marked Private. "But living at the Victorian Cat works out well, because if one of the cats doesn't have company for the night, they can stay with me."

"How often does that happen?"

"We aren't always fully booked during the off-season, but the closer we get to summer, it's rare to have rooms available. We try to have something unique about each of the B and Bs, and returning guests have their favorites. Cat lovers usually pick the Victorian Cat, while railroad buffs prefer the Gold Rail Hotel, and so forth."

"It must be difficult to manage the bookings."

"We have staff dedicated to reservations and

event planning. Poppy Gold Inns is the biggest employer in Glimmer Creek," Tessa said proudly, "and we support other businesses by buying local whenever possible and outsourcing various services."

Gabe nodded as if interested, though it was impossible to tell anything from his face. Honestly, they'd only just met, but it was hard to imagine an emotion daring to crack his iron jaw.

"You appear to have a good many antiques. Do you have live-in staff to keep an eye on things at night? I haven't noticed any video cameras."

It was probably an innocent question, but it seemed odd to Tessa. She'd dealt with a wide range of new employees and eager beavers who asked everything under the sun on their first day, but Gabe's manner seemed more like an IRS auditor than an eager beaver. Not that it was fair to make snap judgments; he was still adjusting to civilian life. Anyway, her father would have run a background check before hiring him.

"Actually, we don't have live-in staff. Security is on duty around the clock, so you won't need to get involved with those issues," she said carefully. "Guest Registration is at Old City Hall, which is located by the original town square park."

"I see."

Tessa firmly escorted Gabe out and locked the

door behind them. "Now, what have you been shown so far?"

"The working areas for Maintenance, including the greenhouses, orchards and vegetable gardens. Also the general employee facility."

"All right, we'll go to Old City Hall next."

They stepped out into the Victorian garden surrounding the large house. Birds twittered in the spring sunshine, splashing in the birdbath and perching on the edge. The California foothills were always beautiful, especially in the historic Gold Country, but spring and summer were the seasons that Tessa particularly loved.

She didn't even mind the hot days. As a kid she'd swum in the creek when the temperature went up, panned for gold dust in the shallows and picnicked along the shore with friends and family. However busy her parents might have been running their bed-and-breakfast business, they'd tried to join her adventures. Lately Tessa didn't have much time for adventures, but someday she hoped to get back to them.

"This way," she said, pointing north.

CAREFUL, GABE WARNED himself as Tessa Connor continued the tour of Poppy Gold. It was a bad idea to ask too many questions. After all, he was supposed to look like a navy vet, working his first job after leaving the service.

Actually, it *was* his first job, but he hadn't applied to Poppy Gold because he needed to make a living. Between his twenty-year retirement from the navy and being a part owner of the family company—Thomas International Products—he had a generous income.

Gabe left running TIP to his younger brother; the thought of being stuck behind a desk all day was more than he could swallow, and doing it for the family company would be that much worse. A muscle in Gabe's jaw twitched. The company was another reminder of his lousy childhood with a work-obsessed father and a vodka-guzzling mother. He'd enlisted when he was eighteen to get away from the misery at home.

Nevertheless, when Rob suspected a problem with industrial espionage, Gabe had insisted on helping. As a former navy SEAL, Gabe had experience in putting together missions and following suspicious activities around the world. And that didn't include the joint operations he'd done with the CIA. Together, he and Rob had narrowed down the most likely location where information leaks could have occurred—Poppy Gold Inns. TIP had been holding executive retreats, training and strategy meetings at the small conference center for the past two years.

They'd contacted the FBI with the information, but the agent had said it was only supposition at this point. "Bring us real evidence and we might be able to do something," the agent had declared.

He and Rob had decided the best way to *get* the necessary evidence was for Gabe to go undercover. In the past two years, the company had lost millions in deals that had fallen through; it couldn't continue.

"This is Glimmer Creek's original city center," Tessa said, stopping and gesturing around a picturesque park, complete with a gazebo-style bandstand and large fountain. "The town has a different center now, of course, in front of the new city hall. Not that it's new any longer since it was built in the 1930s, but that's what it's called."

"Why did they build it instead of using the original building?" Gabe asked, trying to sound more like a new employee than an investigator.

"The story is too long to tell right now, but it's tied up with family history on my father's side. The short version is that my grandfather owned all of the land and buildings in this part of town before he deeded them to my parents to start Poppy Gold. Before that it was nicknamed Connor's Folly."

Connor's Folly? Obviously that was part of the long story Tessa didn't have time to tell him.

"Your grandfather must be well-off."

"Granddad is the owner and president of Connor Enterprises in San Francisco."

Gabe glanced around at the thriving tourist

village—even for a tourist trap, the place was appealing. The extent of preservation reminded him of Colonial Williamsburg in Virginia.

But appealing or not, it was still the most likely source of TIP's problems. Other than Rob's office, Poppy Gold was the only location where certain pieces of company information had been brought together, and the failed contract negotiations had always occurred shortly after a visit to the B and B facility. Rob might have suspected some of his executives were responsible, but different execs had been at the meetings each time, often from divergent areas of the company's operations.

Hacking had also been ruled out because his brother had started keeping data on upcoming deals and contracts off-line. He'd even moved all the files onto a computer that wasn't hooked up to the internet.

He looked back at Tessa Connor. As the manager, she was in the best position to know everything that was going on at the conference center, but whether she was an ally or an enemy was unclear. She could even be the culprit. While Rob thought highly of Tessa, it didn't mean she was innocent.

Gabe almost snorted.

His brother's judgment was probably clouded by Tessa's slim figure and sparkling eyes. For that matter, Rob had a hard time believing anyone would steal from TIP in the first place, which was why it had taken him so long to acknowledge the problem. Gabe, on the other hand, didn't have trouble believing the worst of anyone.

"Come on, I'll show you Poppy Gold's reservation hub," Tessa said.

While the remaining tour of Poppy Gold was thorough, Gabe couldn't pry another shred of personal information from her. He was lousy at chitchat, but it shouldn't have been difficult since Tessa seemed to chatter away with the slightest provocation. She even had conversations with cats.

Still, Gabe noticed that the tour didn't include anything related to security. He just didn't know if the omission meant anything. Working in Poppy Gold's security division would have been his top choice, but naturally they did far more extensive background checks on *those* employees than ones in grounds maintenance. It was likely that his connection to TIP would have been revealed and questioned.

"Have you found a place to live?" Tessa asked after they returned to the maintenance center. Though located in a modern building, it had a Victorian-style facade that blended well with Poppy Gold's ambiance.

"I've rented a furnished studio in town."

"You were lucky to find something local— we don't have many rentals in Glimmer Creek.

I don't see any other employees around. They must all be out working. Did Pop tell you what to do for the rest of the day?"

"Mow the lawns and edge the walkways around these two houses." He pointed to a map on the wall. "I understand you primarily use electric equipment to minimize noise."

"That's right. We have riding mowers for the large areas, like the old city center park, but whenever possible, we coordinate using them around the guest schedule. Have you been given a locker assignment?"

Gabe shook his head.

Tessa unlocked a cabinet, consulted a ledger and gave him a key. "This is to locker 5A—work gloves and other protective gear should be in there already. I'll let you get started, but be sure to take your breaks and lunch. If you have any questions, check with the reservations desk and they'll find me."

She left quickly, and Gabe wondered if she was eager to get rid of him. Not that he'd blame her. She managed the conference center and surely had more urgent responsibilities than giving new-employee tours and evicting ornery felines from rooms where they weren't wanted.

TESSA HURRIED ACROSS Poppy Gold to the Glimmer Creek Train Depot. She tried not to be a micromanager, so she had established her office away from Old City Hall. Since she handled most of the business clients, it was also nice to have the quieter work space.

"Hey, Jamie," she called to her eighteen-year-old cousin, who was dressed in period costume and talking to a group of schoolchildren.

Jamie waved back. Close to half of Poppy Gold's employees were related to Tessa in one way or another. In Jamie's case, she was Tessa's maternal uncle Daniel's daughter and had started working at Poppy Gold Inns right after graduating from Glimmer Creek High. She was rather young for her age, which was why Uncle Daniel and Aunt Emma hadn't pushed her to leave for college immediately.

Tessa's office was on the second floor, and she gazed out the window for a moment, loving the peaceful scene. The abandoned train track had never been torn out, and it ran like a ribbon through the countryside, much overgrown, leading to the old railroad spur turnaround. Only the section that ran along the edge of Poppy Gold was in good condition. On it sat a steam engine and two passenger cars from the 1870s, sparklingly restored, looking as if they had just arrived at the station. Their visitors loved the train, and in peak seasons, the passenger cars were filled with picnickers.

Tessa thought about the lunch baskets available at the general store, packed with fried chicken, baked ham on biscuits, fresh-baked bread and other goodies. The baskets were more Hollywood illusion than authentic flavors from the 1800s, but they were popular. And there might be things Poppy Gold could do to *simulate* a train ride.

She jotted a note in her "idea" book. It was filled with things to do at Poppy Gold, supplementing the plan she'd made in college. Her parents had begun to implement her concept a few years ago, but there was always more to do. In a way it made her feel even more responsible, knowing that turning the business into a conference center was something she'd urged them to try. She'd helped, coming home weekends and spending vacations there, but a lot had fallen on her mom's and dad's shoulders.

Now it was mostly on her.

She pressed a hand to her stomach. Suggesting changes as an eager college student was a lot easier than carrying them out herself. Where *had* all the blind certainty of her youth gone? Maybe the final vestiges had been lost with her mother's death.

"Hey," Jamie said, poking her head through the office doorway. "The school group is gone. Mom made peach pies last night and sent one for you."

She came in holding a Tupperware pie-taker. Tupperware containers were ubiquitous in Glimmer Creek thanks to two of Tessa's maternal great-aunts who'd thrown so many parties to sell the stuff that it was stockpiled in everyone's basements. Glimmer Creek was filled with relatives on her mom's side of the family.

Tessa's mouth watered. Nobody made pies like Aunt Emma. "My taste buds thank her, but my hips aren't so sure."

"Like you need to worry. Can you believe it? Mom even said to eat it with ice cream because you're too skinny. She never says that to *me*."

"I'm not skinny," Tessa denied automatically. Her female relatives kept trying to feed her, claiming she'd lost weight since returning home, but they worried too much.

If they weren't trying to fix her up with a guy, they were urging her to eat more.

"You're skinnier than me."

Jamie tugged at her costume and stuck out her bottom lip in the mock pout she'd perfected as a four-year-old. The same as most Fullerton women, she was a late bloomer and still carried a few childhood pounds she couldn't seem to lose. Tessa had gone through the same phase herself.

"I wouldn't worry about it," Tessa urged.

"That's easy for you to say. My face is so round. I look like a chipmunk that's stuffed its cheeks with nuts."

"Lance doesn't seem to think so."

Jamie's eyes filled with delight at the mention of her boyfriend. "Isn't he wonderful?"

Tessa smiled, though she didn't know a great deal about the young man her dad had hired several months earlier, other than what Jamie had told her.

Lance Beckley was one of the Poppy Gold employees who hadn't grown up in the area. He'd shown up on his motorcycle, wandered around town a couple of days and then applied for a job in the maintenance department. Pop had hired him to clear brush and dig rocks from the area where they hoped to plant two additional orchards. Tessa had been concerned when she heard he was the biker who'd invaded Poppy Gold, roaring up and down the streets, but he hadn't caused any problems since then.

When her cousin had gone back to work, Tessa made calls to several clients, booking a destination wedding for a CEO's daughter, along with three corporate retreats and a class reunion.

At 1:00 p.m. she got up to do her usual quick walk through Old City Hall and around the grounds. At the Mayfair Mansion she stopped and watched Gabe McKinley working in the garden. The lawn at the nearby Calaveras House was already smartly groomed, so he'd obviously started there first.

His shirt stretched over his shoulders, his muscles flexing as he lifted a load of clippings onto a cart, and she felt an unwelcome warmth in her abdomen. She didn't want to be attracted to a guy like Gabe, even in passing.

He noticed her and bobbed his head without stopping his work. Then she noticed he was about to yank one of the plants from behind the sundial.

"No, *wait*," Tessa cried, dashing over. "That's *supposed* to be there."

GABE STARED AT the plant he'd been about to pull. It was supposed to stay? He hadn't touched the flowerbeds since Liam Connor had told him to work on the lawns, but this thing had looked too weedy to leave behind. The gardens in general seemed chaotic, with masses of different flowers crowded together. He guessed it was attractive, but it wouldn't do any harm to impose some order.

Tessa crouched and patted the ground around the base of the weed he'd grabbed, though she seemed to avoid touching the plant itself. "Uh… Pop must have forgotten to say you shouldn't do anything on the flowerbeds until you receive some training."

"Oh." Gabe's instructions from the elder Connor had been distracted, to say the least; Liam gave the impression that his thoughts were somewhere else entirely. Age-related memory problems were also a possibility, despite him seeming too young for senility. "This isn't a weed?"

"No, it's foxglove. This one has already flowered, but wait until you see it next year. I'm not sure foxglove belongs in a true Victorian garden, but we love it."

"Are you a horticulturist, too?"

"Just an enthusiastic amateur. My mother did the research and designed all our gardens and… er…planted most of the perennials and biennials herself. She liked the natural style of the late-Victorian era. Formal gardens wouldn't suit Poppy Gold nearly as well."

Liked. Past tense.

That must mean Liam was a widower. While it was information, it wouldn't have much bearing on his investigation. Gabe shifted restlessly. He preferred direct action to covert activity, but this was something he had to do for Rob. A part of him still felt guilty for escaping to the navy and leaving his younger brother alone with their parents.

"So, what *did* you study in college?" Gabe asked, trying to make the question sound casual. Apparently he didn't succeed, because Tessa became guarded again.

"Business. It looks as if you're almost done here. Since it's your first day, I'm sure Pop won't mind if you take the rest of the afternoon off. Just return the equipment to Maintenance."

"I can't quit early. You know what they say—a day's work for a day's pay. I'll find something to keep me occupied." Gabe was elated. With Liam gone, he would have an ideal chance to poke around and get a better lay of the land.

Her lips tightened. "All right, but don't do anything to the garden beds. I need to get back to my office."

Gabe was almost amused. The only thing he'd learned for certain was that Tessa Connor was protective of the plants her mother had put in the ground. He couldn't imagine being sentimental that way himself, but it was Tessa's business. Of course, his own mother had been pickled with alcohol for most of his childhood, so he was unlikely to get maudlin about her mementos.

The truth was, he knew too much about the dark side of human nature, yet he still found most people incomprehensible.

CHAPTER TWO

TESSA RETURNED TO her office, still not sure what to make of Gabe McKinley. He obviously worked hard—the lawns around the two houses had been cut and trimmed with military precision, without a blade of grass or speck of dirt out of place. Yet she also had the feeling he didn't know anything about the kind of work he'd been hired to do.

There was nothing unusual about having an inexperienced employee, particularly in grounds maintenance, but normally Pop was fierce about warning new staff not to touch his wife's Victorian flowerbeds until they'd been properly trained.

Tessa's stomach rolled.

Fifteen months ago her father had called to say the business was falling apart and he was considering selling Poppy Gold. Though he hadn't asked her to come back, she'd immediately gone to her grandfather's office and resigned. She still didn't know if it had been the right decision... There were so many memories that haunted Liam at Poppy Gold. But she'd been certain he would regret selling the place where he'd fallen in love and spent so many years restoring.

It had also been a little selfish. Tessa couldn't bear the thought of losing Poppy Gold; she missed her mother terribly, and the place was a connection both to Meredith Connor and her own childhood.

The rest of the afternoon passed slowly, and by four o'clock Tessa was on edge, wondering if her father was back from Stockton, and if he was, why he hadn't called. He got depressed, and this time of year was a tough one for him—her parents' thirty-second wedding anniversary was rapidly approaching.

It wasn't fair.

People weren't supposed to die of pneumonia. With modern medicine and all the antibiotics available, it shouldn't have happened. Meredith Connor should still be here, making everyone happy, especially her husband.

Tessa rubbed her aching forehead. She'd always hoped to fall in love like her parents and have children, but after watching her father's agony, she was wary about feeling that much. Not that it mattered—at the moment she was far too busy for romance. She couldn't take the chance that Poppy Gold might fail; too many people depended on them.

Not that she had anything against romance. She'd dated in college and occasionally in San

Francisco, though never to the point of genuinely committing her heart. One of her old boyfriends had complained she was rushing too fast toward her future to think about the present, but she didn't agree. There was so much to do, and she didn't see any harm in graduating high school and college early.

A short time later her father walked in, looking more tired than usual. He sat down with a groan. "Sorry about being late. I got a flat tire. I would have called but my phone was dead."

"That's okay, Pop. Sorry about the tire."

Tessa made a mental note to check the charge on his cell phone when he was taking a day trip out of town, especially if he was taking the 1928 AA truck. He never used to be absent-minded, but a lot had changed in the past eighteen months. It was even possible that he'd spent part of the time down in Stockton just staring into space. The occasions she found him zoned out completely were less frequent now, but they still happened.

"It's just one of those things. How did it go with Gabe?"

"Fine, as far as I know. I showed him around and left him at Maintenance. Later I saw him working on the lawns around the Mayfair Mansion and Calaveras House. Everything was spotless."

Tessa decided not to mention Gabe's attempt

to uproot a foxglove plant; her father didn't need anything else to upset him.

"Good. He seems nice."

Nice?

Maybe she'd missed something.

Tessa knew that two of her worst faults were a quick temper…and a bad habit of making snap decisions about people. Sometimes she was right, sometimes she wasn't. But there was no denying that her first impressions of Gabe McKinley weren't positive.

"What do you know about him?" Tessa asked.

"The usual sort of things from his application. Twenty years in the navy, but no job since getting out. He listed his skills as general mechanic, heavy machinery operation, scuba diving and underwater rescue."

"Scuba diving and underwater rescue? There's so much call for that at Poppy Gold," she muttered wryly. "How about KP or maintenance experience? I thought all servicemen and women had that sort of thing under their belts."

Liam waved his hand. "People don't always like claiming they worked in the mess or scrubbed the officers' head. Gabe didn't list any prior duty assignments, but he has a spotless record—not even a speeding ticket. Do you think there's a problem?"

"Of course not," Tessa said hastily. "I'm just curious. He isn't that personable."

"Give him a chance," Liam urged. "Life is structured in the military. It may take him a while to get accustomed to how we do things."

"I know, Pop. It's just that our guests expect everyone to be friendly and he's rather...poker-faced." Grim and forbidding was a better description, but she didn't want to sound too negative.

"I'll remind him to smile more."

"Is he one of your referrals from Admiral Webster's office?" Over time they'd become acquainted with a high-ranking officer in each of the military branches who now made referrals to Poppy Gold. Sometimes it was for a job, sometimes it was a request to provide a few days at Poppy Gold to service members or their families as a respite from stress or other problems. It had started with one of her father's old army pals who was now a general.

"No referral. Gabe just applied. We ended up talking all afternoon last Saturday. Well, I'd better get over to Maintenance. The nursery got the red astrachan apples we wanted. We should have enough ground prepared in a few days to plant them."

"Shouldn't apples be planted in very early spring or late fall?"

"Yes, but the nursery promised to replace any that don't thrive. Apparently their supplier has trouble getting organic astrachans. Anyhow, I also got a big load of organic fertilizer. I'll unload everything and come over after I clean up."

"Move the truck into the garage and have one of your guys take care of it tomorrow," Tessa urged, frowning. She didn't like her father lifting heavy items by himself. He rarely paid attention to what he was doing—five months ago he'd pulled a hamstring and had suffered minor injuries in other mishaps.

"I'll be fine. When do you want me for dinner?"

"Seven thirty is fine."

"I'll see you then."

Tessa sat for a minute after he left, then jumped up. She headed for Maintenance, stopping only to change into jeans and leave Aunt Emma's peach pie at her apartment in the Victorian Cat. Fortunately she had a separate entrance, so she wasn't delayed by guests wanting to chat.

"Pop?" she called, walking around the end of the main maintenance building. She froze. His antique heavy-duty truck was parked by one of the storage sheds, but instead of one man, she saw two—her father and Gabe McKinley. They were chatting and even chuckled together at one point.

Interesting.

"What are you doing here, Tessajinks?"

Gabe had just hoisted a bag of fertilizer onto his shoulder, but he paused and looked up. "Tessajinks?"

Tessa smiled along with her father, though she was surprised that he'd used her childhood nickname in front of a stranger. "It's from when I was little. You know...jinks, from high jinks."

"My daughter was a carefree, fun-loving toddler," Liam explained, "but very well behaved, of course."

"That's right, I was a perfect angel," Tessa added, relieved that he didn't seem saddened by the recollection from a happier time.

"Yes, it's *now* that she's a handful." Liam shook a finger at her. "She loved to play hide-and-seek, but she would get so excited, she giggled when anyone got near her hiding place. I could tell you stories—"

"But he won't, because you'd just be bored," Tessa interrupted, becoming uncomfortable. She was an only child and knew her fate in life was to be the subject of all of her father's "gab and brag" tales, but her instincts told her to keep revelations at a minimum around Gabe McKinley. Even revelations that were twenty-seven years old.

"To be frank, I'm not a kid person," Gabe said. He barely seemed to notice the heavy load balanced on his shoulder.

"You'll change your mind when you have a family of your own," Liam assured him.

"I'm not going to *have* a family," Gabe replied. His tone and expression suggested it was a carefully considered decision, rather than a casual bachelor's attitude.

Liam shook his head. "That'll change when you meet the right woman. It did for me."

"I'm also not planning to get married." Gabe carried the fertilizer to the shed and set it on a pile of other sacks. He immediately went to the truck and grabbed another bag.

Pop seemed at a loss, and Tessa was annoyed. Her father sometimes offered opinions better kept to himself—she thought of it as small-townitis—but Gabe didn't even seem to realize how curt he'd been. And after all, he was the one who'd volunteered he wasn't a "kid person." But kid person or not, he'd better be nice to the children who visited Poppy Gold.

Eyes narrowed, she went to help, but Gabe let out a sharp "I'll do it" as soon as she reached for one of the bags.

"I may be little, but I'm tough," she informed him, "and I'm sure your shift ended a couple of hours ago."

Liam lifted the bag she'd intended to unload. "That's what I said, but he insisted."

Gabe shrugged. "I'm new to Glimmer Creek, so I don't have much else to do."

"We'll still pay for the extra time," Tessa asserted. Pop sometimes hinted that she was too stubborn. He might be right, but she *had* to be stubborn on fair employment practices.

GABE DIDN'T CARE about a few extra dollars in his paycheck; for that matter, he wasn't comfortable about taking *any* pay since his actions had ulterior motives. As for helping to unload supplies, he'd hoped it would provide another one-on-one opportunity to talk with his new "boss." The Connor name and the family's connection to San Francisco had been bothering him. Later he would research it on the internet and see if anything came up, but he'd hoped to learn something in passing from Liam.

"We don't have much nightlife," Liam said, "but the library is open most evenings, along with several cafés and a country bar. The Gold Shanty is quite popular with our guests."

"Actually, I'm going to check out the weight machines at the staff fitness center. It's available twenty-four-seven, right?"

"Yes. Access it using your employee code," Tessa replied, giving him a cool look. Maybe she thought he was trying to impress her by mentioning working out.

The sooner he found out what was going on at Poppy Gold, the better. Then he wouldn't need to worry about other people's reactions. Ultimately he planned to buy land in the mountains where he'd design and test equipment for the SEALs and other emergency response teams.

Since signing out of work, he'd explored the conference center and learned the location of every feature. It hadn't taken long—he had ample practice memorizing data for his missions. He now had a mental map of the facility and building floor plans securely established in his brain, along with the details of the operations handbook.

"I'll help," hailed a voice as Gabe reached for the next bag in the back of the truck. It was a young man, and he came over with a girl dressed in a Victorian costume.

Gabe gritted his teeth. So much for a private chat with Liam Connor. It was after hours and they weren't in a public area, yet people were popping out of the woodwork.

"This is Lance Beckley," Tessa said, "and my cousin Jamie Fullerton. Lance is in Maintenance, while Jamie works in Guest Services. Lance, Jamie, this is Gabe McKinley. He just started today."

Gabe said hello as Lance jumped into the truck bed and began shifting bags from the front to the back so they could be unloaded more easily. He was probably showing off to his girlfriend, though it hardly seemed necessary since they both looked like lovesick puppies.

It won't last, Gabe thought to himself.

Love was just a series of chemical reactions that didn't survive for long.

JAMIE WATCHED LANCE WORKING, and though they'd been dating for several weeks, excitement went through her. He was the most awesome guy in the world. They got together every afternoon, and on most days she was so anxious to see him that she didn't wait to change out of her costume.

Lance made working at Poppy Gold even better, and she already loved it here. Though his shift started earlier than hers, they could sometimes have lunch together, or just get a chance to say hi.

"How is your class going?" Tessa asked.

"Um…not so good." Jamie squirmed. She was taking a night course in early California history down in Stockton, but lately she hadn't been attending many of the classes. "I might drop it."

"Your mom won't be happy about that."

Her mom wasn't happy about Lance, either. "She just doesn't understand what it's like to have a boyfriend."

"I don't want to sound like an old fuddy-duddy, but she understands better than you think," Tessa told her. "She just wants you to keep your options open."

All of a sudden Jamie remembered that Poppy Gold had paid her tuition, and her face got hot. "I'll pay the money back if I don't finish the class," she said quickly. She hated studying or sitting through lectures when she could be with Lance, but it also bothered her that she hadn't been attending. It was the same as breaking a promise.

"I'm not worried about the tuition, but what about having Lance drive to Stockton with you? He could wait while you're in class, and you'd have the trip down to the valley and back to be together."

"I'll talk to him," Jamie agreed doubtfully.

She was sure her cousin was going to say one of those things like, "If he really cares about you..." but Tessa was looking at Uncle Liam.

Jamie sighed. Sometimes it was sad to see Uncle Liam because he was unhappy so often. Her mom and the rest of the family had worried that he'd leave and they'd never get to see him again. They said it didn't make sense that in-laws sometimes stopped acting like family when their wife or husband died. It was hard enough without Aunt Meredith; if Uncle Liam was gone, too, it would be *awful*. She just wanted him to start smiling more.

"Hey." Tessa nudged her. "What are you looking so gloomy about?"

"Nothing." It wasn't true, but Jamie didn't want to upset her cousin. "Uh, you know, Mom is uptight about Lance. Do you think it's his motorcycle?"

"Could be. Motorcycles make some people

uncomfortable—especially in Glimmer Creek since those two biker gangs got into a fight here a few years ago."

"Lance isn't in a gang."

"I realize that, but take a car to Stockton if he wants to go with you. It'll make Aunt Emma happier, and *I* won't get into as much trouble for suggesting you go together."

Jamie laughed. "Mom could never get mad at you."

"I wouldn't count on that."

Lance dusted his hands and came over. "We're all done, ma'am...I mean, Tessa. Are those the new apples for the orchard?" He pointed to the rows of trees that had come off the truck last.

"Some of them. I understand a section of the ground is nearly ready for cultivation."

"Yes...ma...uh, Tessa. I should be able to start planting by the end of this week."

"Great. Pop will show you what to do when you're ready."

Jamie stepped closer to Lance. He had a hard time calling Tessa and Uncle Liam by their first names, as if he'd get in trouble for doing it or something weird like that. She'd guessed that Lance had gotten into some kind of trouble before coming to Poppy Gold, but Uncle Liam had still hired him. Lance wouldn't talk that much about the past—he could be moody sometimes—but she was crazy about him, anyhow.

"Let's go down by the creek," she whispered. "Unless you're hungry."

"Let's eat later." Lance put his arm around her waist, and they said goodbye.

"It really *is* okay to call them Tessa and Liam," she said, holding up her long skirt as they went to her favorite place along the stream.

"I know."

She took off her shoes and stockings to stick her feet in the water. Her dresses were hot when the weather warmed up, but she loved the costumes, especially the elegant hats. A lot of Poppy Gold employees who worked in areas such as Guest Registration or giving tours liked to wear costumes. The historical society made them, and she got first pick because her mom was the president.

Lance poked around the rocks in the creek with a stick. "I wish that was real gold down there, not pyrite."

"If it was real, it wouldn't be there any longer," Jamie said practically.

"But it—"

Suddenly he slipped on a rock, pitching forward into the water.

A shriek escaped Jamie, and she splashed to his side. "Are you okay?"

"Yeah. Dumbass thing to do," he muttered, rubbing his head. "And you got your costume wet."

"That doesn't matter. Let's go sit down."

"At least we're cooler now," Lance said once they were settled on the creek bank with just their toes in the flowing current.

She laughed and squeezed his hand.

"Does anyone ever find *real* gold in the creek?" Lance asked after a few minutes. "I know there's a place where people pan for it, but I haven't heard that they get any."

"Sometimes they do. And when I was little I heard that someone in California went hiking and kicked a cow patty—only it wasn't a cow patty, it was a big lump of gold. *Pounds and pounds* of it."

Lance's eye widened. "Really?"

"Yeah. People in Glimmer Creek started kicking cow patties for a while after that, but it *is* poop, you know."

"I wouldn't care about the poop if I found that much gold, because then I could really take care of you. And I'm going to. Someday I'll make it big, and you won't have to worry about anything."

It wasn't the first time he'd talked about taking care of her, which was old-fashioned, even in Glimmer Creek, but really cute.

"I'm not worried, so don't start kicking cow poop for me." She put her head on his shoulder, so happy she could cry.

GABE LIFTED WEIGHTS at the fitness center for over an hour before returning to the small studio he'd rented in town. It was actually a cottage, in a cluster that had once been an old 1920s motor court. Despite their age, Glimmer Cottages were well maintained, and they were only a block from Poppy Gold.

In his room, Gabe pulled out his computer and opened his internet browser, linking through his smartphone. Finding the information he wanted didn't take long, and he cursed as he stared at the screen. Tessa was the granddaughter of Patrick Connor, who owned Connor Enterprises, a huge import-export company, just like the one the McKinley family had started two generations back.

Since the two businesses were in the same field, it could certainly help Connor Enterprises to undercut TIP. One of the major agreements that had fallen through for TIP was a deal to import specialty food items from Southeast Asia. In turn, it had caused the failure of a chain of contracts under negotiation, costing TIP a small fortune. According to the Connor Enterprises website, it *also* imported comestibles from Southeast Asia.

Gabe quickly connected with his brother on Skype.

"Hey, bro," Rob answered. He was obviously still at his office at TIP. "Having fun plunging toilets?"

"Very amusing. My duties are limited to grounds

maintenance, but I'm volunteering to be on call for anything else."

Rob's eyebrows shot upward. "Grounds maintenance? You're kidding, right? You can't tell a petunia from an oak tree."

Gabe winced. "Don't remind me. Earlier I was going to pull a weed when Tessa Connor objected—turns out it was something called foxglove that her mother had planted."

"Isn't that stuff poisonous?"

Poisonous? Gabe tucked the information away. It was interesting but not particularly relevant.

"I'll have to look it up. What do you know about an import company called Connor Enterprises?"

His brother's face sobered. "It's only one of TIP's biggest business rivals, that's all. Oh, damn... *Connor.* Surely there isn't a connection."

"Sorry to disappoint you. Tessa is the owner's granddaughter and worked there until a year or so ago. As far as I can tell, she and her father are Patrick Connor's only heirs, aside from his wife."

"I'm surprised Liam isn't working in the family company. Maybe he's a rebel like you."

Gabe ignored the rebel comment. He wasn't a rebel, but it would have gagged him to work for TIP. The only thing he'd regretted about enlisting so young was not being around to look after his younger brother.

"How did Liam end up in Glimmer Creek?" Rob wondered.

"I'll try to find out. Tell me why TIP started coming to Poppy Gold in the first place."

"All I know is that someone in the personnel department recommended it. I'll look into the details, but I can't believe Tessa or her father are involved. They just aren't the type."

Gabe kept his face expressionless. His brother would be much better off if he developed a more realistic outlook on human nature. "It's a fairly big coincidence, so we have to consider the possibility. Can you determine whether Connor Enterprises has profited directly from the information leaks? For example, did they get any of the contracts you lost?"

"I suppose. Are you still confident no one there will connect you with TIP?"

"It's unlikely, provided we act like strangers when you get here. I needed to keep a low profile when I was a SEAL, and the TIP webmaster has never posted my picture or personal history on the company website—"

"Because you refused to allow it," Rob interjected.

"And all TIP business documents identify me as David G. McKinley Jr.," Gabe continued. "In addition, you and I don't look alike."

"True, I'm much better-looking."

"Only in your dreams."

Rob chuckled. He was fair and blue-eyed and possessed a boyishness that charmed women and disarmed opponents. Gabe, on the other hand, was dark-haired, taller, leaner and combat-scarred, and no one had ever accused him of being charming. Yet despite their differences, they'd always gotten along.

"I would have thought you'd crack the case wide open in four or five hours," Rob told him. "Six at the most. I'm a taxpayer, I expect more from all that training you got in the navy. What does it cost to train a SEAL these days, twenty million bucks?"

Gabe snorted. "Not quite."

"Tessa has a lot at stake here, too, since Poppy Gold's reputation could be affected. I know we discussed it already, but it might be easier to simply ask for her help."

"That isn't a good idea. She and her father are logical suspects with their close ties to Connor Enterprises."

"I suppose."

They talked a while longer before logging off.

Skyping had made staying in contact easier over the past few years, though Gabe hadn't always been able to connect in remote locations or when he was in a communications blackout.

Frowning, he reviewed both the town's website and the one for Poppy Gold Inns to be sure he hadn't missed anything in his original research.

There was no information about Poppy Gold's owners on either site, though there were several pages on the history of Glimmer Creek, maintained by the local historical society. The conference center also had a Facebook page with a huge number of "likes" and glowing customer comments. Basically, visitors loved everything from the fresh-baked cinnamon rolls to the distinctive weather vanes on the rooftops.

Gabe absently rubbed his left shoulder where he'd taken a bullet a few months before. It still ached at times, which was partly why he'd retired at thirty-eight instead of staying in the service as a desk jockey. If he couldn't see himself behind a desk at TIP, it would be almost as distasteful in the navy. The navy docs had cleared him for active duty, but he'd known that his arm wasn't quite as strong as it used to be. The difference would matter only in a life-or-death situation... but that was the problem. The risk of letting down a member of his SEAL team was too great.

With a frown, he did a long series of push-ups, hoping to clear his mind of everything else.

TESSA WOKE UP in the middle of the night, a recurring nightmare making her heart race.

"Mrrrooow," cried Mr. Fezziwig, and she reached out a hand to stroke his fur. A low purr rumbled in his chest, gradually growing louder until it resonated like a motorboat.

She let out a breath and tried to shake off the dream. In it, she fell into a dark, nameless depth, and as always, she'd awakened before she could catch herself.

Mr. Fezziwig rolled until his back was snuggled against her chest, and she tucked her chin on top of his head, appreciating his comforting presence. She wished she could keep him in her apartment permanently, but he was a social cat and delighted in the parade of humans through his life.

"Hey," she whispered to Mr. Fezziwig, "why don't you like Gabe McKinley?"

He just purred.

Tessa closed her eyes. Though the occasional whispers of sound through the house usually didn't disturb her, tonight each one seemed magnified. But the most annoying part of not being able to go back to sleep was that she couldn't stop thinking about Poppy Gold Inns' newest employee.

There was something about Gabe that nagged at her. He seemed familiar in a way. She just couldn't figure out why. If she'd met him casually, it wouldn't matter, but anything that affected Poppy Gold was important.

She might have to look him up on the internet. He didn't seem the type for social media, but who knew what she might find?

Stop it, she ordered.

Being in charge was still rather new to her, and she tended to overthink everything. Besides, her father liked Gabe and he usually had good instincts about people. She needed to learn to trust that.

CHAPTER THREE

ON THURSDAY GABE went to the fitness center before dawn as he had the previous two mornings. He always started his day with exercise, but he had also discovered it was a good time to meet other Poppy Gold employees.

While he didn't really need to question them—just listen as they chatted and teased each other—he was drawn into their conversations, regardless. It was the same with the employee lunchroom. They were a gregarious group.

"I heard you just got a new car," he commented to Cheryl Clark as they ran side by side on the treadmills. Poppy Gold employees didn't gossip about the guests, but they made up for it talking about each other. It was a great source of information.

"Yeah, a cherry-red Mercedes," Cheryl said breathlessly. "Picked it up a few weeks ago. Brand-new. A real beauty."

Gabe nearly missed a step. A Mercedes was an expensive vehicle for a low-level housekeeper, and he'd heard she was dating a guy who worked at the local drugstore—unlikely to have any wealth to share with her.

"Mercedes are nice cars," he said. "I'll have to take a look for it in the employee parking area."

"That baby purrs like a kitten. I love it." She switched to a cool-off pace. "That ass, Nate, thinks it's stupid. He says I should have bought a truck like him, but I wanted something that *says* luxury. Besides, what do I need a truck for?"

Nate Dixon worked in the Poppy Gold maintenance division and had just bought a new, fully loaded truck. He'd proudly shown it off in the employee parking lot two days ago during lunch. Then he'd sniggered about Cheryl's "snooty" choice. Before Gabe could ask what kind of car she'd chosen, one of the other employees had mentioned Nate boasting about paying off the house he'd bought a couple of years before.

The conversation had given Gabe two potential suspects—Poppy Gold employees spending well beyond their apparent income. He was still checking them out. There was nothing to explain their spending on the internet, but the local newspaper had only a limited online presence. He'd have to see if there were back issues at the library.

On the other hand, would Cheryl or Nate boast about their acquisitions if they had anything to hide? *Probably.*

He'd dealt with a wide range of people over the years—dictators, spies, technology thieves—anything the navy chose to call on a SEAL to handle. His joint operations with the CIA had given him an even broader scope of experience. And one of the things he'd learned was that people liked to show off, whether it was their money, knowledge or power.

BY FRIDAY MORNING Lance had finished tilling a section of the ground that would be used for the new apple orchard, and he watched carefully as Mr. Connor showed him how to plant the saplings. He was grateful to Poppy Gold for hiring him and didn't want to mess up, though the way they did things seemed weird. Why grow apples when you could just buy them at a grocery store?

"I've never heard of red astrachans," he said.

Mr. Connor smiled. "Most people haven't. They're an heirloom apple. My grandmother grew up on a farm and loved both the red and white varieties. She always claimed they made the best pies. I told Tessa how good they're supposed to be, so she suggested planting them at Poppy Gold."

"You've never tasted one?"

"Afraid not. By the time I came along, my great-grandparents' orchard had become a parking lot for a shopping center." Mr. Connor handed him the shovel. "Think you can take it from here?"

"No problem," Lance assured him.

Planting trees should be a piece of cake compared with cutting brush and digging out rocks. He'd never *seen* so many rocks, and the roots were even tougher to get out. Not that he minded. Doing all that cutting and digging sort of cleared his head.

He was especially proud of the wall he'd built with the rocks. Liam had mentioned they expected to build walls with the extra rocks and had been pleased when Lance had started the job without even being told.

It was weird living in a dinky joint like Glimmer Creek, though. He wasn't even sure why he'd stopped there; he'd just wanted to get away from all the crap in Sacramento. If anything, he would have expected people in such a small town to be even snottier than in the city, figuring they wouldn't like outsiders, but a lot of them were nice. Of course, a few still looked at him funny, especially when they saw his bike.

Jamie's mom was a doctor and didn't seem too sure of him, either—probably because a guy who dug out rocks wasn't that impressive. But he wasn't going to dig holes and cut brush forever; he'd promised Jamie that he would take care of her, and it was exactly what he planned to do.

Now he just had to figure out how.

Lance remembered the story about an old cow patty turning out to be gold and decided Jamie was right; kicking cow droppings probably wasn't going to make him rich.

He'd never known anyone like her. The girls in high school had giggled all the time and teased him about being too quiet. But Jamie didn't mind when he wanted to be quiet; they would just hold hands and take a walk or something.

Not that he'd dated many girls in school. He'd found out that most parents didn't approve of their daughter going out with a foster kid, especially once they heard his dad was in prison. It was as if they thought you were damaged if you didn't have a regular family. The school counselor had claimed he was exaggerating, but Lance didn't think so. He'd never forgotten a story he'd read about how "amazing" it was that some rich guy had succeeded, *despite* growing up in foster homes. He may not have gotten good grades in school, but he wasn't stupid.

Mr. Connor left and Lance began measuring out the proper distance to put between the trees, marking each spot before digging the second hole. Planting each tree took a while, and he was sweating by the time he finished planting the fourth red astrachan.

Just fourteen more to go, he thought, wiping

his forehead. It might be easier to dig big holes than pull out rocks, but it was still hard work. For a moment he felt kind of dizzy, so he gulped down some water. Mr. Connor kept telling him to drink enough fluids, especially on a warm day, and would put extra sports drinks in his pack, just to be sure.

Lance put the bottle away and watered the fourth tree. Then he picked up the shovel and began digging a hole for the next one.

TESSA HURRIED OVER to Old City Hall midmorning. She was playing catch-up on her work as usual, but she wanted to greet the leader of the Talmadge Guild Association before the first meeting. The guild was now on its third visit, and while they could be fussy about their arrangements, they were nice people.

"Hi, Charlotte," she called, spotting the chairwoman getting out of the courtesy shuttle they provided from the perimeter parking areas.

Charlotte Angstrom turned and smiled. "Good morning, Tessa. Did you orchestrate this lovely weather for us?"

Tessa grinned. "Absolutely. The ballroom is arranged for the banquet tonight and the concert hall for this afternoon's meet and greet. Do you need any help getting set up?"

"I'd be happy to assist." The unexpected sound

of Gabe's deep voice made Tessa jump, and she realized he'd come around the corner of Old City Hall, carrying a wide push broom.

Charlotte beamed. "How nice of you to offer. I'm Charlotte Angstrom," she said.

"Gabe McKinley."

"Gabe is a new employee," Tessa explained. "He's always eager to help where needed."

In the four days since Gabe had started with Poppy Gold, he'd been *very* keen to volunteer for anything that needed doing.

"Excellent," Charlotte said briskly. "I'm a tired old lady, so it's wonderful to have a pair of willing hands. Join me upstairs." She turned and strode up the steps of Old City Hall like a general going to war.

"Don't buy that 'tired old lady' bit," Tessa advised Gabe. "Charlotte is the founder of Angel Bite Cookies. She has more drive than both of us put together."

"Is that a big company?"

"They're huge. Angel Bites went from a business started in her kitchen to one of the most popular gourmet cookie-makers in North America."

"Now she leads a crafters' association?"

"Her son convinced her to retire, so she got involved in several organizations. But she still takes time to develop new recipes for the company. You should taste her Little Devils. They debuted last year and are absolutely divine."

"Little Devils from a company called Angel Bites?"

"Mmm, yes. They're a dark chocolate cookie with a hint of hot chili pepper. Incredible."

Amazingly, a smile lurked in Gabe's eyes. "I'll take your word for it. I'd better go assist Ms. Angstrom before I get court-martialed. She reminds me of a commanding officer I once had—he was easy to get along with, provided everything got done his way."

Tessa had to laugh. Charlotte *could* be a challenge.

Gabe went inside Old City Hall, and Tessa started her final review of the arrangements. The guild offered classes on making American patchwork quilts at the annual conference. This year the reservations had skyrocketed, and they were using all the meeting spaces available at Poppy Gold.

The other participants had begun arriving by the time Tessa finished. She was racing from the far side of Poppy Gold toward the concert hall when Gabe made another one of his unexpected appearances.

"Um, hi," Tessa said, her pulse jumping with surprise. For a tall, strong guy, he could move awfully fast.

"Hi. Liam is concerned that you might not have eaten."

Tessa looked at her watch and saw it was after one o'clock. Her dad often had someone track her down to see if she'd eaten lunch, but he usually sent a member of the family.

"Tell him I'll get something after I stop in at the guild meet and greet."

Gabe handed her a covered cup and a straw. "He figured as much, so he made something. I volunteered to bring it over since I was coming this way to do cleanup on the parking areas."

Resigned, she unwrapped the straw and stuck it in the cup. It held one of Liam's special concoctions— blended frozen fruit, yogurt and protein powder. As a teen she'd been very active, hating to stop for meals, so he'd begun making smoothies. Her dad had always been a mother hen, and since it gave him something productive to think about, she didn't object to him fussing at her now.

The biggest problem was when he hinted about grandchildren and suggested she start dating again. She wasn't opposed to the idea, even with her concerns about the risks of falling in love; she just didn't have time. Perhaps in a year or two when things had settled down at Poppy Gold.

Of course, her Glimmer Creek relatives were *also* in full matchmaking mode. Just a few weeks earlier she'd been invited to dinner at her aunt

Polly's house, only to discover Polly had invited the high school principal as well…who just happened to be single. He was a nice guy and had called a couple of times since, but Tessa wasn't interested. *No sparks.*

She started walking toward the concert hall again, and Gabe fell into step next to her. It wasn't uncommon to have employees try to score points with her, but he didn't seem the type.

In spite of her reservations and the lack of information she'd been able to find about him, she couldn't deny that he worked hard. He also seemed to relate well to her father; the previous evening she'd found them in Maintenance, talking away as they poked through the innards of the 1928 pickup. It was Pop's favorite vehicle, and he didn't let just anyone touch it. Then she'd heard they'd gone to dinner together. She would have teased her father about having a bromance, but she didn't think he'd understand.

"Ms. Angstrom mentioned you were business associates in San Francisco before she retired," Gabe commented.

Tessa shrugged. "I made a lot of contacts working for my grandfather. In college, too."

"Those contacts must be helpful now that you're running Poppy Gold. Do many of them book conferences here?"

"Some. We've had corporate retreats, weddings, class reunions, all sorts of stuff. My folks began promoting Poppy Gold as a conference center three years ago, so some of our clients have been coming here since then."

Tessa gulped down the last mouthful of the smoothie and shivered, despite the warm air. She tossed the cup in a trash can near the entrance of the concert hall.

"I've got work to do, and you mentioned needing to work on the parking lots, so you'd better get going," she said firmly.

BEFORE GABE COULD LEAVE, he felt a vibration under his feet.

A truck?

He looked around, expecting to see the antique truck that Liam favored. For the most part Poppy Gold restricted modern vehicles in the old town area, though they used electric golf carts when needed.

The vibration grew more pronounced, and he heard a faint roaring sound.

Visitors began running through the doors of the concert hall crying, "Earthquake!"

Without batting an eye, Tessa directed everyone to the old town square park across the street, at the same time urging them to watch their step and remain calm. When the rush had ended, she got on the radio.

"Central dispatch, this is Tessa. I'm with Gabe McKinley. We're fine. Let's follow Response Plan C. Gabe and I will team up and start checking buildings, beginning with the concert hall, going counterclockwise. Let my father know where Gabe will be for a while."

"Okay, Tessa. I'll take the lead from Old City Hall."

"Thanks, Aunt Polly."

Gabe lifted an eyebrow. Response Plan C had been discussed in the operations handbook and was far more extensive than such a minor event warranted. It included accounting for employees and making a visual sweep of every space in Poppy Gold. There were no preassigned teams, so emergency coordinators called on whoever was available. The goal of the plan was to continue services with as little disruption as possible while checking to ensure both buildings and guests were all right.

"Damage seems unlikely," he said to Tessa. "The quake was minor."

"I know, and all the buildings were reinforced a few years ago, but I want to do a quick check, anyway. Besides..." Tessa continued, dropping her voice, "a number of the conference attendees are older. If any of them have health problems, there's no telling how they'll react, particularly if they've never been in an earthquake. What's minor to us may not be minor to them."

"I understand."

They went inside the concert hall and inspected the main room, restrooms, storage areas and kitchen, ensuring no one was there who might have been injured in the rush to exit the building.

"The concert hall is okay," Tessa reported to her aunt on the radio.

"Got it, Tessa."

Before continuing to the next building, they went out to speak with the guests in the small park, only to have Charlotte Angstrom inform them that she had everything in hand. She had her expert quilters giving impromptu lectures on the history of American patchwork to relax everybody. In the meantime she was marking names on her roster to account for everyone who'd registered.

Tessa nodded. "Thanks, Charlotte. It's fine to go back inside now."

"Heavens, I know that. I've never seen so much drama in my life—one of our guild members from the East Coast yelled for everybody to run outside, and it practically started a stampede. I wouldn't even get out of bed for a quake this small."

"I can't imagine an earthquake daring to wake you up," Tessa teased.

The older woman chuckled and marched off with her clipboard.

"That's a very impressive lady," Gabe murmured.

"She certainly is. I've always—"

"Ms. Connor, where's Jamie? I can't find her," interrupted an anxious voice.

"Take it easy, Lance, Jamie is fine." Tessa patted the young man's arm. "I heard her status reported over the radio. She was giving a tour to a school group and has taken them to the general store for lemonade."

The alarm on Lance Beckley's face began to fade, and his breathing slowed. "Oh." He looked at Gabe. "I wasn't scared, except for Jamie. Honest."

Gabe didn't know why the kid had wanted to make the assertion to *him*—they'd spoken only a few times—but he inclined his head in acknowledgment.

"Lance, I want you to report to Polly Murphy," Tessa said. "She's coordinating in Old City Hall and will let you know if there's something you need to do."

"Okay."

Lance left, and they headed first to the historic church, then to the Gold Rail Hotel. Most of the occupants had gone to the guild's meet and greet, though a few remained in the downstairs parlor—primarily husbands who'd already called their wives to check on them and had returned to relaxing with their newspapers. While focused on the task at hand, Gabe also noted that Tessa carried a master key, giving her access to all rooms in the historic building.

From there they went to the Glimmer Creek Train Depot. It was quiet, with historic re-creations and discreet exhibits about early California railroad history on the ground level.

"The Beckley kid sure overreacted," Gabe commented as they climbed the stairs to the second floor.

"He was worried about Jamie."

"There wasn't any cause for concern. The other day he mentioned growing up in California, so he must have experienced earthquakes."

"I think it's sweet that his first thought was for Jamie's safety," Tessa murmured, opening doors and looking into each office.

She really *was* a sentimentalist, or else putting on a darned good act.

"You don't know it was his first thought," Gabe retorted. "He might have just told you what you wanted to hear."

Her eyes narrowed. "Are you always this cynical?"

"I'm just being realistic."

"That isn't what I call it."

A static burst came over the radio, followed by a report to Tessa that two large pottery planter pots had knocked together and cracked in the garden at the Victorian Cat.

Damage to a garden feature seemed inconsequential, but the expression on Tessa's face tightened. "Thanks, Aunt Polly. How are the cats?"

"They seem to be fine, but Mrs. Canter asked if you could stop by when you have a chance. Moby Dick is hiding, and she wants to be sure that he's all right."

"Will do. The train depot is clear."

"That's everything, then. The city building inspector is doing a walk-through, but he doesn't anticipate any issues," explained the woman on the other end of the radio. "Are you, um, going over to see your dad?"

Tessa pressed a finger to her temple. "After I stop in at the guild's meet and greet and before I check on Moby Dick. Is Pop at the VC?"

"Yes."

"Thanks." Tessa glanced at her watch. "Will you also call Sarah and see if she has additional munchies available to put out at the concert hall? It might improve the mood over there."

"Already done. Talk to you later."

Gabe stayed with Tessa as she walked toward the concert hall again. "Who is Sarah?" he asked.

"What?" Tessa gave him a distracted look. "Oh, one of my cousins. She has a bakery and catering business. We have a contract with her to provide all the food and beverages served at Poppy Gold."

Gabe thought about the interrelations of family working for the conference center. Having so many people intimately connected meant more potential cohorts who might be willing to look the other way in case of wrongdoing. Even when appalled by their behavior, people often hesitated to blow the whistle on a relative.

The old town square park was quiet once more, and they found everyone back in the concert hall. A few were nervously discussing the earthquake, but most were chatting about the upcoming conference and classes. Contrary to what he would have expected, a number of them were fairly young.

"I thought everyone from a craft organization would be a grandmotherly type," he commented when he and Tessa were back outside.

"Don't say that to anyone in there," she advised hastily. "The guild gets all ages. People are fascinated by American patchwork. It's one of the few art forms that originated in the United States. My mom used to have weekly quilting bees, and our guests loved attending."

"You aren't going to revive the custom yourself?"

"When I have more time. Possibly this fall. You should head back to Maintenance now," Tessa suggested as they crossed the street.

"I thought we were teaming up for the rest of the day on earthquake tasks." Gabe tried to make the comment sound innocent. He was having trouble getting a handle on Tessa, so an excuse to spend the afternoon with her was a windfall.

"We were only teamed for the building checks following the earthquake."

"I should still check with your father to see if he wants me to work on the parking lots, or if there's something more critical now."

WHILE IT WAS a valid consideration, frustration welled in Tessa. She wanted to talk to her dad in private. Liam was unpredictable these days, but it was a fair guess that he'd be unhappy about any damage at the Victorian Cat. It had been the first place her parents had restored when they were developing Poppy Gold, and they'd lived in the apartment there until she was four.

On the other hand, maybe it would help to have Gabe around. The two men obviously got along well, though Tessa wasn't sure what Pop saw in the former navy man. They were complete opposites. Her father, despite the realities of running a large bed-and-breakfast business, still had faith in people, while Gabe seemed to be a hard-nosed skeptic with the sensitivity of a bulldozer.

"All right," she acceded reluctantly.

Tessa walked swiftly toward the Victorian Cat. The earthquake, however minor, had disrupted a busy afternoon, but at least the staff's emergency-preparedness training had paid off.

"Hey, Pop," she called as she entered the garden and saw him cutting faded roses from a bush.

He smiled, though he still looked melancholy. The broken ginger jar–style pots were nearby. They were tall and made of fired cobalt pottery. Seven of them surrounded a birdbath, with flowers spilling over the sides. A smug brass cat sat in the middle of the water, as if daring any bird to come for its daily bath.

It was one of the focal points her mother had created in the gardens at Poppy Gold, and a pang went through Tessa. The rounded sides of two pots had smacked together, and nearly identical chunks of pottery had broken off, exposing the soil inside.

"We were lucky—it looks as if this is the only damage," she said, determinedly upbeat. "But it's okay. We can turn the pots so the breaks are pointed toward the birdbath until we get them repaired or replaced. The holes won't be visible once the trailing flowers grow out more."

"Yes, of course. That's what your mother would have done. Did you get your lunch? I worry when you don't eat."

"You don't need to worry, but I drank your smoothie." She kissed his cheek, thinking that he was far more prone to missing meals than her. "Thanks, it was delicious."

"Thank Gabe, he brought it to you."

"Mmm, yes. He wants to know if you have a special work assignment for him," she said.

"If needed, I can stay with Tessa and continue helping with any earthquake-related tasks," Gabe volunteered.

"We're done," Tessa said adamantly. "Checking on Moby Dick and Mrs. Canter is mostly a social call. Pop, wasn't Gabe supposed to be inspecting the parking areas?"

"Oh, yes, he can continue with that," Liam said. He turned back to the roses, his hand shaking as he cut an additional faded bloom from the bush and dropped it in a basket.

Tessa hurried into the Victorian Cat, pleased to be alone. Gabe's watchfulness made her nervous.

Upstairs she knocked on the door of the Tea Party suite and called, "Mrs. Canter, it's Tessa from Poppy Gold management. You wanted me to check on Moby Dick."

A moment later, a white-haired lady opened the door. "The poor dear was sitting on my lap when the earthquake started, but now he's hiding under the bed."

She stepped back, and Tessa crossed to the bed to peer under the edge. Moby Dick stared back at her, blinked and began purring. The little faker. He was a flirt, pretending to be shy when guests arrived, then allowing them to coax him with treats.

He came out and head-butted her leg.

"How wonderful," Mrs. Canter exclaimed. "You have such a way with cats, Tessa. I knew he'd feel better if you reassured him."

Tessa dropped several treats on the ground, and Moby Dick gobbled them up. "We're old buddies. I wouldn't worry about him. He's...um, resourceful."

She'd almost said *manipulative*, but Mrs. Canter was one of those cat lovers who thought they were perfect angels without a devious bone in their bodies. Her twice-a-year visits to Poppy Gold had begun when Tessa was a teenager and Moby Dick was a tiny ball of white fur.

"How are *you* doing, Mrs. Canter?" Tessa asked. "I hope you didn't get shaken up too badly."

The elderly woman chuckled. "Goodness, I live in Tacoma, Washington. I've been through my share of earthquakes, including the Nisqually Quake in 2001. That one was a six point eight, and it cracked the foundation on my house."

"I've only been in minor quakes. Something that powerful must have been frightening."

Mrs. Canter shook her head. "Mostly I was annoyed when a plant upended over my computer keyboard. Potting soil *everywhere*. Fortunately the CPU was under the desk and got spared."

"That's good to hear. I have to go now, but I hope to see you again before you leave."

Out in the hallway, Tessa drew a deep breath.

She'd wanted to make some client phone calls that afternoon, but it might be best to continue making rounds and ensure everything was running smoothly.

CHAPTER FOUR

LANCE DIDN'T GET a chance to talk to Jamie until she finished her shift at 5:00 p.m. When she came out of Old City Hall, he pulled her close.

"I tried to find you after it happened," he said. "Tessa told me you were okay and asked me to report to Mrs. Murphy."

Jamie snuggled in. "I was with a school group."

"Were you scared?"

She tipped her head back and scrunched her nose. "Not really. We don't have many earthquakes around Glimmer Creek, but I was so busy telling the kids it was all right that I didn't think about it."

"Yeah. I got dizzy before it happened, but now I think it was a small tremor before the bigger quake."

Jamie looked worried. "What if it wasn't? You hit your head in the creek on Monday. What if you cracked your skull or something? You know my mom is a doctor and she could—"

"No," Lance interrupted.

He didn't want anything to do with a doctor...

especially if it was Jamie's mother and might involve X-rays or something. A few years ago, the school nurse had insisted he go to the emergency room after one of his "accidents," and they'd asked a bunch of questions. Knowing his foster father would be furious if he told the truth, Lance had lied about falling from a skateboard. After all, it wasn't as if they were going to do anything to keep the creep from knocking his foster kids around, so why make more trouble for himself?

"Please, Jamie, there's nothing wrong with me," he added, seeing hurt in her face.

She didn't understand; her family had asked all sorts of questions the few times they'd met, like what he wanted to do with his life and about his folks. The Fullertons were nice and didn't push when he gave them vague answers, but he wasn't stupid. "Nice" kids had families. If Jamie's parents learned he'd grown up in foster care and about the mess in Sacramento, they might say she had to stop seeing him.

"I just want to go sit by the creek. Okay, Jamie?"

She didn't mention it again, but she still seemed worried as she brushed his hair back from the sore spot on his forehead. It was nothing. He'd gotten worse than that a hundred times.

At the creek they sat down by the water, and he pulled a small box from his pocket. "I got something for you."

Jamie opened the box, and she brightened when she saw the bracelet with a miniature, silver, poppy flower charm attached. "I love it."

He helped her put it on, and she turned her wrist back and forth, admiring the bracelet, before kissing his cheek.

"It's perfect, but you don't have to keep buying me stuff."

"I like to."

"I like giving you presents, too," Jamie said. She reached into her pocket and handed him a bag from the gift emporium on the pedestrian shopping street. Inside was a new pair of sunglasses. "I hope they fit. I know you don't like wearing a hat."

"They're *awesome*."

Lance's chest ached as he put on the sunglasses. He'd hardly ever gotten presents growing up. Sometimes one of his foster mothers had given him a gift for his birthday or Christmas, but it would mostly be stuff she would have bought him anyhow, like a shirt or socks.

But Jamie gave him real presents, not even waiting for his birthday.

He gulped and kissed her.

The idea of losing Jamie was more than he could stand. Somehow he had to find a way to prove to her family that he wasn't a loser on a loud, beat-up motorcycle. They wanted her to go to college, not just take a few night courses the way she was doing now, so they'd never think a maintenance guy at Poppy Gold was good enough.

Jamie leaned against him as he tried to think of ways to make more money.

Poppy Gold paid him okay, and the Connors were the nicest people he'd ever met besides Jamie, but once the orchards got planted, would they be willing to have him do something else? Or would he need to find a way to start over again?

"THANKS, STEPHEN," TESSA said to the city building inspector after he'd given her an all-clear report on Poppy Gold's buildings.

"Wood-frame structures are fairly resilient in small quakes, but it doesn't hurt to check," he said earnestly.

She tried to keep from smiling. Stephen Seibert was an eager beaver—recently out of graduate school—and he relished any opportunity to employ his knowledge.

"Your concern is appreciated," she assured him.

He grinned and left, probably intent on continuing his efforts in the rest of Glimmer Creek.

Tessa had spent the afternoon talking to guests and employees to be sure they weren't worried about the earthquake. You never knew how people would react. A few of their out-of-state visitors had rattled nerves, but on the whole, everybody was calm.

At the end of the day she stepped out of Old City Hall and saw Gabe emptying a trash can in the park.

She sighed and walked over, wondering if she'd been too curt with him earlier.

"Hasn't your shift ended?" she asked.

"I looked at the maintenance checklist and saw a few things that didn't get done today because of the quake. So I told Liam I'd take care of the ones that were highest priority. I'm just finishing up."

"I appreciate it, but be sure to put in for overtime."

Gabe cleared his throat as she started to turn away.

"Tessa, why are the broken ceramic pots a big deal? They're just flowerpots."

She hesitated, unsure he'd understand how it hurt her father to lose anything connected to her mother. She'd never seen two people as close as her parents. They'd lived for each other, and that made it even harder to think about falling in love herself. How could anything live up to the standard her mom and dad had set? At the same time, she really wanted children. She knew she could do that on her own, but if possible, she wanted to give her kids a mom *and* a dad.

"I've mentioned that my mother designed the

gardens. She died unexpectedly a year and a half ago, and Pop is still struggling," Tessa said slowly, trying to ignore the empty sensation in her stomach. "He feels connected to Mom when he's surrounded by the things she loved, so when he found the pots were damaged, it was like losing another little part of her."

"You, too?"

"In a way. Have you ever lost someone who meant that much?"

"I saw death in the navy, but nobody close."

"I'm sure it's still hard to lose someone you've served with or were trying to help."

A strained expression flashed across Gabe's face and was gone so fast she couldn't guess the source. Despite the way he'd dismissed the deaths he'd seen, it seemed to her that few people were genuinely impervious to sorrow. They just pushed it down and refused to acknowledge it existed. Still, whatever pain Gabe might feel, he deserved his privacy.

"You were telling me about your mother," he prompted as he replaced the liner in the trash can he'd emptied.

"My mom got involved in everything, whether it was the church rummage sale or a campaign to buy new books for the library. It seemed impossible she could go so quickly. The whole town was in shock when she died. Everybody adored her."

GABE WAS WILLING to concede that many parents were better than his, but Tessa's mother must have had her share of faults, and putting her on a pedestal couldn't be productive.

It was just one of those strange things that happened with grief.

One of his men had lost his fiancée in a skiing accident, and after he returned from the funeral, he'd called her the most beautiful and talented woman in the world, along with a few other superlatives. He'd also seemed distracted and depressed and had spent a great deal of time reading his fiancée's Bible. Gabe had sent him to the base chaplain for counseling and then put him back on leave.

"How did your parents meet, anyway?" he asked, trying to keep his tone casual. It still seemed curious that Patrick Connor's son had ended up in a town like Glimmer Creek.

"After Pop got out of the army, he didn't want to go into the business right away, so his father sent him to Glimmer Creek to sell the family holdings here. A week after arriving, he met my mom at an ice-cream social, and it was love at first sight. They got married a month later."

"That sounds like the plot of one of those sappy made-for-TV Christmas movies," Gabe muttered, a second later realizing how rude he must have sounded.

Tessa's lips thinned, then she smiled. "It does,

doesn't it? We used to joke about it. Pop would say he wanted Tom Hanks to play him and Meg Ryan to play my mom."

"Did your mother have Meg Ryan's blond hair and blue eyes?"

"Yup, just like me. Only Mom was taller. I'm the shrimp in the family."

"I'm having trouble sorting out your relatives. They seem to be everywhere."

"That isn't surprising. My mom's side of the family is all over Glimmer Creek, and a lot of them work for us."

"But your *paternal* grandfather owned Poppy Gold?"

"That's tied up with the town's history and how Poppy Gold was originally called Connor's Folly. Glimmer Creek was a mining camp during the 1849 Gold Rush, and Seamus O'Connor, my great-great-something grandfather, got rich here."

Gabe tried to recall the California history he'd learned as a kid. "I thought most of the forty-niners barely found enough gold to buy food, much less become wealthy."

"Yeah." Tessa grinned. "That's because they were paying three dollars for a single egg and twenty-five dollars a pound for cheese. Seamus quickly realized he could earn more gold selling groceries to prospectors than by breaking his back panning for it. Eventually he sold supplies from Placerville to Sonora. Made a *fortune*, even by today's standards."

Gabe frowned. "Where does the folly come in?"

"Well, in the late 1880s Seamus dropped the *O* from the beginning of his last name and moved his base of operations to San Francisco. But his great-grandson, James Connor, was a huge believer in preserving cultural heritage...or at least the heritage of the family business. So during the Great Depression, James came back and bought the old part of Glimmer Creek, piece by piece, to preserve it."

"He was buying when everyone else was losing their shirts," Gabe mused.

"That's one way to look at it. James paid top dollar for the Victorians and remaining gold miners' cabins, along with two hotels, the concert hall, courthouse, stores and city hall. Heck, he even purchased the old 1851 jail. Basically, almost everything from the town's historical and cultural heyday. He couldn't get the library that Andrew Carnegie built for Glimmer Creek, but almost everything else went."

"Which is why the townspeople called it Connor's Folly," Gabe guessed.

"Yup, they laughed all the way to the bank. Even more after James bought the train station—trains had long since stopped running through the area. But he gave the town enough funds to build a new city center and modernize the water and sewer system, so Glimmer Creek thought it was worthwhile to relocate their operations."

"Generous of him."

Tessa nodded. "The way everybody saw it, James Connor spent a fortune on worthless land and buildings, and they got the money they needed to survive the Depression. Everybody was happy, though Glimmer Creek often worried that the Connors would eventually sell to developers."

"Which meant they were happy when your father fell in love with a local girl and decided to live here."

"Thrilled."

"So how many relatives do you have?"

"Quite a few, though on the Connor side it's just Pop and my grandparents in San Francisco. Mom, on the other hand, had nine brothers and sisters. Except for Uncle Kurt, all of them have three or more kids, as well. Most live around Glimmer Creek, along with great-aunts and great-uncles and all sorts of first and second cousins."

Gabe suspected that tracking Tessa's relatives could be a challenge. Rob had suggested asking her to help in the investigation, but she was still a suspect. Even if she wasn't guilty, it seemed as if half of Poppy Gold employees were her relatives—and statistics alone suggested that one of them *might* be involved in the information thefts from TIP. Being related to Tessa wouldn't necessarily keep them from seizing an opportunity to make illicit money.

And if *she* was responsible for the thefts, the damage to Poppy Gold Inns would be incalculable.

Before he could say anything else, Tessa straightened her shoulders. "I need to get going. As I said, be sure to put in for overtime. Thanks for your extra effort." Her brisk tone was reminiscent of Charlotte Angstrom's no-nonsense manner. "Have a good evening."

Gabe watched her walk away with wry acceptance, surprised he'd gotten her to talk as much as he had. He just wasn't the sort of guy who grew on people.

After signing out, he found Liam Connor in his office, gazing at a picture, oblivious to everything else. Recalling how the older man's hands had trembled while working on the roses, Gabe looked around, half expecting to see a bottle of whiskey or another alcohol of choice. He'd seen the same tremor in his mother's hands often enough.

"Is everything all right?" he asked finally.

Liam blinked and focused on him. "What? Yes, of course. I was just thinking about how much everything keeps changing, no matter how hard we try to keep it the same."

Gabe sat in one of the chairs and stretched out his legs. For the past few days they'd chatted for a long while after work and had even gone out to eat together, though he still hadn't asked the questions he wanted to ask. Maybe now was a good time.

"Do you miss managing Poppy Gold?" he asked.

"No. My…my wife mostly handled the business end. Things got a bit out of hand when I began running it alone. I considered selling, so Tessa quit her job in San Francisco to come back and take over."

Interesting. Did "out of hand" mean they'd had financial trouble? Yet even as the question formed in Gabe's mind, he dismissed it. Money problems could lead to bad decisions, but Poppy Gold still appeared quite prosperous.

"Tessa seems competent," he said. "She never seems to stop moving."

"She's been that way since she was little. Full of energy, just like her mother. She came up most weekends from San Francisco to help out, even before my wife…" His voice trailed, and pain filled his eyes.

Gabe thought about Liam's nickname for his daughter—Tessajinks. On the wall hung a photo of a mischievous-looking golden-haired toddler—presumably Tessa—who fit the cheeky name. Looking at it gave him an odd sensation.

His years in the service had carried him into every corner of the globe, and he'd encountered children in the worst circumstances. Injured, hungry, sometimes staring into space with blank eyes… His gut clenched, and he forced his thoughts away from the images he could never quite forget.

His cell phone rang, and he pulled it out, seeing his brother's name and number on the display. Talking to him would have to wait; Gabe turned the phone off and returned it to his pocket.

"Does Tessa hope to move back to San Francisco at some point?" he asked casually.

Liam seemed surprised by the question. "I don't think so. She always wanted to run Poppy Gold Inns one day, but after getting her MBA, she went to work for my father's company to gain management experience."

Gabe raised an eyebrow. "She couldn't do that here?"

"Of course. She just thought it would please her grandfather to spend time with him. He's getting on in years."

"He must have hoped she'd step into his shoes when he retired."

Liam let out a snort of laughter. "Patrick Connor will never retire. He enjoys empire building too much."

It didn't sound as if Liam got along any better with his father than Gabe did with his own. "Isn't Poppy Gold an empire?"

"Poppy Gold is modest by comparison to Connor Enterprises, but it doesn't matter. This is our home. After we started the bed-and-breakfast business, I discovered an interest in historical restoration, so that's been my primary focus. I'm grateful to *my* grandfather, James Connor, for preserving the old part of Glimmer Creek. Dad, of course, didn't feel the same. He felt it was a waste of money."

"So he agreed with calling it Connor's Folly."

"That's right. Once Dad was grown they would have arguments about keeping 'useless' property with so much expensive upkeep, though he didn't try selling until James was gone. Sadly, Grandad died in a boating accident soon after handing the company over."

"Maybe that's why your father doesn't believing in retiring."

This time a genuine laugh came from Liam. "Yup, he says it's dangerous. Mostly I think he's seen too many men of his generation retire and die of heart attacks within a year. It's a question of priorities. Don't define yourself by work, Gabe. Family is what matters."

"I'm not that close to my family. Most of them, anyway."

"Sorry to hear it."

Gabe checked his watch; Rob would be getting

impatient, wondering if something was wrong. "I wish I could stay, but I need to make a call."

"Of course. By the way, if you have navy friends who want to visit, they can stay in the John Muir Cottage. We keep it reserved for active service members, as well as veterans and military families going through a rough time. We might have to coordinate visits, but the house is separated into several different spaces, so a room is usually available."

"No."

Liam looked taken aback by the emphatic refusal, and Gabe was annoyed that he'd let down his guard. He didn't know *how* to define the members of his former SEAL team. They were men he'd trusted with his life more times than he could count. At the same time, he couldn't afford to disrupt his investigation.

"That is, I appreciate the offer," he added quickly, "but it isn't necessary. I don't know anyone who could get leave right now, and California is a long way from where they're stationed. It's good to know about the cottage, though. Do service members just ask to stay here?"

"Not exactly. It began with an old friend from the army. We stayed in touch after getting out, and Randall rose quickly through the ranks. When the wife of one of his men was ill and the family needed a break but couldn't afford to go anywhere, he called and asked if they could stay at Poppy Gold for a week. Everything evolved from there. We also get referrals for veterans having trouble finding jobs."

"That's nice." Gabe was impressed. A number of places offered discounts to the military, but Poppy Gold was going beyond that.

"It's the least we can do. Have a good evening, Gabe. Thanks for all the help today."

"Uh, sure." Both Liam and Tessa had a habit of thanking Poppy Gold employees for their work. Gabe was never certain how to respond since he was in Glimmer Creek with ulterior motives.

Back at his studio cottage, he quickly connected with Rob via Skype. "Sorry I didn't answer earlier, I was talking to Liam again," he explained.

"No problem. I understand there was a bit of excitement this afternoon."

"Minor quake, barely worth mentioning."

"Good to hear." Rob leaned closer to the camera on the computer. "I wanted to tell you that my research doesn't show any direct benefit to Connor Enterprises from any of the information leaks."

Gabe was unaccountably relieved, maybe because he didn't want to think Liam was guilty. "That's good. Did you find out who recommended Poppy Gold as a place for TIP's executive retreats?"

"It was through Poppy Gold promotional efforts. The personnel department says they kept getting brochures in the mail, stacks of them, and thought the place looked interesting. Then they got a phone call from the Poppy Gold marketing department, discussing the facility and amenities. It seems innocent enough."

"Except that TIP is an import-export company and the Connors are connected to a company in the same line of business. That's why I wanted to know how you started coming here. Coincidences bother me."

Rob shook his head. "You're still trying to pin this on Liam and Tessa?"

"I'm trying to pin it on whoever is guilty. There's a difference."

"Whatever. What have you discovered on your end?"

Gabe thought back to the last time he and his brother had spoken. "For one, I've learned more about why Tessa returned to Glimmer Creek, rather than staying in San Francisco."

"Anything questionable?" Rob asked.

"No. Tessa's mother died, and her father had trouble running the place alone. I also gather that Liam and his father are radically different."

"I'd say that was like you and Dad, except the two of you might be more alike than you realize."

"Not a snowball's chance," Gabe retorted. "It's okay to be a workaholic if you don't have a family."

"If you say so. What else?"

"I keep thinking that someone in Housekeeping or Maintenance could be our culprit. If one of those employees was found in a guest's rooms, it probably wouldn't be questioned. So I've got an idea for setting a trap."

Quickly he laid out his plan. A small group was coming for the supposed "executive retreat," and Rob had reserved one of the large mansions on one side of Poppy Gold. Gabe wanted his brother to request a last-minute change to a Victorian on the other side of the historic district. That way, the thief might reveal his or her identity by asking for a switch in work assignments. At the very least it would give Gabe someone to investigate.

In the past five days he'd mostly learned about two employees who seemed to be spending more than they earned, though he had to be careful about asking too many questions. He was also compiling a list of Poppy Gold staff from various posted work schedules and would soon have a private security firm do background checks.

"I'd have to come up with a good excuse. Even then, Tessa may not be able to accommodate us," Rob said at length.

"She'll try. From what I've seen, she's obsessed with client satisfaction."

"There's nothing wrong with that."

Gabe narrowed his eyes. His brother seemed

to offer a defense whenever he said something that might be critical of Poppy Gold's manager. "Hey, are you interested in Tessa? I hope not, because that could make things sticky."

Rob chuckled. "She's appealing, but I've got enough to think about without starting anything like that. How about you?"

"Give me a break. Anyway, I'm going to make a copy of the work assignments for when you're here and track any alterations."

"All right. Good night for now."

"Night."

Gabe disconnected. While he'd love to have already solved the case, he hadn't actually expected to learn much before his brother's visit to Poppy Gold. He'd just wanted to spend a few days getting familiar with the facility.

CHAPTER FIVE

ON TUESDAY MORNING Tessa raced into her office and grabbed the phone ringing on her desk. "Poppy Gold Inns," she answered.

"Hi, Tessa. It's Robert McKinley."

"Good morning, Rob. What can I do for you?"

"Well, one of my executives wants to bring her eleven-year-old daughter to the retreat. Normally I'd say no, but Kate is getting a divorce and Natalie is upset about it. The thing is, Natalie loves to swim and her mom doesn't want her at the pool when she's in planning meetings clear across Poppy Gold. I hate asking, but I need to switch our accommodations from the El Dorado Mansion to a house near the recreation area."

Tessa nearly dropped the phone. The weekend had been exceptionally hectic, and she'd just finished saying goodbye to Charlotte Angstrom and the Talmadge Guild Association members. She didn't need any more headaches. "You...uh, are going to be here in a few hours."

"I know, but the weather has been perfect, and it would be great to give Natalie a chance to swim. Naturally I'll pay any expense and surcharges involved. It would mean a lot to me if you could work it out."

Tessa tried not to hyperventilate. How could she refuse? "I'll see if the reservations can be shifted around. What if I can't get one of the Victorians exclusively for your group?"

"It wouldn't be ideal, but we'll work with whatever you can manage."

"Okay, I should know by the time you check in. I can already tell you there isn't another set of rooms available similar to the Joaquin Murrieta suite in the El Dorado. They're all occupied."

"That's okay. I appreciate whatever you can do. See you this afternoon."

Tessa hung up in disbelief.

How was she supposed to move TIP? With the exception of December, late spring and summer were their busiest seasons. They had two family reunions and a large destination wedding in progress, along with dozens of other guests who were either already checked in or due to arrive.

Still, TIP was one of her best repeat clients. The executive retreat this week was smaller than usual, but they'd given Poppy Gold a good deal of business over the past two years. It was worth bending over backward to accommodate them.

Dragging air into her lungs, she hurried to Old City Hall. She could access the reservation system from her office, but it would be easier to do it at the central hub. That way nobody could innocently book guests into rooms she was trying to clear.

"Morning, Aunt Polly," she said, sliding into one of the empty computer stations. She entered a command so no one else could make changes for the current week until she'd finished.

"What's up?"

"TIP wants to move across Poppy Gold to a house near the pool."

Polly blinked. "That's impossible. I know you don't like disappointing anyone, but they arrive today. You'll have to tell them it isn't feasible."

"I'm going to try. One of the execs is bringing her daughter and doesn't want to be so far away when she's swimming."

"We have a lifeguard."

"You'd feel the same if it was *your* kid."

Aunt Polly pressed her lips together and didn't say anything else.

An hour later Tessa finished shuffling reservations. She had a headache and crossed eyes, but she'd found a way to give TIP one of the Victorians closer to the recreation center.

She released control of the system and stretched.

"Done?" Polly asked.

"Done. I just have to move the courtesy fruit basket I put in the TIP president's suite over to the Tofton House."

Aunt Polly sniffed. "I'm not sure he deserves a fruit basket."

"Rob McKinley is a good client," Tessa said, keeping her tone mild. "And I'm sure he'll appreciate the effort."

"What does your grandfather think about TIP using Poppy Gold as their conference center?"

"He just laughed when I told him. Granddad doesn't worry about rivals."

Tessa drove to the El Dorado in one of Poppy Gold's electric golf carts, hoping to get everything moved before their new guests arrived. It wasn't a huge job. Rob had ordered bottles of a special California wine to be placed in each of the rooms, and she needed to retrieve the basket she'd put in his suite earlier.

Upstairs she collected the wine and left it on the front landing before climbing to the private third-floor suite Rob had used on each of his visits to Poppy Gold. She adjusted one of the chairs and made a face; the Joaquin Murrieta suite was lovely and she doubted he'd be as pleased with the new one.

Tessa was headed downstairs when the step abruptly collapsed beneath her right foot, pitching her forward against the railing. An ominous crack sounded, and an involuntary shriek escaped her as the balustrade lurched outward with the force of her fall.

For a moment she dangled in the air over the

open landing, clinging to a length of the polished wood. The next thing she knew, she was sprawled on the floor below.

As soon as she could breathe again, she let loose a string of curses that would have made a longshoreman proud. She wasn't seriously hurt, but she was going to be sore for a while.

This just wasn't her day.

GABE WAS ELATED that his plan seemed to be working. Poppy Gold's employee grapevine was excellent, and he'd heard that Tessa was arranging for the TIP executives to be moved to another location. He'd been certain she would jump through hoops to accommodate Rob's request, and his confidence appeared to be justified.

The radio fastened to his belt let out a burst of static, followed by a report that Tessa needed Maintenance for repairs at the El Dorado Mansion. It was Polly Murphy, and she sounded unusually stressed. He called the dispatcher, saying he'd go. It was almost amusing to see Tessa's expression each time he showed up.

"Tessa?" he called as he opened the front door.

"Up here."

He found her on the floor in the upstairs hallway, toward the back of the house, clutching an elbow and glaring at the smashed fruit scattered around her.

"My God, what happened?"

She pointed, and he saw part of the stair railing hanging precariously over the scene. The rest was nearby, along with a number of the support posts.

"The step tipped, the railing broke and I went flying."

"Hell."

"My sentiments exactly."

She started to get up, but he put a hand on her shoulder, only to see her wince.

"Stay down for a minute." Gabe had advanced first-aid training and checked her quickly. Her elbow would be badly bruised, but she hadn't hit her head, and her other injuries were remarkably minor considering the height of the fall. "It looks like nothing is broken."

"Mostly my dignity is wounded, though my fanny isn't too happy at the moment, either."

The corners of his mouth twitched. "Yeah. Where did all the fruit come from?"

Tessa made a face and shifted, pulling a squashed orange from under her. "This *was* a courtesy basket for the president of Thomas International Products. I was taking it over to the Tofton House."

"I heard they asked to be moved," Gabe said casually. He wondered what, if anything, Tessa would say about the request. "It must have been hard to juggle the reservations with such short notice."

"I managed. Though now I'll need to find new

rooms for the people I moved into this building. We can't have anyone stay here with it looking like this."

"I'm sure someone else can take care of shifting reservations."

A stubborn expression crossed her face, but she didn't say anything. He was helping her into a chair when a horrified exclamation came from behind them.

"Tessa."

"I'm fine, Pop."

Liam's skin was ashen and Gabe gave him a reassuring look. "No need to worry. Tessa was just explaining she had a sore f—"

"Gabe," she interrupted with a glare. Obviously she didn't want him talking about her bruised tailbone with her father.

"Honestly, it's all right," Gabe assured. "All those peaches and grapes broke her fall."

"I see." The color began returning to Liam's face. "That's lucky."

"Yeah. Why don't you take Tessa to your office and call the building inspector, while I handle the mess and evaluate repairs?"

Tessa frowned. "Do you think this was connected to the earthquake? We've had guests in the Murrieta suite on Friday and Saturday, and I was up there earlier this morning."

"You never know."

She stood gingerly, and her father put an arm

around her waist. Gabe's attention was torn between his desire to check the stairs and keeping an eye on their cautious progress down the hallway. After all, the inspector would likely be looking for earthquake damage, while Gabe would be checking for any signs of sabotage. It might just be his suspicious nature, but it seemed odd that the private staircase would collapse the day Rob was supposed to arrive. Still, Tessa was moving very uncomfortably. A split second later, he strode after her and Liam.

Over her protests, he carried her downstairs and put her on the passenger seat of the electric golf cart he'd left near the house.

"Take it easy," he urged, patting Liam's arm. The man looked more rattled than his daughter. "Everything is fine unless you run over a jaywalking gopher."

"That isn't funny," Tessa snapped, only to scrunch her nose. "Sorry. Maybe I broke something after all…like my funny bone."

Gabe grinned as he went back inside. Tessa Connor had grit; few people could have taken a plunge like that without throwing a well-deserved scene. He took the steps up from the ground floor three at a time, any lingering humor fading. Rob had described the El Dorado and the staircase where Tessa had fallen led to the private suite normally assigned to his brother.

It bothered him.

A lot.

He checked the damage, recalling that Tessa had mentioned all the buildings had been reinforced a few years back. The Poppy Gold Victorians were old, but they were well maintained and regularly inspected.

What about the earthquake?

Tessa's thoughts had gone there instantly, but Gabe had his doubts. The quake had been minor, unlikely to break wood or yank out nails. But if it was sabotage, was it necessarily intended for Rob? Industrial sabotage and assault were pretty far apart.

Regardless, he immediately called his brother to explain what had happened.

"Is Tessa okay?" Rob asked.

"Only banged up, though she'll be sore for a few days. Just be careful. I can't tell for certain this was done deliberately, but if it *was* deliberate, you could have been the target. The only reason Tessa was up there again this morning was to move a fruit basket to your new room. Otherwise, you would have been the next one on that staircase. I understand it's a private staircase to the suite that Housekeeping doesn't even use."

"It sounds as if Tessa was lucky."

Something in his brother's tone made Gabe frown. "Is there something you aren't telling me?"

"Er...well, I've gotten a few letters the past week."

A stillness went through Gabe, reminiscent of whenever he'd been in a critical moment of a mission. It was as if time slowed down, letting him think around different sides of a problem to determine the best move. "What *kind* of letters?"

"Anonymous letters with implied threats. I knew you'd overreact, and it isn't as if I haven't gotten them before. It's nothing like Dad's old hate file, which basically filled a whole room."

"What about the postmarks?"

Rob hesitated before answering. "They're from different towns in the San Joaquin Valley."

"Within an easy drive of Glimmer Creek?"

"I suppose."

Gabe cursed. "Go back to that FBI agent and show him everything. And call the police. At least the letters are concrete evidence."

"I'm already at the airport. I'll take care of it when I get back to Los Angeles. But there's nothing to connect the letters to industrial espionage. Personal threats and illegal profiteering are a long way apart."

"Agreed, but it's a pretty big coincidence to get them from a location near Glimmer Creek."

"Coincidences happen a lot more often than you think, big brother. And I don't want to be paranoid. All we have is suspicion."

Gabe eyed the break in the stair railing. "Nev-

ertheless, keep your guard up. It's best to be prepared, and we don't want an innocent bystander
to get caught into this, either." He heard someone walking down the hallway. "I'll have to talk
to you later. *Be careful.*"

Gabe dropped the phone in his pocket as a
young man appeared. "Hello."

"I'm Stephen Seibert, the Glimmer Creek
building inspector." He seemed flustered, an
expression that turned to horror when he saw
the piece of railing that hung over the landing.

"I thought the buildings were safe," he exclaimed. "The earthquake was minor, and I did
an inspection."

"It could have just gotten worse in the few
days since the quake. House settling, that sort
of thing."

"Yes, of course." Stephen's eyes focused. He
began examining the staircase from the bottom
up, breaking his concentration only to bark,
"Don't touch that," when he thought Gabe might
shift the debris.

The reminder didn't annoy Gabe, even though
he hadn't intended to touch anything except the
scattered bits of fruit. The inspector was young,
but he appeared to know what he was doing. He
could be hoping to cover something up, such as
a failure in his own procedures, except there was
nothing in his face or gestures to suggest subter-
fuge. In all, he was fairly easy to read.

Unlike Tessa.

Gabe had received training on analyzing facial cues and body language. Certain expressions were involuntary, even when someone was trying to hide emotions. Still, Tessa's complicated reactions could be nothing more than her attempt to conceal her dislike for him, Gabe thought wryly.

"What do you think?" he asked Stephen after gathering the fruit in the damaged basket, along with the note to his brother on Poppy Gold's letterhead. It was a nasty reminder that it could have been Rob he'd found lying on the floor.

"It's difficult to say. There are breaks in the wood at stress points, which might occur in a quake. I'd have to get seismology reports along with plat maps and the building plan to evaluate…" Stephen's voice trailed and Gabe got the feeling there was something bothering him.

"Is that necessary for an accident?" Gabe asked casually.

Stephen seemed to shake himself. "I just want to be thorough."

TESSA WAS STILL reassuring her father that she didn't need to see a doctor when Great-Uncle Milt arrived.

"Hey, Uncle Milt," she said without surprise. Milton Fullerton had been the Glimmer Creek police chief since before she was born. Her mother had always claimed he possessed a sense of responsibility the size of Texas, so it wasn't unusual that he'd come to check on her.

"Hey, kiddo. I just found out your fall. How are you doing? That was a nasty drop."

Tessa shot her great-uncle a warning glance as her father tensed. "I'm *fine*," she returned firmly. "And the drop wasn't that far. I fell against the railing. It swung out, and I dangled for a minute before it broke, too. Luckily my toes weren't that far above the floor at that point."

"I see. I went over and took a look. No sign of rot in the wood. Any ideas about what happened?"

"None. I went up to the Murrieta suite early this morning and would have sworn the steps were solid." She frowned. "Though come to think of it, there might have been a creak that I haven't heard before. I was distracted and should have checked it out."

"You can't blame yourself. It's just strange that both the stair and railing gave way at the same time. But I suppose the structure could have been weakened with the earthquake and it took a couple of days to show up."

"That's what I've been telling her," Liam asserted. "As soon as I get Tessa home and into bed, I'm checking all the buildings myself again."

"I'm not going to bed—I have work to do," Tessa asserted. "First at Old City Hall and then at my office."

"It can wait."

"No, it can't. Besides, I'd feel like an idiot going to bed after something so minor." Actually, she'd give anything to crawl into bed or a warm bath, but it was important for her father to believe she was back to normal.

"Tessa—"

"Pop," she mimicked back. "It's okay, though I'll accept a ride to Old City Hall."

"All right," he agreed reluctantly. "But I'll leave the cart for you to use. Better yet, call when you want to go back your office or somewhere else. I'll come or send someone else."

"Uh...fine." She'd almost told him to be sure *not* to send Gabe McKinley. Her reservations about Gabe kept growing. He was attractive, resourceful, hardworking...and more cynical than anyone she'd ever met. Reading him was like trying to read a boulder.

"Are you really okay, kiddo?" Great-Uncle Milt asked softly, his blue eyes full of concern. He was a tall man, with a thick head of white hair and a youthful face that belied his age.

"Everybody needs to stop fussing. I just have a couple of bruises."

"You got off darned easy."

Tessa looked at her father, who was talking on the phone. "I realize that," she replied quietly.

Great-Uncle Milt hugged her gently, and she sighed. He was the kind of man everyone depended upon, and she'd cried on his shoulder often in the week after her mother's death. But ever since then, she'd tried to keep her grief hidden to avoid upsetting her father.

Pop had enough to handle without dealing with her heartbreak, too.

TWO HOURS LATER Gabe wasn't surprised to hear Tessa had returned to work in her office, or that she'd personally juggled the reservations once again to move all guests from the El Dorado Mansion.

He'd gotten to work early, so he was able to sign out and head for the train depot. The sun was shining, the grass was green and the flowers were in full bloom. The place was like a Norman Rockwell painting, complete with a white bandstand. But he wasn't sure anything had ever been that innocent. In all honesty, he didn't know *what* to make of Glimmer Creek, though he figured the usual unpleasantness was going on behind their doors.

He'd grown up in the city; small towns were almost as foreign as the remote locations the navy had sent him to over the years. They hadn't been the sort of places to engender faith in humanity, mostly hot spots where people were doing terrible things to each other.

Gabe pushed the thought from his head. He couldn't erase the things he'd seen, but he'd done a small amount of good during his career, no matter how foul the memories might be.

He ran up the steps and knocked on Tessa's office door. "Come in," she called.

A curious blend of emotions crossed her pale face when she saw him. "Hi, Gabe. Thanks for the help earlier."

"No problem."

He carefully closed the door behind him, and her eyebrows shot upward. "Something up?"

"My shift is over, and I wanted to ask a few questions about what happened. But I don't want to risk your father coming in. He didn't look good when he saw you'd fallen."

"Pop worries about me."

"Yeah. I wanted to ask if you went upstairs on the inside or the outside of the steps."

She blinked in apparent surprise. "On the inside."

"Makes sense," he said absently. "People generally follow rules of the road, even when they aren't driving. Even when they're alone. Always stay to the right—road, sidewalk, staircase."

"I'm also right-handed. I broke my ankle a few years ago and prefer holding the rail." Tessa lifted her right hand, only to wince. Her elbow had swollen and was turning blue. "Guess I'll be going up and down on the left for a while. But you already knew I hold the railing with my right hand, didn't you?"

"Yeah. I noticed when we inspected after the earthquake."

"That's an odd thing to notice."

"The navy taught me to be an observer."

Tessa smiled enigmatically. "Is that so? What sort of work did you do?"

"I was in Special Forces, though it isn't something I enjoy talking about," he said. "But the reality is that anyone stationed in the Middle East needs to be vigilant about their surroundings. By the way, I hope nobody was staying in the El Dorado last night. I didn't see anyone around after you fell."

Her lips pressed together, then relaxed. "Actually, the whole house was reserved for the night. Seven couples, plus eight teenagers, who each wanted separate rooms. But they were no-shows."

"Whoa. Does that happen often?"

She tossed her pen on the desk, only to wince at the movement. "Not usually, but it isn't unheard of. Cancellations are required by three in the afternoon, though we're lenient when there's a good reason. The couples were caravanning as a group, and the reservations were held with the same credit card. Nobody called and the charges for all the rooms were run at midnight."

"I see."

"Gabe, why are you so curious? You're in maintenance, not security."

"It's just a habit, left over from my navy days. Poppy Gold is fortunate that it wasn't a guest who fell on that staircase. You must be glad you won't have a lawsuit on your hands, especially with all your safety checks," he said, figuring the comment would distract her.

Anger flashed in Tessa's eyes. "Of *course* I'm glad it wasn't a guest. Or an employee. I'd hate for anyone to get hurt, but not because of a lawsuit. Poppy Gold is a family, and we take care of family."

Curiously, Gabe believed her. Concern about possible tort claims didn't mean businesspeople lacked compassion for injured clients or employees, but it was a reality of the modern world.

"It must help that so many of your employees actually *are* family."

"I won't apologize for that," Tessa said evenly. "We'd have a hard time staffing Poppy Gold if we didn't hire relatives. But everybody is considered for promotions, irrespective of their filial connection."

"Even maintenance guys who tick you off?"

Understanding seemed to dawn in her face. "I get it. You want to work on the security team, don't you? That's why you asked those questions the day you started. Why didn't you apply for a security job to begin with? If you were in Special Forces, you probably have the skills we need."

Gabe shrugged. He still couldn't apply for a

job with Poppy Gold security, even if there *was* an opening. As a former navy SEAL, he'd be a viable candidate for a position, but he was even more convinced that the extensive background checks would reveal his connection to Rob and TIP. He'd seen the application; it was thorough and included a warning that applicants were rigorously screened.

"I needed a break," Gabe said, "with work that's less intense than what I used to do in the navy. But I can't help springing into action mode when something happens. Analyzing a situation and asking questions is instinctive at this point."

Tessa nodded. "Working outdoors is healing, but if you change your mind about applying for a security position, be as specific as possible about your skills and training on the application."

"Of course."

She shifted in her chair, plainly in physical discomfort, and regret went through Gabe. He hated thinking she may have been caught in a trap that had been set for Rob. He needed to find out more about the letters his brother had received, not to mention yell at him for keeping them to himself.

Maybe Rob was right and he should have been honest with the Connors from the beginning. They could have worked together with local law enforcement to catch the culprit, though it was hard to see the Glimmer Creek police force being *that* effective in uncovering an industrial spy.

His head began to churn with all the possibilities. Supposedly hindsight was twenty-twenty, but not in this case. He *hadn't* told Tessa or Liam, and now he would have to deal with their reactions once they learned the truth. And that was even presuming they were innocent, which his instincts told him they were. After all, if Tessa was responsible for the damage to the stairs, she hardly would have forgotten and taken them herself.

CHAPTER SIX

THE PHONE ON Tessa's desk rang. Caller ID showed the call was from Guest Registration, and she picked up the receiver, keeping a careful eye on Gabe. Everything he'd said made sense, but she was still unsure how she felt about him.

"Tessa Connor," she answered.

"It's me," said Aunt Polly. "You wanted to be notified when the TIP president arrived. He's being driven to the Tofton House now."

"How about the wine and the replacement fruit basket?" Tessa hadn't found the energy to move the bottles herself and had asked Aunt Polly to arrange it. Aunt Polly was a shift manager, but in many ways she was also a de facto assistant manager, keeping an eye on everything and willing to step in whenever Tessa wasn't available.

"The wine has been moved, and a runner from Sarah's Sweet Treats just brought the new fruit basket to Reception. I'll have someone make the delivery right away."

"I'll deliver it myself. See you in a few minutes."

Tessa pocketed the envelope addressed to Rob and stood carefully, her bruised muscles protesting.

"Sorry, I have to go now," she told Gabe politely.

He observed her slow progress around the desk. "I'd better drive you."

The offer reminded Tessa that her father had asked her to call for a driver if she wanted to go somewhere.

"Fine," she agreed. "I need to stop at Old City Hall and then go to the Tofton House."

She made her way to the first floor, painfully conscious of Gabe by her side. He'd carried her down the steps at the El Dorado, which had annoyed her on two fronts. For one thing, she wasn't a damsel in distress, and for another... every cell in her body had gone on alert. However irritating and cynical, he was a sexy guy who oozed masculine heat. She disliked responding to him that way, though it wasn't surprising considering her social life had been on hold for over a year.

Guests were wandering around the depot; some were looking at the historical displays, while others pretended to wait for a train, picnic baskets in hand. The recorded sound of an old steam engine grew louder, and a whistle reverberated through the waiting area. Poppy Gold had even installed a device to send vibrations through the floor, simulating the arrival of a passenger train.

Tessa paused, loving the excitement on everyone's faces. Several small groups with picnic baskets or pails got up, chattering about their upcoming "destination." Usually even the most jaded tourists were delighted by the modifications, and train buffs were over the moon.

Gabe insisted she stay in the electric cart while he fetched the basket in Old City Hall. A moment later he strode out and deposited it in the cargo area, then drove across Poppy Gold.

"You're quiet. Is something wrong?" he asked as he parked in front of the Tofton House.

"Just debating the right thing to do."

"Meaning?"

"Nothing you need to worry about."

He helped her down and grabbed the basket. Tessa was secretly grateful; walking was painful, and it would be worse carrying something. She tucked the envelope from her pocket between two peaches. They found Robert McKinley in the front parlor. He was looking through a stack of papers, and she smiled when he looked up.

"Welcome back to Poppy Gold," she said.

"It's good to see you, Tessa. Are you all right? You seem pale."

She swallowed. "I'm fine. I just had a little accident earlier."

"Are you certain nothing is wrong? Falls can be very serious."

Gabe cleared his throat as Tessa frowned thoughtfully. She hadn't mentioned falling and doubted the employees at Guest Registration would have, either.

"I have a few bruises, that's all." She took the basket from Gabe with her left hand and passed it to Rob. "I apologize this wasn't in your room when you arrived. Please let us know if there's anything we can do to make your visit better."

"Thank you. We always enjoy coming to Poppy Gold."

His face looked more strained than usual. Tessa had gotten the feeling on his last trip that something was bothering him, and the impression came back stronger now. It was possible he was considering going to another conference center, but presidents of major companies didn't hesitate when making that kind of decision, no matter how personable they might be. If it happened, it happened. She just didn't want it to be because of poor service.

They shook hands, and she left with Gabe, still musing about what might be going on with the TIP president.

"OHMIGOSH, DID YOU hear what happened to Tessa?" Jamie asked when she met Lance in front of the ice-cream shop after her shift.

"Yeah, but she's okay. I saw her at Maintenance."

Jamie felt awful. Except for Aunt Meredith, the only other member of the family who'd died was Uncle Tate; he'd been killed in the navy when she was little. She hated to think about something happening to Tessa, too.

"Uncle Milt came over and checked things," she murmured. "He even talked to the housekeeper about when the rooms were cleaned and if anyone noticed anything weird. It's almost as if they think something is strange about the accident."

"Who'd wanna hurt Tessa?"

"Nobody, I guess. Did Uncle Milt talk to you?"

Lance's face tightened. "Why would he talk to me?"

"I just wondered. Why are you getting defensive?"

"Well, he didn't. I'm going. I have to wash my clothes."

She put her hand on his arm. "I could help or do them for you."

"That's okay—I can handle it. I'll see you tomorrow."

Frustration filled Jamie as he walked away. It was as if he thought she'd accused him of doing something wrong, but she'd never do that. Great-Uncle Milt had talked to a *bunch* of people, including her, even though she hadn't gone into the El Dorado Mansion since they'd moved her from

Housekeeping to Guest Services. He was just being careful; everybody was saying the earthquake had caused the problem with the staircase, especially with Great-Uncle Milt telling everyone to inspect their own homes for hidden damage.

Jamie straightened the sleeve on her costume. She'd hoped to share a Gold Miner's Special with Lance at the soda parlor…coffee ice cream topped with hot fudge, toasted almonds and whipped cream. But it wouldn't be any fun without him, and she shouldn't be eating so much, anyhow.

She turned and viewed her reflected profile in the window. The costume was pretty, but no matter what her dad or Tessa or Lance said, she was sort of round and soft and unfinished, like she hadn't finished growing up. It was fine for everyone to claim she was a late bloomer, but eighteen seemed awfully late to bloom.

She saw her dad's father, Grandpa George, turn the corner. "Hey, Grandpa."

"You look awfully serious, darling," he said, kissing her forehead. "You must need an ice-cream cone."

"Maybe a diet soda," Jamie said, thinking about her reflection in the window.

He shuddered. "I can't abide fake sweeteners. Have cold milk instead."

Jamie wanted to laugh. Grandpa George was

tall and thin like Great-Uncle Milt and didn't need to worry about counting calories.

"Where's that young man of yours?" Grandpa George asked when they were standing in line at the counter.

"He had stuff to do. You know, laundry and all."

They moved to the front of the line, and the cashier gave them a smile. "May I help you, Pastor Fullerton?"

Everybody knew Grandpa George because he was the preacher at the community church.

"I'll have a double scoop of roasted almond mocha on a waffle cone. How about you, Jamie? My treat."

Jamie debated and finally said she'd take a single scoop of lemon sherbet. Maybe she should start using the employee gym. That might help. She could go before work, then shower and change in the locker room. That way she wouldn't miss any time with Lance.

She and Grandpa George walked down the street licking their cones. Several visitors took pictures, exclaiming over how cute her costume looked. It *was* great. Whenever she worked at the train depot doing living history, she wore one of the travel costumes, with her hair piled high and a fancy hat perched on top of her head.

"Mom doesn't approve of Lance," she murmured.

"I'm not so sure about that. Daniel tells me

that Lance is respectful, and I understand he's hardworking."

"He is," she agreed eagerly. "Uncle Liam says he's never seen anyone work so hard."

"What does his family do?"

"Uh...I don't know. He doesn't talk about his childhood that much." Jamie didn't want to mention that she thought things hadn't been very nice when Lance was growing up. Not that he'd complained or told her anything, but that was partly why she thought so. He never talked much about family or friends, even when she asked, and he didn't want to go back to Sacramento. *Ever.*

She wasn't sure what it meant if Lance didn't care about anybody where he'd lived most of his life. What if he decided he'd had enough of Glimmer Creek and wanted to go somewhere else? Would he leave and not look back, the way he'd left Sacramento? Jamie thought he loved her, and he'd talked about taking care of her, but sometimes talk was just talk.

"What *do* you and Lance chat about, then?" Grandpa asked.

She licked a drip of lemon sherbet. "Mostly about Poppy Gold or the things we're going to do one day. He wants to make it big so he can take care of me."

"Hmm. I don't know how a modern gal like you puts up with him. That's a very old-fashioned boy."

"It takes one to know one." Jamie tossed her cone in a trash can and hooked elbows with her grandfather. "What is Grandma making for the ice-cream social on Saturday? Mom is making blackberry pie and vanilla ice cream."

"Trying to change the subject?"

"Uh-huh." She'd love to confide in someone, but things were too mixed up right now.

In the past she'd gone to Aunt Meredith or called Tessa, but Aunt Meredith was gone and Tessa was busy with Poppy Gold; it didn't seem fair to load any other problems on her.

LANCE WALKED FOR over an hour. The long grass covering the hillsides was already turning golden in the unseasonable heat, but this late in the day it wasn't as hot. He even looked for dried-up cow patties to kick, but he didn't see any. Finding a big heap of gold would fix a bunch of problems.

He shouldn't have gotten uptight with Jamie. It wasn't her fault that he didn't like having policemen ask questions. The stuff in Sacramento was still on his record, and if the Glimmer Creek cops found out about it, who knew what they'd do? To some people, being accused of something was almost the same as being guilty. Heck, his boss at the restaurant had *fired* him because of it. He'd made an excuse, but Lance had overheard him talking to one of the waitresses, saying, "Where there's smoke, there's fire."

Finally Lance headed back into town to do his laundry. Digging rocks and holes and other stuff was dirty, sweaty work, so there was always a lot to wash. There were two washing machines available for the tenants of Glimmer Cottages, and he pushed everything into the first one.

"Hello, Lance."

The voice was so startling that he jumped and his knee whacked the machine. He spun around and automatically straightened. "Uh, hello, Mr. McKinley."

"It's Gabe." Gabe put an armload of clothes into the other washer and pulled money from his pocket. "You were deep in thought. Is something bothering you?"

"Just stuff with my girlfriend."

"Women can be trouble."

"I suppose. You were in the navy, weren't you?"

Gabe poured detergent into the tub and fed coins into the slots to start the machine. "Twenty years. I enlisted on my eighteenth birthday."

"Did you make good money? I mean, like, enough for a wife and stuff?"

"Can't say since I never had one. Are you thinking about getting married?"

"Someday. Jamie is pretty special." Lance started his own washer. "I bet you earn more as an officer," he said, rather than asking what he really wanted to know—why Gabe had taken early retirement. The guy was intimidating. Nobody could get away with pushing him around. Even though he was new, the other men in Maintenance already respected him.

"Sure, officers are in higher pay grades. Do you want to enlist?"

"Naw, just curious. I'd probably get seasick." Enlisting sounded good, but Lance wasn't sure if the navy would feel the same way as his old boss at the restaurant did. It might be okay if he knew how things worked, but he didn't, and he'd have to *tell* someone what had happened to find out.

"There are ways to deal with motion sickness, and the navy can use people with a variety of skills," Gabe said. "I've noticed you work on your motorcycle. Mechanical ability is useful in the service."

"I guess. Did you hear about Tessa falling today? Jamie was awfully upset about it." Lance wasn't sure why he'd mentioned the subject, especially since it was partly why he'd gotten weird with her.

Gabe's eyes narrowed. "I got to the El Dorado Mansion soon after it happened. It was just one of those things."

"But she isn't hurt bad, right?"

"A little bruised, is all. Wasn't that included in the scuttlebutt going around?"

"Scuttlebutt?"

"Gossip. That's what we call it in the navy."

"Oh. I asked because Jamie was still worried. Nobody would want to hurt Tessa, would they? I mean, like someone who works at Poppy Gold." Lance didn't know why he was pushing, but there was something odd about Gabe's expression.

Gabe frowned. "An unhappy employee? I doubt it, though anything is possible. The Connors are decent employers and I haven't heard that anyone has a grudge against them."

"Me, either," Lance agreed, feeling relieved. "And I'm sure Jamie would have told me if she'd heard anything. She says Tessa is more like her sister than a cousin."

"Yeah." Gabe checked his watch. "I'd better get going—I need to make a phone call."

"Should I put your load in the dryer when it's done?"

"Sure. Take this." Gabe gave him a handful of quarters. "Let me know if you have more questions about the navy. It's a good career, Lance."

Lance nodded. "Thanks."

When he was alone, he carefully counted the change Gabe had given him and put it in his pocket, then jumped onto the washing machine to sit and wait for his clothes to finish. He probably didn't need to stay, but back in the city he hadn't dared leave anything at the Laundromat, or else it got stolen. Of course, he didn't think Gabe McKinley needed to worry about replacing a few ratty shorts and T-shirts. The guy drove a brand-new SUV that was loaded with extras like leather seats.

After a while both machines started spinning.

A deep sigh came from Lance's gut.

He'd gotten used to spending his free time with Jamie after work and it was lonely without her. Being alone wasn't new; he'd always been alone. But until he'd met Jamie, he'd never had anyone who truly cared about him, either.

"YOU DON'T NEED to say it," Rob announced when he answered Gabe's call. "I nearly blew your cover with Tessa. I'm sorry."

"Yeah, well, you may be right that I should have told her the truth from the beginning and asked her to work with us. If she'd believed us, she could have easily gotten the local police involved. It turns out that she's the police chief's great-niece."

"There's no time like the present."

Gabe's jaw hardened. "Don't quote Dad to me."

A sigh came through the phone. "I'm not quoting Dad, I'm quoting Grandmother Ada. I saw her a good deal after she moved back from Boston."

"Then Dad was quoting her."

"Something like that. I know you don't want to believe it, but he's changed."

"Mostly because he divorced Mom and remarried," Gabe added. Their parents had finally gone their separate ways, but David McKinley had simply exchanged work for other obsessions—parasailing and pretending he was the same age as his twentysomething second wife. "Did you get the email suggesting we call him Dave now?"

"That may have been Shellie's idea."

Shellie was their "stepmother." She was a blonde dingbat who lived in bikinis and probably didn't know the difference between a prenuptial agreement and a battleship. On the other hand, she was pleasant and seemed genuinely fond of her husband.

"Do you honestly think she cares what Dad's grown sons call him?"

Rob chuckled. "I just know she makes him happy."

"Yeah, and meeting her convinced him to retire and let you run the company without interference. But back on the important subject, a kid working in Maintenance asked if someone might have a grudge against Tessa."

"Change your mind about me being the target?"

"I'm considering options, that's all. That's a private staircase to the suite. Tessa's pattern is predictable—she personally delivers all courtesy baskets for her group clients. The step could have been intended to collapse on her first visit this morning and just happened to do it the second time. Maybe the vandal got lucky that you asked for the switch."

"You have the jolliest ideas."

Gabe moved restlessly around his small studio cottage. "I'm just keeping an open mind, despite the hate mail you received. Tessa used to work at her grandfather's company, and I'm sure Patrick Connor has more than his share of enemies. She may even have made a few of her own when she was in San Francisco."

His brother didn't say anything for a long moment. "I don't remember you being this pessimistic about people when we were kids."

Gabe's mouth tightened. Tessa had accused him of cynicism, and now his brother was calling him pessimistic. He didn't see it either way, though the criticism wasn't new. "Ask Mom if I've changed," Gabe advised his brother. "I tried tough love a few times when she was drunk, and she called me a coldhearted monster like Dad."

There was another long silence. "At least you had the guts to try. I slept at a friend's house whenever she'd had too much."

The old regret went through Gabe that he hadn't been there enough for his brother. Early in his career, while stationed in Virginia, he'd asked if Rob could spend his last year in high school back East with him, but his parents had refused, still bitter that their eldest son had enlisted instead of doing what they'd wanted him to do.

Gabe's mother remained angry, though she seemed to have stopped drinking and was living in Arizona in an exclusive housing development on a golf course.

"Does Mom bother you much these days?" he asked.

"She calls once in a while, usually when she wants money. She's hoping to enter a senior golf tournament. Do you want me to give her your cell number?"

"Perish the thought. You don't have to talk to her, either, and you certainly shouldn't be giving her money. I'm sure she got plenty in the divorce."

"Still trying to protect me? I'm all grown up now, you know."

"It's a habit," Gabe muttered. The *only* reason he was at Poppy Gold, pretending to know something about petunias and lawn mowers, was because he was still trying to take care of his little brother. Would he always feel guilty for leaving Rob alone with their parents?

He shook himself.

"Anyway, about the staircase," he said, "I'm not rejecting any possibility. I'll tell you something interesting, though… A group was supposed to check into the El Dorado Mansion last night. But they didn't show or call to cancel."

"It would have offered the opportunity to rig the stairs."

"That's what I think." Gabe frowned. "Why didn't you tell me about those letters as soon you started getting them?"

"Because there's nothing unusual about the president of a large, international company getting hate mail. If we import a product that's also made in the United States, somebody accuses me of *not* supporting American workers. If a food product isn't organic, I get letters saying I'm poisoning children. There are a lot of people out there, with a lot of opinions."

"But TIP makes every effort to import fair-trade products."

"Doesn't matter. Are you warning Tessa, too?"

"I'm going over again tonight, and I'll look for a way to suggest staying on her guard. But when I get a chance I may also talk with the Glimmer Creek police chief. He's already suspicious about what happened—he was questioning employees right and left today, which will probably make the culprit hunker down for a little bit. Nonetheless, be alert and careful."

"Local police involvement might be best, though they may feel the same way about the lack of evidence as the FBI."

"Threatening letters are evidence, so I need copies."

"When I get home. They're in my office safe."

Gabe got off, wishing he could find out who had reserved the mansion for the night. The name on the credit card might give him a jump in his investigation, but getting the information from Tessa was bound to be a challenge. On the other hand, it was most likely a case of identity theft.

If he could just find some convincing evidence, the FBI would probably be able take over the investigation. In the meantime, he had to keep searching.

CHAPTER SEVEN

TESSA LAY ON her couch, resting her shoulder on a hot water bottle and clutching an ice pack to her elbow, wondering if dragging herself to bed was worth the trouble. It was, after all, a very comfortable couch.

Aunt Emma had stopped and checked her injuries, but she hadn't been amused when Tessa tossed out a joke about doctors who made house calls. She'd scolded her niece for not visiting the medical clinic before finally admitting that nothing seemed to be seriously amiss.

The doorbell rang again, and Tessa groaned. Immediately after Aunt Emma left, Great-Uncle Milt had shown up again asking questions, though he'd refused to explain why he was so curious. Then her father had arrived with dinner, solicitously offering to spend the night to look after her. She'd convinced him to leave, but maybe he'd come back.

"Coming," she called, hoping it was just a Poppy Gold guest. Her apartment at the Victorian Cat had an outside entrance from the garden clearly marked "private," but that didn't prevent them from occasionally ringing the bell.

To her astonishment, it was Gabe McKinley on her step.

"Uh, hi, Gabe."

"How are you doing?" he asked.

Tessa didn't feel like keeping a stiff upper lip, but she forced a smile. "I'm fine." It was a response she'd given all day. The concern was nice, but every time someone asked, it made her stomach plunge.

"I doubt it," he said bluntly. "Sorry for intruding, but I've got a few more questions about what happened today."

Tessa's eyes narrowed, her patience at an end. "Gabe, if you want a security job, apply for it. But don't try to impress me this way. I'm tired and sore and don't feel like talking. Good night."

She closed the door firmly and limped back to the couch. It was bad enough to have fallen, but did everyone have to keep talking about it?

Yet she frowned as she put the ice pack back on her elbow, reminded that Gabe had seemed familiar to her since the day he'd started working at Poppy Gold. *It's his eyes*, she thought, only to realize that Gabe reminded her of Rob McKinley.

McKinley?

No, there couldn't be a connection. Her imagination was just working overtime.

GABE CONSIDERED KNOCKING AGAIN, but unless he told Tessa everything, he probably wouldn't get far.

The sun was low on the horizon, and he thought about going to the Tofton House to see Rob, but there was too much chance of someone questioning why he was there.

His presence at Tessa's apartment might also raise eyebrows, though it could prompt a different sort of question. After all, she was a beautiful woman.

Very beautiful.

Back at his studio cottage, he found a paper sack in front of his door, filled with the clothes he'd left in the laundry room. An envelope held the extra change he'd given Lance, with a careful note showing how much had been used to dry the load, along with the remaining balance.

It was almost as if the young man was concerned someone would question his honesty, but Gabe pushed the thought aside. Little was known about Lance Beckley other than he kept to himself, drove a motorcycle the town wasn't crazy about and was dating Jamie Fullerton. And that he gave her frequent gifts. Supposedly the girl's parents were wary of the relationship.

The money Lance was spending on Jamie was a question mark, but he'd started working at Poppy Gold after the thefts from TIP began.

While that didn't automatically mean he wasn't involved, it was a factor in his favor.

Filled with restless energy, Gabe started doing push-ups. Despite his shoulder giving him less trouble the past week, he knew he tended to work harder on his right side. A fleeting wish went through him that he hadn't retired from the navy, but maybe it had been time, anyway. Like athletes, a SEAL had a short active career. Even before he'd gotten shot, his superiors had been making noises about moving him into an administrative position, which he would have hated almost as much as working at TIP.

Still, it was more than restless energy driving him. He was trying to suppress his attraction to Tessa. It didn't make sense. She wasn't even his type; his tastes leaned toward earthier women. He liked sexual partners who were tall, experienced with casual affairs and deaf to the ticking of their biological clock.

Sitting at the small table, Gabe pulled out the new housekeeping schedule he'd copied at the employee center and began comparing it with the original schedule. Several other houses showed minor staffing adjustments, just none to the Tofton House. The changes were to be expected; Tessa had closed the El Dorado for repairs, so its staff had been transferred to other assignments.

Frustrated, Gabe shoved the papers away. The staffing assignments for Rob's prior visits to Poppy Gold might reveal whether any employee had routinely worked in the El Dorado, except the old schedules weren't available to him. All he'd been able to get were the ones posted in the employee lounge. So once again there wasn't anything to latch on to; nothing to help catch whoever was stealing information.

TIP was unimportant compared with Rob's well-being, but Gabe didn't even know if the person stealing company secrets was connected to the damaged staircase. Or if they'd sent the threatening letters.

Gabe clenched his fingers into a fist, whispers of warning going through his head. The sense of time running out was difficult to escape.

LANCE KNEW HE was being paranoid, but he'd watched from behind his curtain to be sure no one disturbed Gabe McKinley's laundry before he came home.

Seeing him take it inside had been a relief.

Lance paced around his studio thinking about Jamie. She was the sweetest, most generous person he'd ever known and had a quirky little smile that turned him inside out. She also seemed so *good*. Well, that wasn't quite right. Jamie made him want to be better. When he'd gotten out of high school, he'd just figured he would take any job and make enough to get by. But now things were different. It was like she made him see there was more.

Finally he couldn't stand it any longer. He went outside and started walking again.

Glimmer Creek wasn't bad. None of it seemed run-down or dangerous, even around the country bar that stayed open late. He'd had a fake ID for years, but he wouldn't have tried going into the Gold Shanty, no matter what. After all, word might get back to Jamie's parents, and the Fullertons didn't drink. Maybe he ought to get rid of the ID. It wouldn't be honest to use it, and he was over eighteen now, so he didn't need it to apply for jobs with people who didn't want to hire a minor.

The neighborhood where Jamie lived with her folks was especially nice, and he walked down the street. Most of the lights on the houses were off because people went to bed early in Glimmer Creek. The Fullertons' house was a sturdy place with wide porches, a big lawn and curtains on every single window. It was a world he'd never known before—pretty and clean, with everything in its place.

Jamie had told him her bedroom was on the side, but he didn't dare go around to see if her light was on in case her dad caught him. So he just stood outside and looked at the dark house, thinking that no matter what, maybe he'd always be on the outside.

That was what it was like to be a foster kid. You lived as if you were outside a candy shop you couldn't go in. He supposed some foster homes were better, especially if they wanted to adopt you, but he'd never been in one. Maybe it was because his dad was in prison and people were scared he'd turn out the same way.

But he'd never steal or try to hurt someone. He couldn't even dissect a frog in high school biology, much less do something worse.

A shadow moved on the porch, and a second later he saw it was Jamie.

"I figured you were asleep," he muttered.

"I was sitting on the swing. I'm sorry I upset you, Lance."

"You didn't do anything. It was my fault." He drew a deep breath, thinking he should tell her *part* of the truth at least. "The cops used to hassle me back in Sacramento. You know, because of the bike. And I don't think they like it much here, either. Honest, I don't try to make it loud— it just *is* loud."

"I know that." Jamie threw her arms around his neck, and he held her tight. "I love you," she whispered in his ear. "Forever and ever."

She'd told him the thing he wanted to hear most, and his throat got so tight he couldn't say anything.

"Come on, let's go sit on the porch," she urged,

pulling him toward the house. They sat on the porch swing, and she rested her head on his arm.

"Uh, I got you something," Lance said, pulling out the bag he'd intended to give her earlier.

The paper crackled, and a minute later Jamie giggled. "It's a charm for my bracelet, right? But there isn't enough light to tell what it's supposed to be."

"Guess."

"Well…it feels like a cow patty."

The idea made him laugh, too. "It's meant to look like gold in a gold miner's pan, so that's close enough."

"Cool."

She put her head back on his shoulder and he kicked the porch floor with his foot to rock the swing. They'd been out there a couple of times when her parents were around, but never in the dark, and he'd always sat upright and very proper in case somebody saw them.

"Are your mom and dad in bed?" he asked.

"Yeah."

If she'd been one of the few girls Lance had dated in high school, he might have considered it a convenient chance to angle for more than cuddling and a few kisses. Jamie was different, though. Special. He couldn't quite explain, even to himself, but he didn't want to go too fast. She was too important to him to make it all about sex.

Under the streetlight on the corner he saw a cat strolling around as if it owned the planet. It'd be nice to feel that way, Lance thought. He yawned and closed his eyes, enjoying the breeze that was cooling the air. A dog barked in the distance, but the only nearby sound was the faint creak of the swing, slowly moving back and forth.

JAMIE FELT FUNNY as she woke up, comfortable, just not as if she was in bed.

Then all at once she realized the sun had risen and she'd fallen asleep on the porch swing with Lance.

She looked up and saw her mother. Embarrassment went through her, but she hadn't done anything wrong. She and Lance had barely kissed, much less done anything more than that. And what if they had? She was eighteen, not fifteen.

Straightening, she eased off the swing. Her chin lifted as she gazed into her mom's face. She didn't want to be defiant, but she wasn't a child any longer.

"Good morning," she whispered.

"Good morning. I'll have breakfast ready in a few minutes," her mother whispered back. "Doesn't Lance usually go to work on the orchard by six because of the heat?"

"Yes."

As Emma Fullerton went back inside, Jamie shook Lance's shoulder. She doubted he'd want to eat with her parents, but it would be nice if he did.

"Wh-what?" Lance mumbled, yawning widely.

"We fell asleep."

He bolted to his feet as if stung by a bee. He looked around wildly. "Your folks... I'd better get out of here."

"Mom says breakfast is nearly ready."

"She *saw* us?"

Jamie shrugged. "She was worried you'd oversleep. Come on, you should eat before going to work, and there isn't time to go back to your studio."

It was up to him. She didn't say anything else, just turned and went inside. Paper crinkled in her pocket, and she took out the small bag Lance had given her the night before. She shook out the little charm. It was darling, and she laughed about thinking it felt like a cow patty.

She walked into the kitchen and dropped a kiss on her father's forehead. He was reading a book by C. S. Lewis. "*Prince Caspian?* Cool, Dad."

"I've always enjoyed the Narnia Chronicles, and I like them much better than the Twilight series you made me read," he grumbled.

"You're the one who says a youth pastor should know what kids are reading and seeing at the movies," Jamie reminded him. "You liked *Divergent* and the new *Star Trek* films, even the guy playing Mr. Spock."

His eyes twinkled at her. "I don't have a problem with the Twilight stuff—I'm just not into vampires."

"Me, either. Anything I can do to help, Mom?" she asked brightly.

"Thanks, but I'm almost done. Lance is eating with us, isn't he?"

"I'm here, Mrs. Fullerton," Lance said from the doorway, sounding awkward. "Uh, sorry, I mean *Dr.* Fullerton."

Jamie's heart thumped painfully. He was *so* uncomfortable with people. With her, too, in the beginning. She didn't believe women had to wait for guys to ask them out, which was a good thing because it might have taken Lance *forever* to do it himself. Of course, she wondered sometimes if he'd gone out with her the first time because he didn't know how to say no. But it was okay. Now he was talking about everything they'd do in the future.

"Please call me Emma," her mother urged him. "Have a seat, Lance. Do you drink coffee?"

"Yes, ma...uh, yes."

Clearly, calling his girlfriend's mother by her first name was more than he could handle. The breakfast Mom had cooked was fancier than usual, and Jamie hoped it was because she wanted to be nice to Lance. He was very polite, taking a serving of everything, even a bowl of oatmeal, which she knew he hated. He added brown sugar and cream before resolutely stuffing a spoonful into his mouth.

A smile broke out on his face. "Wow, this doesn't taste like glue." He promptly turned red. "Uh, sorry."

Dad chuckled. "You've been a victim of vicious propaganda, young man. Everyone seems to think oatmeal should be creamy, but we like steel-cut oats, barely cooked so we have something to chew. Emma knows how to do it right."

"So do you, Daniel," Mom said pointedly. "Cooking isn't solely a woman's province."

"I'd cook if you let me near the stove."

"Maybe I would if you hadn't burned up two of my favorite pots after we got married. How you could destroy quality stainless steel cookware is beyond me."

"Excuses, excuses."

After breakfast Lance waited while Jamie changed into her costume. It was too early for her to start work, but she wanted to walk to Poppy Gold with him.

Lance was quiet for several blocks, and then he glanced at her. "Don't you hate it when your folks argue like that?"

Jamie blinked. "Argue?"

"That stuff about your dad burning up pots and all."

She grinned. "That was a joke. Mom had a superwoman complex when they got married…

as if she could go to medical school, have babies and still do all the cooking and cleaning. It took a while to sort everything out, but now they have fun teasing each other."

"Your mom doesn't do all the cooking?"

"Nah. They both work, so Mom usually handles breakfast, while Dad makes dinner. I take turns, too. But since Mom loves to bake, she does all the bread and pies and junk, though she doesn't make as much now that my two brothers have gone to college."

"I never knew anybody who could make bread."

Lance didn't say anything else, and Jamie wished she knew what he was thinking. She knew tons of people who baked bread; one of her cousins had even opened a sweet shop and was catering all the food for Poppy Gold.

Jamie thought about it. Perhaps *she* ought to learn how to bake, but not just to please her boyfriend. As for college… Mom and Dad wanted her to start in the fall, but she wasn't so sure. One of her brothers was already in medical school, and the other wanted to be a veterinarian. But she didn't know what she wanted to do, and right now being with Lance seemed the most important thing of all.

Still, while she lived with her parents, she was an adult now. She had a job, and when she said she'd do something, she'd darned well better do it. The niggling guilt she'd been feeling about her college class got even stronger.

She kissed Lance goodbye, then got out her phone and pulled up the number for her professor's office down in Stockton. Studying history was dull compared with the excitement of falling in love, but she'd started the class and it wasn't right to keep blowing it off.

Jamie pulled in a deep breath when the recorded voice told her to leave a message. "Hello, Professor Wendell, this is Jamie Fullerton. I'm a student in your Early California History night course. I know I haven't been in class lately, but I'm calling to see if there's any way I can make it up. I'm willing to do extra work or whatever it takes."

She gave her phone number and disconnected.

It would mean missing time with Lance to attend classes and study and write papers, but she'd feel better if she finished the course.

CHAPTER EIGHT

GABE HAD VOLUNTEERED for lawn and garden maintenance on the Victorians around the Tofton House, and he kept a close watch the next morning.

Apparently a group of ghost hunters was staying in the Mill Race Cottage across the street. They *looked* normal, but he questioned the sanity of anyone who believed in spirits. Nevertheless, the only time he saw them was when Sarah's Sweet Treats and Catering delivered breakfast.

Later he saw Tessa drive up in one of Poppy Gold's electric carts, rather than walking as usual. Obviously she was still suffering from her fall, and he watched as she limped first to the Tofton House and then to the Mill Race Cottage.

He was waiting by the cart when she returned from talking to the ghost hunters.

"Did the Ghostbusters find anything interesting?" he asked.

"Go ask them yourself."

"I prefer staying away from crazy people."

Tessa shook her head as she got into the cart.

"Opinion polls suggest that thirty to fifty percent of the people in the United States believe in ghosts. They can't all be crazy."

"Maybe, though it isn't reassuring to hear about presidents having séances in the White House. They have too much power to be listening to unseen spirits."

"I don't think that's happened for a while."

"I've heard that Abraham Lincoln had séances during the Civil War."

Tessa jerked and a curious expression flitted across her face. "Actually, it was Lincoln's wife who hosted the séances after one of their sons died of typhoid. I believe Abraham attended at least one to make Mary Todd happy, only to discover it was a political liability."

"Yup. That much more proof that wives just get men in trouble."

"And *that* comment is more proof that you're a cynic," she said crisply. "Now, if you'll excuse me, we both have to things to do."

An unaccustomed grin split Gabe's face as she drove away.

TESSA FUMED AS she parked the cart behind the train depot. Dealing with Gabe McKinley seemed to remove all of her verbal sensors. He didn't guard his tongue, either, but that was no excuse. On the other hand, maybe she should be pleased that he was confident their tense exchanges wouldn't affect his job with her father.

Yet Tessa frowned as she went up the rear stairs to her office. Gabe's remark about Lincoln was curious. She'd had a number of discussions with *Rob* McKinley about Abraham Lincoln. They both admired the martyred president, and she'd even put a copy of her favorite Lincoln biography in one of his courtesy welcome baskets.

Still, since Abraham Lincoln was one of the most admired men in American history, it wasn't totally bizarre that his name would come up in conversation.

AFTER SIGNING OUT for the day, Gabe walked nonchalantly toward the historic shopping street. There were various stores, all offering products with a Victorian flair, and a large number of people were still out shopping. It had seemed a likely place to engineer a "casual" encounter with his brother.

He looked into various store windows and finally stopped in front of the Glimmer Creek Mercantile as planned. Bolts of fabric were displayed along with other artifacts, some of which looked quite old, including a kerosene lamp. O'Connor Dry Goods was stenciled on a burlap sack and several other items.

"Do you think there was a store like this in 1849?" asked a voice.

Gabe cast a sideways look at his brother. "I understand the O'Connors largely sold their supplies from the back of a wagon, but Glimmer Creek was their home base. Of course, if they *had* a store, it probably started out as a cramped log cabin."

"You could be right."

Gabe waited until the chattering group of tourists surrounding them had gone by. "Have you seen anything questionable?" he asked softly. "Anyone around the Tofton House who shouldn't be there, or someone who comes at odd times?"

"Nothing out of the ordinary so far."

"No papers disturbed or luggage out of place?" Gabe pushed.

They were gazing through the window and not at each other, but Gabe saw Rob's head shake in the reflection. "Nope."

"We found out someone might be trying to hurt you. That's valuable. It's safer to know than to be surprised. I'd feel a lot better if you had an emergency and left early."

"Then you've dismissed the possibility that Tessa could have been a target?"

"Pretty much."

Gabe tried to read his brother's expression, but the image in the glass wasn't distinct enough. "She's popular and hasn't fired any employees since taking over at Poppy Gold. Now that I've thought about it more, it also seems unlikely that anything would have followed her from San Francisco."

Gabe deliberately turned his back to Rob and checked his watch, then looked up and down the street as if searching for someone before facing the window display again. "Have you checked into getting a bodyguard?" he asked. "One of the men I used to command has a personal security company. He might even do the job himself. He's tough and reliable."

"That means he's an action guy. A businessman's life is too dull to interest someone like that—he'd skip town within a week. There are no adrenaline rushes in my line of work."

It was the first time Gabe had heard a hint of dissatisfaction from his brother about running TIP. "Are you bored? You could get somebody else to run the company and do whatever you want."

"We aren't all cut out for glorious heroism like you."

Images flashed through Gabe's mind of injured and starving children in war-ravaged countries. "I'm not a hero, and there was nothing glorious about what I used to do," he said bluntly. "Somebody has to take care of messes, so that's what I did."

"I guess there's more than one way to look at something."

"Yeah, and you're deflecting. I'll text KJ's number to you. His company is on the East Coast, but he sends his guys all over the world."

"I'll think about it." Rob didn't sound enthusiastic about the idea, which meant he probably *wouldn't* consider a personal security guard.

Another group of tourists came out of the mercantile, so they fell silent again, still trying to gaze at the window display with fascination.

"THANKS FOR THE HELP," Ollie told Tessa. Ollie ran the general store, and Tessa was helping him carry a load of empty picnic baskets back from the train depot.

Tessa went warm with embarrassment. "No problem." She'd offered after seeing Gabe head across Poppy Gold and down the pedestrian shopping street. He wasn't the type for touristy activities, and she'd gotten curious. "How are the picnic baskets doing?"

"We sell out every day. I've asked Sarah's Sweet Treats to increase our order three times already. Fried chicken is our bestseller, but the baked ham and biscuits are popular, too."

"That's nice," Tessa said absently, keeping an eye on two distinct figures ahead on the brick sidewalk—Gabe and Rob McKinley, standing next to each other in front of the mercantile.

Ollie turned into the general store, and Tessa reluctantly followed.

"Here you go." She handed the collection of baskets she carried to Ollie's wife.

"Thanks, Tessa," said Virginia. She would wash the cotton linings and sanitize the wicker for use the next day. Tin pails, the contents covered with red-checkered cloths, were also popular with picnickers, who were able to return either container to a variety of locations throughout Poppy Gold.

Tessa gazed around the crowded store, noisy with the cheerful babble of tourists deciding on postcards and other souvenirs. "You're certainly busy."

"Isn't it wonderful? We've had tour buses stopping all day long," Virginia explained before bustling away to help a customer.

Ollie and Virginia were relative newcomers to Glimmer Creek, but they'd embraced the spirit of the community. Both of them were plump and cheerful, and they never failed to dress in the garb of Victorian storekeepers; Virginia even removed her long white apron and donned a bonnet whenever she went out during business hours.

Tessa stepped out into the sunlight again and saw that Gabe and Rob were still standing in front of the Glimmer Creek Mercantile. Though they weren't facing each other, she could swear they were talking.

Interesting. While Gabe was taller and more strongly built, they shared a similar body type. Broad shoulders, erect posture, powerful legs in a wide stance...

She determinedly walked over. "Hello, gentlemen. Do you mind telling me what's going on?"

Rob whirled around with a distinctly guilty expression. Gabe turned more slowly and gave her a calculating look. "Hi, Tessa. How are you recovering so far?"

Tessa shrugged. She was still sore and the skin around her elbow was a glorious purple, along with a few other places, but she was okay.

"Limping some, but I'm all right."

"I've noticed you're wearing long sleeves, despite the hot weather. I assume it's to conceal your bruises from Liam."

Gabe's perception put Tessa's teeth on edge, maybe because it was so hard to read anything from him in return. "It also hides the elbow brace," she explained. Aunt Emma had told her to wear a light support for a few days.

"I see." Gabe checked his watch. "It's late, I'd better be going."

Tessa shook her head. "You can't get away that easily. Rob, *what* is going on?"

"Uh..." Robert McKinley shot a glance at

Gabe, similar to the one Tessa had seen the previous day, and it confirmed her suspicions.

"Maybe we should talk somewhere else," Gabe suggested.

"Maybe you should explain why you're pretending you don't know each other."

"Not *here*," Gabe ordered in a low, urgent tone that didn't brook disagreement. "I'll talk to you later, Rob. Watch your back."

Robert McKinley walked away as Tessa pondered the "watch your back" warning. Gabe gestured toward the park with a sharp jerk of the head and started walking without even checking to see if she followed. She stayed put. After a few steps he turned and glared.

She smiled sweetly as he stomped back.

"We need privacy," he snarled.

"Perhaps, but I'll choose where we get it."

Tessa began walking toward the more modern part of Glimmer Creek. After a moment Gabe caught up and matched her pace, frustration radiating from him. At the new city park, she stopped. They were in full view of the buildings along the street, but far enough away they could talk without being overheard.

"Give me a break," Gabe muttered, looking pointedly at the police station sign. "Do you honestly think I'm a threat?"

"I don't know what to think except that something hasn't added up from the very beginning."

A flicker of emotion flitted across his face. If it had been anyone else, Tessa would have guessed chagrin, but he was probably too arrogant for that.

"Rob is my brother," he admitted.

"That explains the resemblance around your eyes. Are you really retired from the navy?"

"Yes. I didn't lie on my job application."

"But you obviously didn't tell us everything. Why are you in Glimmer Creek?"

GABE GLANCED AROUND. Tessa had chosen her spot well. They were visible to traffic from two sides of the park, yet no one was around—possibly because, however pleasant, it lacked the picture-postcard appeal of the original city center in Poppy Gold.

"Someone has been stealing information from Thomas International Products," he said grudgingly. "Data on pending contracts, future acquisition plans, that sort of thing. They're using the information to sabotage TIP, or at least to make a profit elsewhere."

Tessa regarded him narrowly. "I'm sorry to hear that, but… *Oh, my God*, you think someone at Poppy Gold is doing it, don't you?"

"This is the only place where all the information has been together outside Rob's office. And when something happens, it's right after TIP has had executive training or planning sessions here. The company has lost a great deal of money."

Her mouth opened and closed, then opened again. "Why didn't Rob talk to me about this?"

"I advised against it."

"Wise of you. After all, I might be involved."

Gabe waited while the other shoe dropped. Tessa was upset and still recovering from her fall, or she would have gotten it earlier.

"Damn it," she exclaimed a second later. "That's *exactly* what you think. Do you actually believe I'd steal business secrets from one our clients? If something like that came out, it would destroy Poppy Gold Inns."

Yeah, *now* Gabe understood her devotion to the bed-and-breakfast complex. She was practically obsessed with making it a premier visitor and conference center.

"It isn't that far-fetched," he defended. "You're Patrick Connor's granddaughter and worked as an executive with Connor Enterprises until fairly recently. Basically, you and Liam are the only heirs of a company in direct competition with TIP."

"You mean my father is a suspect, too."

"That isn't what—"

"You're insane," Tessa interrupted. "My dad could never cheat, and Granddad would be appalled at the thought of using stolen information."

"You can't believe that. Patrick Connor is a ruthless businessman."

She breathed hard for a moment, visibly trying to control her temper. "Grandfather is a *good* businessman. That doesn't mean he's ruthless. What sort of people have you been associating with? I've always thought men and women who served their country must be pretty decent on the whole. But maybe you *weren't* in the navy."

"I told you, I didn't lie on my job application," Gabe ground out. "I'm a retired navy SEAL. We don't advertise ourselves, even after getting out of the service."

"You also didn't say that you'd come to spy on us. To think Dad actually told me to give you a chance. He said it takes a while for a veteran to adjust to civilian life, but you've been playing us the entire time."

"Give me a chance? I thought Liam was my boss, not you."

"He is, but I wasn't thrilled about you having contact with guests, so we discussed it. Or do you think we don't talk to each other about Poppy Gold?"

"Of course not." Gabe frowned. "Why didn't you think I should be around guests?"

"Because we're in the hospitality business, and your personality is less than stellar. In fact, most of the time you're stiff and look surly."

"Oh."

Tessa let out an exasperated breath. "Did it ever occur to you that spying is unethical? You have a lot of nerve accusing my grandfather of being ruthless." She pointed across the street at the police department. "We're going right over to tell my great-uncle about this. He's the police chief. He'll start a full investigation, and Poppy Gold will cooperate fully."

"Fine, but it needs to stay confidential. Public trust is involved for both Thomas International Products and Poppy Gold Inns. You won't get far as a conference center if executives are worried their information will be stolen here."

Some of the anger faded from Tessa's face. "Uncle Milt won't tell anyone." She sank onto a bench, looking as if the wind had been knocked out of her sails. "But the news will come out at some point, even if only when an arrest is made."

"Except that will mean the problem has been resolved. TIP is owned by the family, so we don't answer to any stockholders, but other companies will be reluctant to do business with us if they think they're at risk of being undermined. The company has lost a ton of money since this started. Rob has put all acquisitions and new contracts on hold right now because of it."

"That can't go on forever."

"No, it can't. Rob and I talked to the FBI, but there wasn't any evidence to give them. Frankly, they acted as if we were paranoid. That's why I came here to see if there was any way to track down what was happening. I figured that if I could present evidence or point to a specific suspect, they might be willing to take the investigation further."

TESSA'S STOMACH ROILED and she could barely think. She'd been too uncomfortable and upset the previous night to sleep, realizing that her fall could have been fatal.

Now this?

"Why were you so curious about my accident at the El Dorado?" she asked finally.

"Frankly, it seems suspicious. That's a private staircase to the suite. Housekeeping normally uses the back stairs, right?"

She blinked. "Yes, and only by key access. My parents built the deluxe suite seven years ago. Obviously, we can't have penthouse elevators in historic buildings, but the idea was to give a sense of exclusive luxury. It's also good for—"

"Hell," Gabe exclaimed, cutting her off.

Tessa looked up and saw Great-Uncle Milt coming toward them. He must have spotted her from his office window. His proximity was why she'd chosen the park as a place to speak with Gabe.

Milt Fullerton inspired confidence. He'd looked after Glimmer Creek for decades, and everyone was dreading his retirement in a few months.

"Hey, Uncle Milt."

"Is everything all right?"

She exchanged a look with Gabe. Their choice was to talk in the park or follow her great-uncle into the police station and make people wonder what was going on. "Not exactly. This is Gabe McKinley. He has something to discuss with you."

She kept an eye out for anyone who might overhear them, while Gabe laid out why he'd come to Glimmer Creek and his suspicions that someone had tampered with the staircase.

Great-Uncle Milt had looked grim when he joined them, and his expression darkened as Gabe spoke.

"So we have two problems, possibly related," he said finally. "Stephen Seibert talked to me yesterday, Tessa. He's suspicious about your accident. The stair riser that collapsed is a different type of wood from the rest of the steps, and a piece appears to be missing. The damage to the railing is also strange. It might be completely innocent, but I've sent everything to the state crime lab for analysis."

Tessa's pulse skipped. "Normally I use the rear stairs to deliver the courtesy baskets, but nobody was checked in at the mansion and I was in a huge rush."

Great-Uncle Milt shook his head. "It's unlikely anyone would target you. I have to agree the intended victim was probably Mr. McKinley's brother, particularly with the increased number of threats against him. The postmarks from town close to Glimmer Creek are too big a coincidence to ignore."

Tessa let out a breath. "I don't know, industrial espionage *and* attempted murder? That doesn't make sense to me. It's a huge leap to go from white-collar theft to killing someone," she said at length.

"Any thoughts on that, Mr. McKinley?"

Gabe shrugged. "Rob claims he's gotten other hate mail in the past, but I think it's possible that somebody is trying to hurt him or TIP for personal reasons. Maybe they're getting impatient or decided economic damage isn't enough. I told him to take the letters either to the police in Los Angeles or to the FBI agent we spoke to a few weeks ago."

"I'd like copies, as well. Have there been any other suspicious accidents?" asked Great-Uncle Milt.

"No, just the letters."

"But why turn violent all of a sudden?" Tessa interjected.

"Opportunistic crime, prompted by the earthquake," Gabe said. "The saboteur could have hoped everyone would assume it was freak damage. I realize it sounds paranoid, but they would have had the whole night to rig the steps. And that business of someone reserving the whole house and not showing up or canceling is questionable, as well."

Tessa rubbed her forehead, still trying to process everything. It *did* sound paranoid, but what was the saying—just because you're paranoid, it doesn't mean everyone *isn't* out to get you? Besides, if the step *had* been sabotaged, who else could be the target?

"Gabe, was Rob's request to move to another house in Poppy Gold part of your investigation?"

"I asked him to do it. I keep thinking the thief could be in Housekeeping because it wouldn't be overly suspicious if they're seen entering a suite at odd hours, say with a load of fresh towels. So I told Rob to ask for a change of accommodation, hoping someone on the housekeeping staff would ask to switch assignments, as well."

Tessa raised her chin. "Why couldn't it be an outsider, posing as one of our housekeepers?" The idea that an employee might be behind this made her nauseous.

"They'd need keys. Besides, surely a stranger would be noticed," Gabe argued. "It has to be someone who works here, or else hired a person who does. Either way, there's nothing you could have done."

It seemed uncharacteristic for Gabe to try to make her feel better, but it didn't matter. Tessa *felt* responsible. A good manager ought to know when something fishy was going on. And she still needed to consider whether somebody might be stealing from any of her other corporate clients, not just TIP.

"What do we do now, Uncle Milt?" she asked. Perhaps she'd get an idea later, but right now her brain seemed stuffed with cotton wool.

"I'm already in place," Gabe said quickly. "And confidentiality is critical, not only to TIP, but for Poppy Gold's reputation. I'm an ex-SEAL. I can take care of myself and obviously have the necessary skills."

Great-Uncle Milt gazed at him for a long moment. "Loath as I am to go along with someone who suspected my great-niece of being an industrial spy, I'm inclined to agree with you. I can't go in myself or send one of my officers without it being obvious."

Tessa was annoyed to see a faintly smug expression on Gabe's face.

"I'll help, too," she declared.

"No," both men said simultaneously.

"Yes," she shot back. "If the FBI investigated and didn't think I was involved, they'd almost certainly come to me for help as an inside contact, or whatever they call it. Poppy Gold is my responsibility and I have to do whatever is necessary. Gabe can be the brawn, and you and I will be the brains."

Gabe scowled while her great-uncle laughed. "I'll think about it," Milt declared.

"While you're thinking about something I've already decided to do, I'm going back to work." Tessa got up slowly from the park bench and walked away.

GABE TURNED, PLANNING to follow Tessa.

"Stay right here, Mr. McKinley," Milt Fullerton ordered sternly.

Gabe turned and raised an eyebrow. "Yes?"

"I don't appreciate being backed into a corner, young man. Tessa means the world to me, and I refuse to let her get hurt."

"I tried to keep her out of it."

The police chief snorted. "You weren't protecting her—you were deciding if she was guilty or not. That girl wouldn't steal a paper clip."

"I don't suspect her any longer, but frankly, most people don't believe a relative could be guilty."

"I'm not just anybody. I've kept the law around here since long before Tessa was born."

Gabe liked Milt Fullerton, but the old guy couldn't have much investigative experience. The local police were probably fine with traffic stops and petty theft, but industrial espionage was another matter. Maybe that was even part of the reason the spy had set up shop at Poppy Gold.

It would be easy to spot anyone investigating in such a small, tight-knit community.

"Are you going to tell any of your officers about what's going on?" Gabe asked instead of challenging Milt.

"Not at the moment. And I'll have to decide what to do if any search warrants are needed. You're right about one thing—this needs to stay confidential, and very little stays private around Glimmer Creek. It's a good thing I decided to come over to check on Tessa. Everybody is used to me being nosy, but if you'd come to my office, there would have been even *more* talk."

Gabe sighed, missing the anonymity that large cities offered. The average citizen of Glimmer Creek could probably tell a tourist and a local from a mile away.

More than once he'd heard someone exclaim, "You're that new guy," when he walked into a store or restaurant.

"What are they going to think after seeing us together in the town park?"

"The truth—that I was checking up on you. They might even speculate that you and Tessa are involved, but that won't hurt anybody. So let's shake hands and pretend we're getting along."

"Aren't we getting along?" Gabe asked, putting out his hand. Milt Fullerton's grip was surprisingly strong and firm.

"Time will tell, young man. Time will tell."

RETURNING ALONG THE pedestrian shopping street gave Tessa a strange sensation, and she realized it stemmed from Gabe's revelations. What if someone had seen her talking to Rob and Gabe? What if she and Gabe had been seen talking to Great-Uncle Milt? What if she went to the Tofton House to see Rob, and the thief thought there was something suspicious about it?

There were a thousand "what-ifs," and she shook the thought away. She had to be careful or else she'd start seeing sinister motives in everything. Nevertheless, she wanted to speak with Robert McKinley and see what he had to say.

First she stopped at her office to get a flyer about upcoming Glimmer Creek community events. While she didn't need an excuse to visit one of her top clients, it would look better if she arrived with a purpose. She answered a phone call before leaving, only to see Rob at the office door as she hung up the receiver. Maybe he'd been thinking the same way.

He gave her a sheepish look. "I hope you don't mind—one of the employees let me come up here. May I come in?"

"Of course. I was just about to go look for you."

He closed the door, and she motioned to the small seating area at the end of the room. They'd met in her office before, discussing various upcoming TIP visits to Poppy Gold, but it was different now that she knew what was going on. When they were both comfortable, Rob leaned toward her with an earnest expression.

"I'm so sorry about the deception, Tessa. Gabe genuinely thought it would be best for him to get a job here without anybody knowing he's my brother."

"How serious are the thefts?"

"Serious. Several major deals have fallen through, enough to have a substantial impact on our profits. If we had a board of directors, they'd be screaming for my head."

"I don't understand why you suspect someone at Poppy Gold, rather than one of your own employees. I'm not an expert on industrial espionage, but surely that's more likely than one of my housekeepers or other staff."

"Other than me, no single person at TIP has had all the information. Deals have always fallen apart immediately after one of our executive sessions here, but it hasn't been the same executives involved each time. I've tracked it. One time it will be a group from LA, another from the East Coast or Asia. The *only* common factor is Poppy Gold."

"Not necessarily." Tessa looked at the computer on her desk. Her brain was beginning to work faster, the way she wished it had worked when she'd been talking to Gabe and Great-Uncle Milt. "What about cybertheft? Anyone with the right know-how can break into a computer, no matter where they are."

"Agreed, but most of the information has never *gone* on a computer with internet access, especially after the first leak became obvious. Anything committed to paper has stayed with me, and I never leave it, or my laptop, behind at the office or home."

Tessa released a breath. She kept hoping Poppy Gold wouldn't have any role in the thefts and wanted to suggest Rob's phone had been tapped or another option, but she would just be grasping at straws. It was important for Robert McKinley to know she was taking things seriously.

Rob touched her hand. "Tessa, please understand. I never seriously thought you had anything to do with this, even after Gabe told me you were connected to Connor Enterprises."

"He was spying on us, Rob." A renewed surge of anger swept through her. *"Spying."*

"I'm sorry. And I know it bothered Gabe. He's honorable and decent, the finest man I've ever known, so please don't think too badly of him because of it."

Tessa tried to regain her equilibrium, remembering Rob might be the target of more than information thefts—his life might be at risk. Curiously, it was easier to forgive him than Gabe.

"What's done is done," she said, forcing a smile.

"It must be strange to have a brother who went into such different work than you. A navy SEAL?"

"Our childhood was complicated, and our folks were furious when he enlisted instead of going to college. I don't know why he took his twenty-year retirement. I'm just glad he's out. He really got banged up in the service."

In more ways than one, Tessa thought. Gabe's faith in human nature must have taken a major beating. Or maybe he'd been born mistrustful. Some people seemed naturally skeptical, and no matter what they experienced, they never changed.

"Well, right now you're the one who needs to be careful," she murmured. "I understand my fall may not have been an accident, after all."

Regret filled Rob's eyes. "It's a possibility. You'll probably be glad to see me leave for Los Angeles in a couple of days."

Only if you take your cynical brother with you, Tessa wanted to say, but she forced another smile. "Don't worry about it."

"That's very generous. I, uh… What are the chances of my returning with some of my executives in June? Gabe wants to set up another sting operation and would prefer not waiting until the retreat scheduled for August."

Great. Another potential disaster.

"I'll do my best," she said, "but I know we don't have an open block of rooms then. The best possibility will be to track cancellations and hold rooms as they become available. You might have to come on short notice."

"This isn't a problem. Put any expenses on my business account. Thanks for all your help."

Rob left quickly before she could say anything, and she wondered if his brother had told him about the tongue-lashing he'd received earlier. Probably not. A man like Gabe McKinley wouldn't care about anything she'd said.

Lord, a navy SEAL?

That was like having a combination of Darth Vader and Obi-Wan Kenobi working for Poppy Gold, though she wasn't convinced that wisdom and insight were lurking beneath Gabe's rhinoceros hide. The only redeeming trait she'd seen in him was concern for his brother.

To think she'd actually felt a flash of heat as the louse had carried her down the steps of the El Dorado, when all the while he was trying to decide if she was a criminal. Her reaction had come largely from adrenaline and the survival instinct, of course, but it was still annoying. She didn't like Gabe McKinley enough to warrant wayward impulses.

The ceiling fan cooled Tessa's face as she began mapping out a plan of action. While she was furious that Gabe had been spying on them, the worst part was knowing someone may have stolen from their clients. Poppy Gold wasn't just a business, it was home. Most of her aunts and uncles and cousins were connected to it in some way, so if somebody hurt Poppy Gold Inns, they hurt her family, as well.

Nobody was getting away with that.

Gabe and Great-Uncle Milt probably still hoped to keep her in a sideline role in the investigation, but that wasn't going to happen.

This was war.

CHAPTER NINE

GABE EXERCISED FOR an hour at the employee fitness center, running on the treadmill followed by a lengthy session lifting weights to release his frustration.

Telling Tessa about the information thefts would have been better than having her figure out the connection between him and Rob and learning it that way. But she was smart and like a lioness when it came to Poppy Gold, so her protective instincts had probably tipped her off that something was going on.

Though Gabe preferred hard evidence, he had a healthy regard for instincts. The survival instinct was one of the most powerful forces in nature. He scratched the scar on his left shoulder. According to the surgeon, the wound should have killed him. Instead he'd rendezvoused with his team in time for their helicopter pickup. Survival at its most basic.

Dodging bullets was part of the job, but the thing that haunted Gabe was the civilian who'd stumbled into the mess. Innocent bystanders weren't supposed to die. Unfortunately drug cartels didn't follow any rules of engagement, and they didn't like witnesses.

There was no way he could let Tessa get involved in the investigation. It was dangerous. While they would need to wait for proof about the staircase, his gut told him it had been a trap for his brother.

If Tessa had gone over the railing headfirst…

He lowered the weight bar, not wanting to think how Liam would have reacted if his daughter had been hurt worse. Father and daughter appeared quite devoted to each other. Not being close to his own father, Gabe didn't understand the relationship, but Liam was also a different kind of man from David McKinley.

Gabe flipped the top of his water bottle and drank down half the contents.

He knew Rob had gone to talk with Tessa and was now back in his suite at the Tofton House. They'd spoken briefly on the phone, and his brother had flatly refused a bodyguard, saying it would just tip off the thief. He was both right and wrong. Catching the culprit *after* more violence had occurred wouldn't help anyone.

Gabe headed for the men's locker room. Tessa had sent him a text message to meet at her apartment, and he should shower before going. He would have preferred to set the time and place himself, but in light of everything, it would be best to go along.

Half an hour later he rang her doorbell.

Tessa opened the door, and her forehead crinkled when she spotted the flowers in his hand. "Are those supposed to make people think you're coming here for romance?"

"Don't you have a social life?"

"Not lately." She stepped aside to let him in. "I should also point out that you aren't exactly the romantic type. So your bringing me Western coneflowers is going to attract more attention than anything else. Especially if one of the employees saw you picking them from a Poppy Gold garden."

Disconcerted, Gabe dropped the blooms on a side table. "I thought they were strange-looking daisies."

"They aren't."

"Are they poisonous like foxglove?"

She gave him a quizzical look. "Foxglove isn't exactly poisonous. It contains digoxin, which affects the heart, so it's important to handle the plants carefully."

"Which means it *could* be poisonous."

"Presumably if administered the right way, but historically, Native Americans have used both foxglove and Western coneflower to treat their various illnesses." Tessa retrieved the blossoms and stuck them in a small vase. "Next time skip the bouquet."

"Are you embarrassed that someone might think we're involved, or do you think your father wouldn't approve?"

"Neither. I'm sure Pop would prefer not thinking about me being sexually active, but he isn't a prude. On the other hand, he might be concerned because you're *so* not my type."

"Okay, I'll bite. What are five things you look for in a man?"

Tessa shrugged. "These aren't necessarily the *top* five, but intelligence, a sense of humor, someone who wants children, who shares my values and likes small towns." She reeled off the list as if she'd given it serious thought.

Nothing on the list was surprising, particularly the part about wanting children. He'd discovered a lot of women felt strongly on the subject.

"Not that I'm promoting myself as a boyfriend, but I'm intelligent," Gabe pointed out.

"One in five doesn't cut it, and I doubt you'd do better on the next five, either."

Gabe doubted it, as well.

"What's so great about small towns?" he asked, hoping to change the subject he'd foolishly introduced. "I can't wait to get out of Glimmer Creek."

"A lot of things, but if you don't already understand, it isn't likely you ever will." Tessa sat carefully on a chair and grabbed a pad and pencil sitting next to it. "Now, what's your great idea for a sting operation on TIP's next visit to Poppy Gold? I'll give Uncle Milt the details the next time we talk."

"There isn't a plan. I simply asked my brother to set up another executive retreat while I'm devising a strategy."

She tapped the tip of her pencil on the paper. "Anything we come up with has to be safe for my employees and guests."

Gabe was annoyed as he dropped onto the couch...though he was mostly annoyed that he couldn't stop the surge of heat through his groin. She'd changed from her work clothes into a pair of light pants and a thin T-shirt, two garments that emphasized her petite figure in exactly the right places.

"I'm concerned about safety, too," he muttered, "but there isn't any 'we.' You can't get involved— it could be dangerous. Milt Fullerton obviously agrees."

"You aren't doing it without me. Poppy Gold is *my* family business. And since spying on us was practically an accusation, I want to be fully involved in the investigation."

His jaw clenched. "I didn't accuse you. I simply thought it was best to get the lay of the land without anyone being the wiser."

"Call it what you want, but you're still stuck

with my help. I've had a few self-defense classes, if that's what you're worried about."

Swell. That was like a kitten sticking out its claws and declaring, *I can protect myself.*

Investigating Poppy Gold was already a nightmare. It was the town's biggest employer, which meant most people in Glimmer Creek had a vested interest in the business, whether they worked there or not. Guests and day tourists wandered in and out of the historic district, shopping, eating and taking pictures. And that didn't include the large number of employees and subcontractors with access.

Trying to work with Tessa on this investigation would just make it worse. And now they'd be coordinating everything with her great-uncle.

"Tessa, listen to me. I have experience handling a range of risky situations. You don't."

She waved her hand dismissively. "You're overdramatizing. Everything should be fine with proper precautions. Maybe I can temporarily increase the security staff. We already hire off-duty police officers whenever needed."

"No," Gabe refused sharply. "Look, I have contacts who can help—men I trust. We can bring some of them in as undercover guests, with full disclosure to your great-uncle, of course. I know you hold rooms back for contingencies."

Tessa began laughing.

He glowered. "What's so funny?"

"Your contacts won't fool anybody if they're like you."

"What is that supposed to mean?"

"People visit Poppy Gold to have fun and enjoy the atmosphere. Unlike you, they're usually people who enjoy small towns, or at least are open-minded about them. As a rule, they *aren't* six-foot-three commandos with military haircuts, rigid postures and sudden death in their hands."

"You've watched too many movies," he scoffed.

She rolled her eyes. "I'm not an expert, but I know SEALs are an elite unit with some of the best training possible. I presume most of your contacts are ex-SEALS, as well. Actually, learning about your former career explains a lot."

Gabe wanted to be annoyed, but Tessa was right that he didn't fit in around here. Small towns remained a mystery to him.

"Fine, maybe I don't blend in that well," he conceded, "but these guys have been out of the service longer than me. One of my men started a personal security and investigative business several years ago. The company has protected everyone from rock stars to ambassadors. They know how to blend. Surely you don't think I'd knowingly put my brother at risk?"

Tessa regarded him for a long minute. "All right, we can work out the details later. Poppy Gold is pretty well booked from Memorial Day on, so I'm still trying to figure out a way for TIP to come back." She held up a hand when he opened his mouth. "And no, I can't cancel another group. It wouldn't be fair, and besides, it would look suspicious."

Once again, Tessa was right. If she did something out of character in favor of Thomas International Products, it would raise questions.

"Okay."

"So where do we go from here?" Tessa asked. "There must be something we can check before TIP returns."

"For one, see if anybody regularly works in Housekeeping when Rob and his executives stay at Poppy Gold. Are those records available?"

"The work schedules are kept on the computer system. I'll do some checking."

"Excellent. I've asked Rob how they found out about Poppy Gold. He said they got brochures in the mail. Do you have any records of which companies have received promotional materials?"

"Why is that important?"

"Mostly for my curiosity, though it's rather coincidental that your grandfather is in the same line of business as Thomas International Products. It could be that someone hoped to muddy the waters by diverting suspicion onto your family. The TIP personnel department received dozens of Poppy Gold brochures and then got a call from your marketing department."

Tessa frowned. "When TIP booked their first executive retreat at Poppy Gold I was still in San Francisco, but I was coordinating all the business marketing for my parents. Becoming a conference center had been my idea, and I was determined to make it succeed. Initially I concentrated on companies in Northern California, so I was delighted when a Los Angeles firm made reservations. I thought they'd heard about us through word of mouth since I hadn't expanded the mailing list yet."

"Is there any chance that your mother or father called TIP?"

"Unlikely. And they certainly wouldn't have claimed to be from the marketing department since we didn't *have* one. I also can't see sending that many brochures to a single company."

It certainly seemed that someone had tried to lure TIP into coming to Poppy Gold. Then something else occurred to Gabe, and he cocked his head.

"Tell me something—why didn't you put Rob and his executives into the Mill Race Cottage when you moved them? It's closest to the pool and around the same size as the Tofton House. You could have shifted the guests out of there just as easily."

"I would have, but the ghost-hunting group had specifically booked the Mill Race."

Gabe stared. "What difference did it make where they stay? That paranormal stuff is nonsense."

TESSA WAS ANNOYED. "They came to Poppy Gold because the Mill Race has a reputation for spooky happenings."

"You can't honestly believe that stuff."

"Maybe I do a little. But it doesn't matter, anyway. Their money is just as good as anyone else's, and they specifically asked for the Mill Race *before* Rob made his request."

Marley, one of the Victorian Cat's feline residents, jumped onto the couch next to Tessa and mewled, apparently picking up on the tension. She scratched his neck until he curled next to her, though the tip of his tail continued to twitch.

"It's okay, Marley," she soothed.

Marley was a pleasant cat but not as much comfort as Mr. Fezziwig, who seemed to understand when someone wasn't feeling well or was sad and tried to comfort them.

"Look, Gabe, I understand you don't have faith in anything you can't see for yourself. I can't imagine what you saw as a SEAL, but it isn't so clear-cut for me. Part of me wants ghosts to be real, because maybe…" She stopped and swallowed. "Maybe my mother might be able to visit sometimes. I really miss her being here."

A spasm crossed Gabe's face and vanished. "I'm sorry about your mom. She sounds like a great person."

"Thank you."

Tessa petted Marley again, trying to push down the flood of unexpected emotion. For some reason it meant a lot that a man like Gabe, hardened by life, wasn't telling her to stop feeling bad or to cheer up. People meant well, but the grief never went away; she just hoped that in time, happier memories would come before the memory of loss.

GABE WATCHED TESSA, silently acknowledging that he could have handled things better...from the moment he'd arrived at Poppy Gold. He rarely wasted energy on regret, but he knew when he'd made mistakes. Knowing how to correct his mistakes with her was another matter.

"What did you call this cat?" he asked.

"Marley. From the Dickens novel *A Christmas Carol*."

Gabe was struck by the irony. "Wasn't old Marley a ghost?"

"Yup."

She put her head back, looking exhausted, and he was reminded that she'd had a nasty fall less than forty-eight hours ago. And now she was faced with something that could have a terrible impact on Poppy Gold.

"Tessa, I know you're tired and I'll get out of here in a minute, but I'm curious about the people who'd booked the El Dorado the night before TIP was supposed to arrive. When were the reservations made, and did they specifically request that building? Having the place empty would have given someone the entire night to sabotage the staircase."

"I'll check. I'm sure Uncle Milt will ask the same question, too."

She absently ran a finger beneath the elasticized brace on her right elbow, drawing Gabe's attention. Purple bruises extended below the brace, and various other bruises were also visible. He'd also noticed she kept sitting down with caution, which suggested her tailbone remained tender.

Tailbone?

The thought was a reminder that Tessa had a very attractive rear end. Gabe shifted on the couch, fighting his response; she might not be his usual type, but she was still a desirable woman. Yet even if she'd been interested in pursuing something, she wasn't up for any kind of vigorous activity, horizontal or otherwise.

"I'll go now," he said. "You need to rest."

"We haven't resolved anything."

"And we aren't going to tonight. But it would

be great if you could check that housekeeping schedule tomorrow. Let me know so we can get together and talk. Maybe we could conference your great-uncle in on the phone."

TESSA WRINKLED HER nose and wondered if allowing Gabe to go home was letting him off too easy. He *had*, after all, suspected her of industrial espionage.

On the other hand, she felt as if a truck had run over her.

She stood up. "I'll call when I have anything. I also want to analyze any patterns related to my other business clients."

Gabe followed her to the door, and she opened it.

"I apologize for suspecting you," he murmured.

"Since you seem to suspect everyone, it might not be as big of an insult as I thought," she returned in the same low tone. "So I…"

A movement caught her attention on the other side of the garden, a dark figure in the shadows. It probably wasn't anything, but a chill crept over her.

"Tessa?"

"I, um…"

She hated feeling vulnerable and questioning things that were most likely innocent. More than three hundred people were registered at Poppy Gold for the night, and the gardens were public space. But what if somebody was watching them? It wasn't impossible; their argument at the new city park could have been observed, along with Great-Uncle Milt's presence. Perhaps even more critical, she'd drawn attention to Gabe's and Rob's presence together on the pedestrian shopping street.

Unable to think of anything else to divert suspicion, she rose on her toes and pressed close to Gabe.

"Tessa?" he whispered again, this time against her mouth.

"Human-shaped shadow across the way," she mumbled.

Instantly he pulled her into his arms. He turned, making their profiles more visible to the garden, and gave her a thorough kiss.

A minute later he released her, and Tessa grabbed the door frame for support. Gabe McKinley's social skills might be rusty, but he knew how to kiss in *no* uncertain terms.

"I'd love to stay, but you need to rest," he said in a louder voice than he'd used before. "Get better soon, okay?"

"Okay."

He touched her lips with the tip of his finger. "Sleep well."

His eyes glittered in the light spilling out from the living room, and Tessa could have sworn it was from laughter. Except this was Gabe McKinley, and from what she'd seen, his sense of humor sucked. He barely knew how to crack a smile. If anything, he was just having fun at her expense.

"You, too."

She stepped back inside, grateful the awkward paranoid moment was over. It was all Gabe's fault. Picking flowers on his way over to her apartment? If someone *had* been watching from the garden, it was probably an employee wondering if they should report him for inappropriate behavior. While guests sometimes plucked a few blooms, employees didn't. Heck, there wasn't any need. Uncle Kurt grew so many cutting flowers for use in the facility, there were plenty available for the asking.

Tessa's mood mellowed as she thought about Uncle Kurt. He looked like he should belong in a motorcycle gang, but instead he was a devoted father, grew amazing flowers, had a garage where he specialized in repairing diesel motors and drove a late-model pickup.

Where were men like that today?

She took the vase of Western coneflowers into her small kitchen and trimmed off the raw ends before putting them back in water. If Gabe hadn't shown up, flowers in hand, she wouldn't have gotten the idea to pretend they were more than friends while saying good-night at her door. Of course, he was also the one who'd made her jumpy about shadows in the garden.

But as she set the vase on a shelf, Tessa's wry humor asserted itself. It was just as well she wasn't interested in Gabe McKinley, since this small bouquet would probably be the last one she ever received from him. He wasn't the type to send flowers, offer romantic trinkets *or* go for long, moonlit walks.

When she crawled into bed a few minutes later, she expected to think about how complicated her life had become with the revelations about industrial espionage and attempted murder.

Instead, she thought about Gabe.

And about how her pulse had raced when he kissed her.

GABE WENT STRAIGHT back to the fitness center and the treadmill. The sensation of Tessa's mouth against his had destroyed the benefit of his earlier workout. He was now even more wired than before.

Mile after mile ticked by. He increased the speed and incline, pushing his body further. As far as he was concerned, sex was merely a case of scratching an itch with a like-minded partner.

Gabe finally looked at the clock on the wall and went into a cool-down pace. When his breathing had slowed, he stopped the treadmill and wiped his face.

Nobody had been at the fitness room when he'd arrived, and he didn't think anyone had come in since then. By and large, Poppy Gold employees seemed to be the same early-to-bed sort as the rest of the town. Still, there were still the graveyard and swing shifts, so he searched the premises to be sure he was alone. Then keeping an eye on the entrance, he dialed KJ. KJ was short for Kyle John Bermann, though KJ hated his given name so much, it was rarely used.

"Commander, you're lucky I wasn't in bed with somebody," a low voice growled.

Gabe's eyebrow shot up. "You're in bed?"

"It's after two in this part of the country, what do you think?"

Gabe almost smiled. "I didn't think you slept. Ever."

"Only on nights I spend alone. Which isn't often. What do you want?"

"I may have a job for you. Is there anyone you trust available?"

KJ snorted. "It's a security business. My butt is on the line if anybody screws up, so if I don't trust them, they don't work for me. What's up?"

Gabe explained quickly. "Rob is refusing protection," he concluded, "so it'll have to be long-range unless I can make him see sense. Even then it would need to be hush-hush to avoid tipping anyone off. The local police are involved, but they can't assign anyone or put him in protective custody for the same reason."

"Is Rob as hardheaded as you?"

"In his own way, but it's masked by charm."

"Doesn't sound like he'll change his mind. I can send a couple of guys right away, but I need the particulars."

Gabe gave a concise description of the thefts at Poppy Gold and threats to Rob before reeling off the details needed to watch his brother covertly. Rob's schedule was utterly predictable, which just made him an easier target.

"It'll be a boring job," KJ said at length.

"Yeah, but Rob and a group of his executives are returning to Poppy Gold as soon as Tessa Connor makes the arrangements. That's when things may get more interesting. I'd like some of your people to come posing as guests at the same time, with staggered arrivals to avoid suspicion. They should be very casual and low-key, as if they're going to a Victorian Disneyland."

"Since it's you, Commander, I'll come myself. In fact, I'll do a reconnaissance trip first. That way it will be less questionable if I'm also there at the same time as your brother."

Some of Gabe's tension eased as faint sounds of typing came over the wire. KJ had been one of the best SEALs he'd ever commanded. The business he'd started did a little bit of everything, including consulting on almost any security issue that arose. Nevertheless, he refused to be called a private detective.

"Got it," KJ said. "A week from Friday, plane

tickets and reservations for one at the Gold Rail Hotel. Say, I can't find a picture of Tessa Connor on the Poppy Gold website. What's she like?"

"Pint-size and never stops moving," Gabe said reluctantly. KJ was a ladies' man and his cover commonly included chasing any single woman under sixty.

"Is she built?"

"She's petite."

"That's okay, I'm open-minded. How do I meet her?"

The question annoyed Gabe for some reason. "That's up to you, but she does a quick visit in the reception area between one and two each afternoon. She's one of those managers who talks to the troops every day."

"She sounds interesting. I'll text you after I get in."

A faint beep sounded, indicating the end of the call; it was typical of KJ to disconnect without warning. Gabe dropped the phone into his pocket. With the potential threat to Rob, getting KJ involved was the safest move.

Gabe grabbed his athletic bag and slung it over his shoulder. Morning came quickly, and he ought to get a couple of hours of sleep before reporting to work.

He would have to tell Tessa about KJ tomorrow, and she could tell Milt Fullerton; it wouldn't be worth the grief to hide anything else from her.

Yet as Gabe walked back to his studio cottage, he wondered whether he should also warn her about KJ's womanizing. KJ didn't pretend to be looking for more than a night or two of fun, but women still fell for him.

After all the things they'd seen as SEALs, KJ was a fatalist; he believed when your number came up, that was it, and he had every intention of enjoying life in the meantime.

For Gabe, believing in fate would mean believing in destiny. He didn't. It wasn't that he had any faith in humanity, but he couldn't see some great power beyond, either. At the same time, KJ's behavior bothered him; it was too much like using other people.

Brief liaisons with women who shared Gabe's views about marriage were one thing, but not with someone who still might have hopes and dreams. He'd leave it to other people to smash them. He wasn't going to be part of it himself.

Still, he probably didn't need to warn Tessa; she was smart and dedicated to Poppy Gold. If anything, KJ would likely just annoy her.

CHAPTER TEN

LANCE HAD A funny expression on his face when Jamie told him at lunch that she was going to start attending her class in Stockton again.

"Uh, okay," he said.

"Is something wrong?" she asked.

"No, of course not. I just… It's nice when we can get together after work, that's all. But I know you want to finish."

"I just have to go to a few more classes and write an extra term paper to make up for the time I missed. It won't be that long."

He still seemed distracted, and she kissed his cheek.

"I wish you'd tell me what's bothering you." Until now she'd mostly stayed quiet when he was quiet, but sometimes people *had* to talk.

"Are you going away to college this fall?"

"I'll start taking more classes in Stockton, but I'm going to keep working at Poppy Gold. We'll still have lots of time together, Lance, I promise. And maybe we could *both* take some classes."

Lance shifted his feet and looked even more

miserable. "I'm not like you, Jamie. I should have told you before, but my grades were lousy in high school. Nobody expected a kid like me to go to college or do anything important, so it never seemed worth the trouble."

Jamie didn't know what "a kid like me" meant, but she knew Lance was smart and good and could do whatever he wanted, no matter where he'd grown up.

"Do you *want* to go to college?" she asked cautiously.

"I never thought about it."

"Well, if it's what you *want*, I think you can take classes at a junior college, even without good grades. Besides, you're supersmart. Look at how you put the stone wall together next to the orchard. The rocks fit together and it's really straight, even though the ground is so uneven. I couldn't have done it for a million bucks."

He began to smile a little. "That didn't take brains, just muscle."

"I don't know. I'm terrible at math, but Mom says you must be really good in geometry and stuff."

His shoulders straightened. "Your mom said that?"

"Yeah. I showed her and Dad the wall on Sunday morning before church. I wanted them to see how hard you worked on it and the orchard." The clock on top of Old City Hall bonged, and she hurriedly gave Lance a kiss. "I have to go back to work. Talk to you later at the creek."

At the train depot, Jamie went around to the back of the building. She climbed onto the second passenger car and moved forward, talking to picnicking tourists. When the train whistle sounded, she stepped out onto the platform as if she'd just arrived from a journey. It was part of her living history act.

Poppy Gold employees and volunteers did living history on Fridays and weekends, and it was Jamie's favorite work assignment. She loved dressing in costumes and pretending to live in the late 1890s. The character she played was Isabelle Douglas, a real girl who'd been born in Glimmer Creek, though nobody knew what had happened to her after she ran off with a handsome gold miner headed to the Klondike.

That is…nobody in Glimmer Creek knew. *Somebody* had to know, and Jamie was trying to find the answer by writing to historical societies in Alaska and checking old census records. Isabelle's story had always seemed romantic, but lately Jamie was starting to wonder how much fun it would have been to live in a tent and crouch for hours panning gold in freezing-cold water. Chapped hands and woolen long johns didn't sound romantic *or* sexy.

The waiting room was crowded when Jamie went inside. She smiled, aware that she was the center of attention in her costume. For several minutes she wandered around talking to people, and then a man stepped up to her, gesturing toward the high ceiling.

"You can't tell me they had ceiling fans back in the 1800s," he announced loudly. Clearly he wasn't pretending to be anything except a tourist in plaid shorts. "If you're going to have anachronisms in a historic building, it ought to be air-conditioning."

"Honey, it wouldn't kill you to play along," scolded the woman next to him.

"I'd rather be golfing."

Jamie gave them both an earnest look. "Sir, some people in Glimmer Creek think it would be more modern to put those electric ceiling fans into the railroad station, but my father disagrees. He believes the ones that use water are quieter."

The golf enthusiast frowned. "Water?"

Other guests had perked up their ears and were coming closer, as well.

"Well, *yes*," Jamie said, pleased. "A stream of water turns this… Oh, dear, I'm not educated about such things. Gentlemen know so much more about mechanics. It isn't like a mill's waterwheel, but it's something else that turns. Do you know what it might be, sir?"

"Gears… *No*, a turbine," the man said, plainly determined to trump the ideas being thrown out by other gentlemen in the crowd around him.

"Goodness, you're clever," Jamie exclaimed.
She loved it when people were interested, even
when she had to play dumb to get their attention. "The turbine makes the belts turn, which
then spin the two blades. Papa says that *all* the
fans in this part of the depot run off the same
turbine. He owns stock in the railroad, so he
should know."

The visitors gazed upward at the high ceiling where the fans turned lazily. They were the
real, honest-to-gosh fans installed in the 1870s
and were still powered by water. The system
had been refurbished, of course, but the Connors were really proud of it.

Jamie had met Lance two months ago while
explaining how the ceiling fans worked, so they
were extra special to her for that reason alone.

GABE STOOD ON one side of the depot waiting
room, watching Jamie Fullerton chatter to the
tourists. She was an excellent actress and art-
lessly wove a wide range of information into her
spiel.

After a while he heard the sound of clopping
hooves outside, and soon an older man stepped
inside the depot, dressed in the elegant garb of
a Victorian gentleman.

"So sorry I'm late, my dear," he said, coming
over and kissing her forehead.

"I don't mind, Papa. I've been talking to these

nice people. They're waiting for a train. Everyone, this is my father, Eberhard Douglas."

"Delighted." "Eberhard" offered a very correct bow. "I hope you've enjoyed your visit to our community."

A murmur of assent ran through the crowd. They all appeared drawn into the moment.

"We've been talking," Jamie explained. "An opinion has been expressed that the new electric ceiling fans might be best in the depot, to keep up with modern times. After all, it *is* 1895. We wouldn't want anyone to think we're backward in Glimmer Creek."

"Nonsense," her pretend father snorted. "And I certainly hope you haven't brought up any of the suffrage tomfoolery that your aunt holds to. Women shouldn't vote. It isn't natural."

"Whatever you say, Papa." Jamie sounded demure and obedient, but chuckles rippled through the waiting room.

She was good. She pulled her audience right in and got them to play along. Even without saying anything overt, she made everyone believe that she harbored different opinions from her father. It was easy to picture her character sneaking off to suffrage rallies and handing out ribbons without her father's knowledge.

Jamie was talented, and Gabe remembered Lance's questions about being able to support a wife if he enlisted. At their age, would they know what they were getting into, or was Lance just thinking about possibilities for the future?

"Come along, Isabelle," urged Jamie's pretend father. "The stationmaster has placed your bag in my carriage, and your mother needs help. I do believe she's invited half the town to tea."

Jamie said goodbye and took his arm. En masse, the crowd followed to watch as Eberhard helped her into an elegant carriage being drawn by two black horses.

It was a highly polished performance. Jamie put up a parasol and waved to the waiting "passengers" as her father slapped the reins. Gabe knew she'd return in a couple of hours and they'd repeat the routine. In the meantime they were going to the Douglas House, where high tea would be served to guests who'd bought tickets for the event.

It was quite a production, and people seemed to eat it up. Finally he accessed the front staircase to Tessa's office and walked upstairs to knock on her door.

"Come in," she called.

Gabe stepped inside. "Hello, darling. I'm so glad to see you."

Tessa gave him a dark look. "Don't even think it."

"Hey, you're the one who kissed me."

Her face was pale, as if she hadn't slept well. "Actually, I *didn't* kiss you," she said. "I just *pretended* to kiss you because I thought some-one might be watching. You're the one who took it further. And may I add, the idea that someone was watching wouldn't have occurred to me if you hadn't spied on us in the first place."

He couldn't deny the spying part; he *had* spied on Tessa and Liam. True, he'd felt qualms about doing it and intended to return his paychecks at the right opportunity, but he'd done what he thought was necessary.

"Anyway," Tessa continued, "you gave me the idea about a fake kiss when you brought flow-ers. I'm just glad you didn't pick poppies. That's illegal, you know."

Gabe turned one of the chairs around by her desk and sat, straddling it. The act was deliber-ate since Tessa had suggested he was too stiff to fit into the relaxed atmosphere of Glimmer Creek. "I remember a grammar school teacher saying that, but I don't understand why. Unless it's because of their opium content."

"Opium poppies are different from California poppies." Tessa seemed to reflect on the idea. "Actually, I think picking them is only illegal on state or public property. Maybe because they're the California state flower."

"That makes more sense." Regardless, it was time to get this conversation back on track. He rested his arms on the chair. "Apparently we're pretending to be lovers during the investigation."

Tessa had been typing something into her computer. She backspaced and typed something else before looking at him again. "I've thought about that, and I don't think anyone would believe we're involved."

"Why not? Opposites attract, and we need a cover story to explain why we're spending time together. Besides, it fits in with something your great-uncle said."

Tessa stared. "What?"

"He mentioned that people might wonder if we were involved after seeing us in the park. Not that it seems like a bad idea to have a cover story for meeting together." A wicked idea to tease Tessa occurred to Gabe. "It's too bad there isn't a costume ball coming up at Poppy Gold. We could go as Antony and Cleopatra."

"You *would* pick two lovers who came to a tragic end."

"I suppose you'd prefer going as Prince Charming and Cinderella."

"I don't prefer anything when it comes to you," she snapped. "But if I *had* a costume suggestion, it would be Ebenezer Scrooge and the Ghost of Christmas Future. Dickens's description of Ebenezer is perfect for you. Let's see…hard and sharp as flint. Secret and self-contained. Solitary as an oyster. Sound familiar?"

Gabe shifted uncomfortably, though it was

an accurate portrayal. "I guess a costume ball wouldn't be the best idea, after all."

"That's probably the first thing we've agreed upon." She stopped and sighed. "Sorry, I'm not in the best mood. I keep worrying if all my business clients are at risk, not just Rob."

"It seems unlikely, especially if someone went to so much trouble getting TIP to come here."

"But there are no guarantees. Luckily we don't have any business conferences coming here in the next few weeks. It's mostly weddings and reunions, along with our usual vacationing tourists. So we have to find the answer *quickly*."

The urgency Gabe had been feeling swept through him with renewed intensity. It was the best explanation for his lack of restraint with Tessa. The previous night he'd wanted to keep kissing her until it led to something more. It didn't matter that she would have stopped him before it got that far; he should have kept a better lid on his response.

"Did you check the housekeeping schedules for the other times TIP has visited?" he asked.

"I loaded everything into a database and ran a comparison, but I didn't find any patterns. If I get a list of the times Rob believes a leak occurred, I'll check again. I've also looked for patterns with other businesses that have had conferences here, but nothing stands out. No employees have consistently worked at a house where clients were staying more than any other."

"Nothing has happened with TIP's latest visit, other than the collapsing staircase," Gabe mused. "If the culprit pinned their hopes on getting back at Rob that way and it failed, they may be afraid to try something else in case suspicions were raised."

Tessa smiled faintly. "Uncle Milt was at Poppy Gold all day Tuesday after the accident, questioning people. That probably would have scared anyone off. Has Rob observed anything suspicious at the Tofton House?"

"No. I gave him two high-tech video cams to catch anyone going in and out of the room or hanging around the desk—very small and hard to detect—but Rob didn't see anything unusual in the recordings from yesterday. He brought old documents with him, nothing confidential, and spread them out on the desk in his suite. The housekeeping staff did their thing, but nothing appeared suspicious."

Tessa looked at him grimly. "You didn't tell Great-Uncle Milt about the camera, and *don't* tell me it slipped your mind. You aren't the Lone Ranger on this investigation any longer. There's a much better chance of catching the thief and getting a conviction if all the legalities are observed."

"Glimmer Creek doesn't have the resources for

a major investigation *or* for the high-tech gadgetry we might need."

She made a derisive sound. "Poppy Gold will pay for anything that's needed, high or low tech. But why don't you admit the real problem…that you don't think an aging police chief from a small town can be of any real help? You think you ought to be able to handle it yourself."

Gabe heaved a deep sigh.

Maybe he *was* guilty of playing Lone Ranger… of wanting to be the hero for his brother. There were too many things in the world that couldn't be fixed, but this situation shouldn't be one of them.

"Were you planning a little primitive justice for the guilty party and can't now with Uncle Milt involved?" Tessa continued, and he narrowed his eyes.

"I always planned to give any evidence to the authorities," he said crisply. "Don't forget we tried to get the FBI to investigate before we ever started this, though I don't blame them for being skeptical about our claims. For that matter, the only reason Milt Fullerton is taking it seriously is because of your accident on the staircase."

"Did you tell the FBI that you'd ruled out hacking?"

"Of course. But Rob doubted it could be that from the start. His IT security team would have immediately notified him of any attacks on the company's firewall. Nevertheless, to rule out an internal breech, he simply disconnected the information from any hackable source."

"What about the cameras you set up? Are you going to review the recordings yourself?"

"Rob is going to hand them off to me before he leaves tomorrow. He'll call later tonight if he sees anything from the ones today."

Tessa shook her head. "Another casual meeting? He'd better give them to me. There's nothing unusual about the Poppy Gold manager talking to guests, and I can get everything to my great-uncle without it looking suspicious."

Gabe supposed he'd better get used to things going through Milt Fullerton.

"What about the people who were supposed to stay at the El Dorado Mansion Monday night?"

"I checked, and they made the reservations *after* the earthquake, specifically asking for the El Dorado. It couldn't have sounded suspicious at the time. Groups often ask to stay together in a particular house, and since so many of the weekend guests leave on Sunday, the house was available. I already let Uncle Milt know." Tessa gestured to her computer. "I've also been looking at the calendar. I'll do whatever I can to get enough rooms for TIP to come back in June."

The phone rang, and Gabe watched Tessa's

face as she dealt with an inquiry from someone wanting to book an autumn class reunion at Poppy Gold. She searched three possible dates before finding enough available rooms.

He wished she wasn't so determined to get involved in the investigation. It would be best for him to coordinate with Milt Fullerton and keep her on the periphery, but she clearly wasn't going to cooperate.

Besides, something about Tessa got to him. She was intelligent, beautiful, sexy and her personality was a force of nature. And while it might be misplaced, her loyalty was admirable. Her relatives could easily be taking advantage, but she was more likely to suspect the Easter Bunny than any of them.

"Sorry," Tessa said after her call ended.

"That's okay. Shall I come over tonight? We have more to discuss, and we can have Milt conference in."

"Sorry, there's a wedding and reception booked for this evening. I need to be on hand for it."

"Have you ever heard of delegating?"

"Have you ever heard of minding your own business?"

Gabe got up. "While I'd love to stay and debate the question with you, my lunch break is almost over. I need to get back to my weeding and lawn mowing."

TESSA CLENCHED HER JAW, wanting to throw something at the door after Gabe had closed it behind him. Her work habits weren't any of his business.

On the other hand, it might be wise to get extra rest. She also needed to call her grandfather and didn't want to do it where there was any chance of being overheard or interrupted.

Back at her apartment in the Victorian Cat, she dialed Patrick Connor's private line.

"Hey, Granddad."

"*Tessa.* How wonderful to hear your voice. I just got out of a meeting."

"Ouch." Tessa remembered the Connor Enterprises executive meetings. They were deadly dull. "In that case, I wish I was calling for a better reason."

"Oh?"

Quickly she explained what she'd learned from both Gabe and Rob and that the situation may have escalated into violence.

"Liam told me you fell, but I didn't realize it was something like this," Patrick exclaimed.

"Pop doesn't know, and I don't *want* him to know unless absolutely necessary. You know what a worrywart he can be."

"Yes. I'm glad Milt Fullerton is on the case."

Tessa made a face. "I'm sure Gabe wishes Uncle Milt was a young, aggressive FBI agent, but apparently the FBI wouldn't get involved because of the lack of evidence. Uncle Milt will be great, and he'll be sure to keep the investigation confidential. Oh, and in case Pop says anything to you or Grams, Gabe and I are pretending to date. It's a cover to explain any time we spend together."

"I understand. Promise you'll be careful," Granddad urged.

"Of course. But Uncle Milt is very protective, and Gabe is a retired navy SEAL, so I'll be fine. One Connor worrywart is enough, and Pop has dibs."

"I'm glad this McKinley fellow is capable. What can I do to help?"

Glad about Gabe? Tessa wasn't so sure, but she had a great deal of faith in the US Navy to train an effective SEAL. According to their reputation, SEALs were able to do anything.

"I wanted to find out if anyone has attempted to pass insider information to Connor Enterprises. At any level. I know it's SOP to refer anything like that to the security staff."

"I haven't received anything myself, but I'll check with my security chief and let you know."

"Thanks. How is Grams?"

"Busy as always. She wants a rooftop garden. I refused, so naturally we have landscape architects submitting proposals. We're leaning toward one with a water feature."

Tessa smiled. While Granddad was radically different from his son, he and Liam shared at least one trait—unshakable devotion to the women in their lives.

After they talked for another few minutes, Tessa sent her love to her grandmother and got off. She'd hoped Granddad would have more information, but it still had been a relief to tell someone else what was happening.

Gabe would likely go ballistic, but she trusted Patrick Connor and didn't need permission to enlist his help.

CHAPTER ELEVEN

LANCE DUG IN the ground, trying not to think about what Jamie had said at lunch. College wasn't something he'd ever considered.

His shovel hit a rock, but as he felt around the edges to lever it out, he realized it was practically a boulder. He began digging around it, the effort making everything else go away in his head for a while.

Finally he used a lever to lift it out of the hole and then rolled it over to the pile of rocks he'd already dug out. He took off the sunglasses Jamie had given him and carefully put them in a pocket before wiping his face with a bandanna. He wasn't too sure about the bandannas—they seemed kind of folksy—but she was always putting them around his neck to keep him from getting sunburned, so he didn't object.

"How are you doing?" called Liam as he came up the hill.

"I haven't gotten much done because of this rock," Lance said, nudging the boulder with his shoe.

"Digging that out was plenty. It's bigger than a beach ball."

Lance nodded. He hadn't seen many beach balls—on a beach at least—but it *was* a big rock.

"Here's something to cool you off," Liam said, handing him a huge bottle of a sports drink. "I don't want you getting heatstroke."

"Thanks." Lance took off the lid and chugged down a bunch. In the beginning he'd been wary when Liam brought him food or something to drink, thinking it would come out of his paycheck, but Jamie had told him the Connors were nice to everyone.

He liked Liam.

Sometimes the guy was absentminded and didn't seem to hear stuff, but everybody said it was because he missed his wife.

Lance got it.

If he ever lost Jamie, it would be the worst thing in the world.

"We don't see much hot spring weather like this," Liam murmured. "It's unusual even for summer. I've been thinking we should find something else for you to do in the afternoons until the weather breaks."

"I don't mind the heat," Lance said quickly.

"Are you sure? We'll have to reassign you once the second orchard is planted, anyhow."

"Will I still be able to take care of the trees?"

It felt silly, but Lance was protective of the small apple orchard he'd planted.

"Certainly, but I also want you to learn how to maintain our antique vehicles. At first I thought you could work with my brother-in-law in the greenhouses, but Gabe McKinley mentioned that you seem to be mechanical. That would be better for you because it pays a bit more."

Pride and relief swelled in Lance, both because Mr. McKinley had spoken up for him and because his job at Poppy Gold seemed safe. As for a pay raise? Except for the gifts he got for Jamie, he lived cheaply and was saving as much money as possible, but anything more would help.

"That's awesome," he said, his throat tight. He'd gone to work as a restaurant busboy after high school because nobody else would give him a chance. Now he might get a promotion.

"Excellent. Are you sure you're all right out here?"

"I'm fine." It would take a long time to finish clearing the brush and digging out the new orchard, but Lance wanted the Connors to know he'd finish the job.

"All right." Liam pulled two more bottles of sports drink from his pack. "Bring these back empty," he ordered.

Lance grinned. "Yes, sir."

He went back to digging. When there were enough rocks to pick and choose from, he planned to build another stone wall. On the first one he'd used a quick-setting concrete in the center, to be sure it wouldn't fall down, but nobody could tell—it looked just like the old walls he'd seen on the internet. A wall was sure better than piles of rocks where snakes could hide; he'd already surprised several rattlesnakes.

The apples he'd planted were growing. The Connors planned to install a drip irrigation system, but until then, the trees had to be watered by hand.

Lance looked over at the new orchard. He'd check the trees again before he left. He hoped the weather got cooler; he didn't mind bringing water out on the little handcart, but the heat seemed hard on the saplings.

He wiped his face again, still wishing he knew what Jamie's suggestion about them taking classes together meant. If she just wanted them to spend time together, that was cool. But maybe she'd decided she didn't want to date a guy whose life might not be going anywhere.

The truth was he didn't know how to be with a girl like Jamie. He needed her a lot more than she needed him, and he worried all the time that she'd decide he wasn't good enough. And the hardest part was knowing that he really *wasn't*.

AFTER WORK JAMIE changed out of her costume and raced down to the creek. Lance wasn't there yet, and she hoped he wasn't unhappy about her taking the time to finish her class.

Surely not, though *something* had been bugging him lately. She was glad that he'd told her about his grades and the other stuff. In the beginning everything had been dreamy and romantic with Lance, but according to her mom, *falling* in love was a lot easier than *being* in love.

Jamie took her shoes off and put her feet in the cool water. While she didn't want to bother Tessa, maybe she *should* talk to her. Her cousin was older and had more experience with dating, so she might understand what was bothering Lance.

She bent over and looked at the rippling currents in the water. She loved Glimmer Creek and didn't want to leave. Her parents wanted her to go away to college in the fall, so she figured working at Poppy Gold and taking more classes down in Stockton was a compromise. Mom didn't entirely agree; she kept saying it was only for a while, but four years was *forever*.

Dad understood a little better.

He'd grown up in Glimmer Creek and had convinced Mom to do her residency in family medicine with Dr. Romano, saying if she hated living there, they'd discuss going somewhere else. Twenty years later, they were discussing whether they wanted to buy a house outside the town where they could keep a couple of horses and some chickens.

Jamie dug a toe into the soft sand of the creek bed. Maybe she should check and see if Lance was okay. He liked to shower and change his clothes before they got together, but what if he wasn't feeling well? What if he'd gotten heat-stroke or something from working outside this afternoon? It was the hottest day they'd had so far.

Suddenly worried, Jamie got up, only to see Lance coming down the path.

"Hey," he said. "Sorry I'm late. I had to make two extra trips for water to give to the apple trees."

"That's okay." Jamie brushed the hair away from his forehead to see if the bruise was gone; it was hard to tell with his dark tan, but she thought so. "Should we sit down or go for a walk?"

"Let's sit."

Jamie happily sat down again. She wanted to ask if she was right, that something was bother-ing him, and about other things, too, like why he didn't push for more than kissing, but right now it was enough that they were together.

LATE IN THE afternoon Tessa returned home fol-lowing a visit with Uncle Milt at the ice-cream parlor on the pedestrian shopping street. They'd arranged to meet there so she could casually hand off the video recordings and copies of the threatening letters Rob McKinley had received.

The letters were disturbing, pieced together from clips from magazines and newspapers, ugly in tone and sounding a little unhinged. How Rob could be so cool about it she didn't know.

Back at her apartment in the Victorian Cat, Tessa hastily changed into something appropriate for a wedding. She did her hair in a French braid and headed for the old town square park. The rows of chairs for the guests were already in place, and two industrial-sized misting machines had been set up, blowing water-cooled air over the area.

While they weren't the most attractive pieces of equipment, she had a feeling they'd be quite popular with the guests and bridal couple. Nobody had expected such a heat wave in May.

Satisfied, she went to check the staff's progress on setting up for the reception. Luckily they had air-conditioning in the concert hall.

Inside, Aunt Polly turned around as she approached and smiled. "You look lovely, dear. I think the worst part about these things is figuring out what to wear."

"I've been thinking about that," Tessa said. "Maybe we should have a standard employee uniform for formal events. Then nobody would have to keep a black skirt or pants and a white top in their wardrobe and we'd all be more easily identified. I'm not sure the sky blue armbands are enough."

Yet Tessa's heart thumped painfully. Her mother had always resisted uniforms for employees other than the maintenance and housekeeping staffs, preferring to rely on a dress code and name tags. When Tessa had first taken over management of Poppy Gold, she'd instituted the armbands, but even *that* had felt as if she was stomping on Meredith Connor's legacy.

"Excellent idea," Aunt Polly affirmed.

To Tessa's annoyance, Gabe's comment about delegating floated through her head. He was a fine one to talk about delegating; he was a one-man demolition team.

"Uh, yeah. Do you want to come up with something?" Tessa asked. "Maybe with a Victorian flair, but comfortable and practical?"

Aunt Polly seemed pleased. "I'll do several sketches and see where we could have them made. Something might even be available already with the uniform companies, so I'll check them out, as well. But…uh…how about uniforms the rest of the time? I know my sister didn't care for them, but you have to do things your own way."

Tessa let out a breath. "Sure. Come up with a proposal, and we'll discuss how extensive to make it."

"Sounds good."

A chair clattered to the floor from a trolley, and Tessa jumped...mostly from realizing it was *Gabe* pushing the trolley. She hadn't recognized him at first; he was wearing black shoes and pants and a long-sleeved white shirt, adorned with the usual sky blue armband. He looked entirely too tall and sexy for comfort.

She hurried over. "Gabe, what are you doing here?"

"Maintenance, naturally. One of the guys scheduled for tonight didn't feel well, and I volunteered to fill in."

"Don't you have *other* things to do?" she asked pointedly.

"Not that I can think of. After all, you're working and I'm lonely."

Lord. She didn't want to pretend they were socializing, but other employees might well wonder why they were spending so much time together. Romance was a reasonable cover story. As for the investigation, Rob had left that morning, so Gabe was probably bored and at loose ends.

She stepped even closer. "I'm going to play along, but you're going to stay lonely," she said in a very, *very* low tone.

"Please don't tell me we're having our first fight," Gabe replied, except his voice was loud enough that others in the concert hall might be able to overhear.

Tessa regarded him blackly. With anyone else

she might have suspected it was a twisted joke, but with Gabe McKinley, it was probably just part of the act.

"Sorry, I have work to do."

She headed for the kitchen, only to have him call after her, "Tessa, are you sure it's going to be too late for me to come over after the reception?"

She froze.

Finally she turned and looked back, wanting to tell him that having fun at someone else's expense wasn't the same as having a sense of humor.

"Yes, Gabe, I'm *absolutely* positive."

To her everlasting annoyance, he actually smiled.

CHAPTER TWELVE

TESSA ROLLED OVER in bed on Saturday morning, luxuriating in the one day a week she allowed herself an extra hour.

The wedding had gone well, in spite of Gabe's unexpected presence. He'd helped quite a bit, shifting chairs to expand the dance floor, etc. He'd tried to be unobtrusive, but one of the bridesmaids had tried coaxing him to dance. He must have been tempted—she'd been tall, slender and well-endowed in her low-cut gown. She also hadn't seemed to be looking for more than a night of fun.

Whether Gabe had succumbed was another question. At one point Tessa had spotted the other woman slip something into his pocket. A key? An invitation? Either way, it wasn't her business, though he probably hadn't because of the investigation.

Tessa had just closed her eyes again when the doorbell rang. The only person likely to visit this early on a Saturday morning was her father, so she threw a wrap over her nightgown and ran downstairs. Pop got depressed when they had weddings at Poppy Gold, so she'd begun telling him to stay away from the events. She didn't think it was because he begrudged anyone else their happiness; weddings were just another reminder that the love of his life was gone.

"Hey, Pop, want some breakfast?" she said as she opened the door.

Only it wasn't Liam Connor standing there. It was Gabe McKinley.

"You shouldn't answer doors without checking who's on the other side," he advised, looking her up and down. "Especially dressed like that."

Tessa determinedly kept from blushing. Her light cotton nightdress wasn't provocative. It was cool and comfortable and far less revealing than swimwear.

"That's none of your concern."

Gabe stepped past her into the apartment, and she scowled, irritated by the flash of feminine heat he provoked.

"It's customary to wait for an invitation. Were you raised in a barnyard?" she asked, shutting the door more firmly than necessary.

"Nope, but I had a vodka-guzzling mother and work-obsessed father, so I'm afraid the social niceties were left out of my education." The blunt response seemed typical of him.

"I don't think you're afraid of anything."

"Just of my brother getting hurt."

"Fair enough. Where did *Rob* learn his manners?" Tessa asked, heading for the kitchen. She needed coffee to deal with Gabe McKinley, the stronger the better.

"From one of our grandmothers. Grandma Ada moved back to Los Angeles soon after I enlisted. She's a true, old-style Bostonian. Quite proper and correct."

Tessa ground coffee beans and started them brewing. "My mom's parents are here in Glimmer Creek, but I still miss my Connor grandparents in San Francisco. Things are so busy I don't get to see them often enough. Oh, I called my grandfather yesterday to tell him about the problems with TIP," she added casually.

Gabe stared. "You did *what*?"

"I talked to Granddad, which is something granddaughters do occasionally. But don't worry—he won't say anything to my dad about the staircase or the thefts."

"Who cares about that? You just told the enemy that TIP has a problem."

"No, I told my *grandfather*. I asked if anyone has approached him or Connor Enterprises with offers of insider information. He doesn't know of any, but he'll check with his security staff."

Gabe paced the length of the small kitchen with the energy of a caged panther. "This isn't a fairy tale, Tessa. He'll use this against TIP. We may as well advertise it in the *New York Times*."

Tessa took eggs and cheese from the refrigerator, realizing Gabe genuinely didn't understand that decent people vastly outnumbered the bad.

"Calm down before you have a stroke," she advised. "I'll put this in terms you should understand—Granddad won't say or do anything, if for no other reason than it would devastate Poppy Gold Inns."

"Poppy Gold stole both you and your father away from working with him," Gabe snapped. "I'm sure he doesn't harbor any fondness for the place."

"Nobody stole anything. My father was never happy until he met my mom," Tessa said, feeling the familiar stab of grief. Would thinking about her mother always hurt this much? "Grandfather deeded Connor's Folly to my parents because he knew Glimmer Creek was the right place for his son. He also knew I expected to manage Poppy Gold when my parents retired and was glad to have me in San Francisco for however long I could stay. He's never once done anything to make me feel guilty for leaving."

"What about his empire?"

"Maybe I'll have a child who wants to run it someday."

Gabe's expression turned even grimmer. "It's irresponsible to bring children into such a screwed-up world."

Tessa began breaking eggs into a bowl, unsure of how to react. She'd heard men spout the same sentiment as if repeating something they'd read and used as a toss-off line to warn a date they weren't looking for anything permanent. *It isn't right to bring kids into this kind of world*, usually delivered in a smug, self-satisfied tone.

But with Gabe, it was real and personal. He *didn't* want children for the exact reason he'd given.

"The world isn't going to get better if people stop having kids," she said finally. "Every child represents hope. They could become a Mother Teresa or brilliant doctor, or just a good person who adds to the decency in the world."

"Yeah, well you haven't seen the things I've seen. Hideous, backbreaking poverty. Brutality at the most vicious level. Ruthless killing that doesn't care about life, much less innocence." He delivered the words in a clipped, almost emotionless tone, yet the rigidity in his posture spoke volumes. This was a man who'd seen the darkest parts of human nature and was still bleeding inside from them. "There isn't much hope in any of that."

Tessa drew a shaky breath and began beating the eggs. Gabe had reasons for being such a cynic. Pop had also seen dreadful things while serving in the army…some so awful he still had intense dreams about them. It was partly why they tried to assist military men and women and their families.

The coffee finished brewing, and she poured two cups, wordlessly handing one to Gabe. He stood at the kitchen window, staring into the garden. The Victorian gardens at Poppy Gold were lushly, romantically beautiful—an idyllic delight, enticing butterflies and birds to visit. Yet Tessa wondered if Gabe was seeing something else entirely.

A pang went through her. Anyone who could have such deep wounds in his soul over the hurts and injustices of the world had to have a larger heart than he'd probably admit to having. Trying not to think about it, she swallowed a mouthful of coffee and put two skillets to heat on the stove. When they were ready, she poured in the egg mixture.

"I'll bet all those cats upstairs would love to get outside," Gabe murmured after a long silence. "Lots of birds to catch. Or do you think Mr. Fezziwig would leave them alone because you asked him to be nice?"

It was an obvious attempt to get a rise out of her, but Tessa wasn't biting. "We keep the cats inside because it's safer and healthier for them, but I'm sure they'd chase birds if given an opportunity."

"Then all they have to hunt are dust bunnies."

"We have a dedicated housekeeping staff, so I hope the cats don't have *those* to hunt, either. However, they have toys in their rooms and lots of company."

Tessa added fillings to the omelets before dropping slices of bread in the toaster.

"Do you want cream or sugar for your coffee?" she asked, noticing he hadn't drunk any.

"Neither. I prefer it black."

She shrugged and poured milk into her own cup. A few minutes later she cleared her throat. "Come and get it. I'm hungry, even if you aren't."

GABE TURNED AND blinked at the golden omelets sitting on the breakfast table. Without fuss, Tessa had produced breakfast for two. With another woman he might have wondered if she was trying to impress him, but Tessa's low opinion of him wasn't a secret.

He liked that.

He also liked that she wasn't fussing about being in her nightgown. It was white, feminine and full to the ground. What she probably didn't know was that despite the floaty thing she wore over it, the fabric was transparent enough to reveal hints of her figure. Curiously, it was just as provocative as a more revealing garment.

"I didn't expect you to feed me."

She shrugged and spooned jam on her toast. "Are you here to tell me something?"

"Yes." Gabe put his cup on the table and sat in a chair. "I told you that I have security contacts. One of them is coming next Friday for a few days. He owns a security business that does a little bit of everything, including private investigations."

"So he's coming to do a reconnaissance."

"Exactly. I didn't want KJ to arrive without your knowledge. I also figured you'd want to tell Milt about him."

Tessa hiked an eyebrow. "That sounds very self-righteous for somebody who's been spying on us."

"Are you ever going to let that go?"

She ate a bit of toast before answering. "Probably not. Is KJ another ex-SEAL?"

"Yeah."

"Married?"

"Definitely not."

"Too bad. He might not stand out so much if he had a wife with him."

Gabe ate a bite of omelet. It was tasty, though that didn't surprise him. Tessa was a pint-size dynamo who seemed capable of anything. Even after almost getting killed, she'd worked a full day and kept things moving at Poppy Gold.

"I don't think KJ will stand out, at least not in the way you think," he said.

"Now I'm curious."

"You'll figure it out when he gets here," Gabe told her. It was almost guaranteed that KJ would hit on Tessa.

They finished breakfast in silence.

"I suppose you're working today," Gabe said when she got up and put their plates in the sink.

"This morning. Later this afternoon there's an ice-cream social at the Veterans Memorial Hall, and I'm trying to convince Pop to go."

"Why wouldn't he?"

Tessa seemed to hesitate. "Remember I told you he met my mother at an ice-cream social? The memories are hard for him, and he gets emotional. So what are *you* going to do with your weekend?"

"Something you won't like—I'm researching the employees at Poppy Gold. I've identified several people who seem to be big spenders. You know, fancy cars, big homes or other purchases that suggest hidden income."

"I told you—"

"I know what you told me," he interrupted, "but it's the only action I can take right now, and it's amazing how much information is available on the internet and through gossip."

TESSA LOOKED AT the clock on her stove. It was past the usual time she got to her office on Saturday morning. Except…maybe it would be better to deal with Gabe now, rather than later.

"All right, what are the names?"

His eyebrows went up. "I thought you needed to work."

"What I *need* is to make sure you don't point a finger at somebody for no good reason. Believe it or not, people deserve their privacy. We'll call Uncle Milt if I agree that something sounds questionable."

"I don't have the list with me. How about taking a drive? That's a nice thing for people to do when they're getting to know each other. And there wouldn't be any chance of being overheard."

"Fine," she agreed. "I'll get dressed and make a few phone calls. When and where should I meet you?"

"Let's say ten o'clock near that Sarah's Treat place."

"Sarah's Sweet Treats," Tessa corrected automatically. Her cousin's bakery and catering business was near the pedestrian shopping street. She could take care of a few things and get there quickly.

"Whatever. Wear something that looks like we're going out on a date, not what you normally wear to work."

"My clothes are my business. Anyhow, I doubt you know how to have fun. By the way, you had some nerve suggesting I work too many hours the other day. Aren't navy SEALs a dedicated lot?"

Gabe looked chagrined. "Yes. But I don't have a family at home."

"Neither do I. So do me a favor and stuff your double-standard attitudes."

She saw Gabe out, stepping back quickly when she suspected he intended to give her another kiss at the door. There weren't any suspicious shadows in the early morning sunlight, and she didn't want an unnecessary repeat of something that had kept her awake for hours every night since then.

Drat him, anyhow.

She didn't sleep around, but with one kiss, Gabe had turned her into a sex-crazed woman who had trouble thinking about anything except ripping his shirt off. Surely it was just because he was different from every other man she'd met.

He was mysterious, strong, dangerous, and the darkness in his eyes held a deep pain…

Furious for even thinking about it, she went upstairs and threw her nightgown on the bed. She looked at herself in the mirror, turning back and forth in the reflection. So, Gabe wanted her to dress for a date. Tessa smiled and decided to accommodate him. She pulled out shorts, a lacy, camisole-style top and strappy sandals.

The other night Gabe had pulled her against him as they kissed, and there hadn't been any doubt that he'd become aroused. But he wouldn't be thinking about sex today...not with so much of her skin an unsightly patchwork of yellowing bruises.

GABE WAITED NEAR the bakery, uncomfortable in the cheerful throng of tourists. He half expected Tessa not to show up, but he still kept looking for her.

A shapely pair of legs caught his attention, and he watched with appreciation. Not overly long, but shapely. On her feet were the type of ridiculously impractical sandals that women sometimes wore, with a loop over the big toe and a thin band around the ankle. Her naturally golden skin was nice, with plenty of it displayed since she also wore a skimpy top that revealed her midriff.

Gabe's gaze moved upward again, and his jaw dropped.

Tessa?

"Hey," she said, smiling provocatively. "I hope you didn't have to wait long." Rising up on her toes, she pressed a light kiss on his mouth. "Do I look all right?"

She turned slowly, and Gabe suddenly understood her transformation. The bruises from her fall were quite evident, and he was torn between wanting to drag her into bed and concern for what she'd gone through.

He cleared his throat. "You look great."

"Why, *thank* you, Gabe," she returned in an overly sweet tone. "Shall we go?"

"Yeah."

In his SUV, she put on her seat belt with a satisfied look on her face.

"Was that necessary?" Gabe asked.

"I don't know what you're talking about."

"Your outfit."

"You wanted me to wear something other than my work clothes." Her expression was pure innocence.

"I didn't say... Oh, never mind."

Tessa had a wicked sense of humor, but if she thought a few bruises would turn him off, she was greatly mistaken. Instead, they'd made him start thinking about positions in bed that would put less pressure on her discolored bottom. Well, he didn't *know* her bottom was discolored...other than the bruises he could see extending from beneath her very short shorts.

Frustrated, he headed out of town, taking the shortest possible route onto the small highway.

"Not that I want to be a backseat driver, but you're driving as if the hounds of hell are chasing us," Tessa advised.

Gabe lifted his foot off the accelerator, but it was too late. Lights flashed behind him, and he pulled over to the side of the road. Pain instantly throbbed in his temples.

The cruiser stopped behind him, and an officer got out, walking up to the driver's window. He looked inside, and his face split into a smile. "Whoa, Tessa, you're dressed to kill."

"It's a hot day, Howie. A girl's gotta do what a girl's gotta do. I heard your mother's sciatica is acting up. How is she?"

"She's back on her feet and should be at the ice-cream social later. Are you going?"

"Unless you arrest me."

The deputy grinned wider. "The way you're dressed, I ought to bring you in for something, but I'll let you off with a warning." He sobered when he looked at Gabe. "Sir, may I have your driver's license, vehicle registration and insurance card?"

Keeping his expression as neutral as possible, Gabe dug them out. Howie examined each carefully before taking them to his cruiser.

Gabe glanced at Tessa. "Another cousin?"

"High school boyfriend."

Of course.

Howie came back a few minutes later and returned the documents. "I won't give you a ticket today, Mr. McKinley, but please stay within the speed limit from now on." He tipped his hat to Tessa. "Nice to see you, Tessa."

"Same here, Howie."

Gabe waited until the cruiser had U-turned and was driving back toward Glimmer Creek. "Don't say anything," he warned.

Tessa gave him a smug smile. "You know *that* isn't going to happen. Now everyone will believe we're out on a joyride. Howie will make sure of it."

"We had to run into your old boyfriend."

"There are worse things—it could have been Uncle Milt. Not that he won't hear about it. Speeding with his great-niece in the car won't endear you to him."

Sheesh. Gabe checked for traffic and pulled onto the road again.

"So, who are your current suspects?" Tessa asked after they'd driven several more miles.

"The first is Cheryl Clark. She's low on the housekeeping staff but recently bought a new Mercedes. She isn't married and doesn't seem to have a rich boyfriend."

From the corner of his eye, he saw Tessa shake her head. "Cheryl inherited money a few years ago from her grandparents. She probably could quit but seems to prefer working. She's dated our local pharmacist for years. They have a very unusual relationship. Quite inventive, as a matter of fact."

"That sounds like an interesting story."

"Let's just say they enjoy creative role-playing and don't mind going public with it." Her voice was amused. "Who else are you suspicious about?"

Gabe spotted a historical marker at the side of the road and pulled off again to park under a tree. He took his list from his pocket and reviewed it. "Nate Dixon on the maintenance crew has paid off the home he just bought two years ago. He also just purchased a new truck, loaded with every possible accessory."

"Let me guess, Pablo Garcia, Penny Cox and Wes Sunderland are also on that sheet of paper."

Gabe nodded, hoping he was finally making progress.

"Sorry," Tessa said instead. "They won the lottery together ten months ago. It was a nice payout, even after taxes. Who else?"

Losing his best suspects was exasperating, but on the other hand, he wouldn't waste any more time on the wrong people. Perhaps Tessa was going to be more help than he'd thought…and drive him to distraction in the process.

"Jodi Wilcox in Housekeeping. She was talking in the employee break room about going on a cruise this autumn. Frankly, she's the nondescript sort nobody would notice going in and out of guest rooms."

"Jodi isn't a saint, but she works hard and will turn in a dime if she finds it on the street. Her daughter and son-in-law are taking her on a cruise to Alaska for her birthday."

Tessa wiggled in her seat and stretched out her legs. It hiked her shorts even higher, and Gabe nearly lost track of the conversation. She really *did* have nice skin, bruises notwithstanding.

"Uh, okay," he muttered. "The last two are Celina Noble and Lance Beckley."

"Why Lance?"

"He's new in town and spends a fair amount of money on Jamie Fullerton. He's also mentioned wanting to make it big."

"Ambition isn't a crime."

"No, but someone might try to exploit it. What can you tell me about Celina?"

Tessa's face was thoughtful. "Not a great deal. She didn't grow up in Glimmer Creek and has a reputation for being a loner. It's no secret that she prefers working the night shift in Guest Registration."

"She has expensive taste in jewelry."

"Again, not a crime. We can mention her to Uncle Milt, but she could have inherited, saved, be buying on credit or any number of other perfectly innocent alternatives. For all we know, she's related to someone who runs a large international company and is investigating industrial espionage."

Gabe's headache got worse. "How many times will I have to apologize for that?" he asked.

"Until I think you mean it."

ON THE DRIVE back to Glimmer Creek, Tessa reflected that trying to fake a romantic relationship was rather like having rabbits—one thing led to another until you were ankle-deep in bunnies.

She'd agreed to lunch so they'd be away long enough to look as if it had been a genuine outing, then Gabe had decided she should walk back through Poppy Gold carrying something "fun," similar to returning from a carnival with a stuffed animal. She'd wryly suggested balloons, and he'd taken her seriously.

"Where is your brain? I'm not eight," she'd said in exasperation.

As a compromise she'd bought a pair of glove stretchers at Beecher's Antique Mall; their bags were printed with a bold drawing of a gold miner holding up a nugget and yelling, "Eureka."

"Under the circumstances, shouldn't we go to the ice-cream social together?" Gabe asked as he parked near the bakery again.

"*No.* We have nothing else to discuss, and you just want to give me a hard time. But don't let me stop you from going."

"It might be a good place to learn more about the locals, but I'm not the kind of guy who goes to that sort of thing alone," Gabe argued. "It would be better to have people speculating about who I'm with than something else."

Tessa pursed her lips.

The bunnies were now hopping up to her knees.

If she went to the ice-cream social with Gabe, her father might think that she was starting to look for a serious relationship. Yet if she told Pop about the problems with TIP and the possible connection to her accident on the staircase, he'd worry himself sick.

Pop would rather close Poppy Gold Inns forever than risk his daughter getting hurt.

"Tessa?" Gabe prompted.

"I was just thinking about my father," she said slowly. "I don't like lying to him."

"Not correcting a wrong impression isn't exactly a lie, and you're already trying to avoid telling him about the information thefts."

She frowned unhappily. "All right, I'll tell him we're seeing each other, but that it's very casual since we don't think we're compatible. Maybe I can tell him that I'm mostly trying to get you to loosen up so you're more approachable for our guests."

"I did okay last night at the wedding."

"That's because one of the bridesmaids wanted to sleep with you and didn't intend to take no for answer."

GABE DIDN'T BOTHER wondering if Tessa had been jealous; her tone was too unconcerned. If she hadn't liked the other woman's behavior, she was keeping it hidden.

He parked near the pedestrian shopping street and got out to open the door for Tessa.

"When should I pick you up this afternoon?" he asked.

"I'll meet you. Or *we'll* meet you, provided I

can talk Pop into going. Four o'clock at the Glimmer Creek Veterans Memorial Hall. That's up Carson Street on the right."

"Gotcha."

Tessa slid down from the high seat of the SUV, avoiding the hand he extended to help her. She grabbed her shopping bag and neatly ducked as he stepped closer for a kiss.

"Just pretend we had an argument about the bridesmaid," she advised him.

Damn, she was sharp.

Tessa walked away, and he watched appreciatively. She packed a lot of punch in her petite frame, swinging her hips with just the right amount of sass.

Cool it, he ordered silently.

Tessa Connor had already proved to be a handful, and she was the wrong kind of woman for a casual affair.

The bridesmaid on the other hand?

She'd definitely been looking for a one-nighter, but only to get back at her boyfriend, who hadn't been able to attend the wedding. Distaste filled Gabe. He might have a dim view of marriage and long-term relationships, but he wouldn't help someone cheat, for revenge or otherwise.

CHAPTER THIRTEEN

TESSA WAS GLAD she didn't meet anyone she knew well on the walk back to the Victorian Cat. She wasn't embarrassed about her clothes, but she hadn't worn such skimpy garments in Glimmer Creek since becoming the manager of Poppy Gold Inns.

She changed into a T-shirt and pair of capris before heading over to see her father with a container of fruit compote. He'd moved out of the house he'd shared with her mother and was staying in an apartment above the maintenance building, claiming it was best to be readily available for the crew. But he hadn't fooled either of them; he just hadn't been able to live with the memories.

The best thing about the apartment above Maintenance was a rooftop garden that looked across the hills. Liam spent most of his time out there when he wasn't working. Tessa was glad; as she'd told Gabe, she believed in the healing strength of nature.

"Hi, Pop," she said after climbing the outside

stairs and spotting him with a watering can in hand. "I thought you had a spigot and garden hose up here."

"I do." Liam kissed her. "But the hose doesn't stretch this far."

She made a mental note to get another hose. He'd never remember to buy one on his own. "Have you eaten?" she asked.

"I had something earlier."

Tessa knew his "something" was probably a cup of coffee. "I'll fix you a meal."

She went inside, first plugging his cell phone in to charge. There wasn't much food left in the kitchen, but she found cheese, a package of chicken strips and a loaf of bread in the freezer. While the chicken was thawing in a skillet, she threw a load of laundry into the washer and made a list of groceries. Pop was great at nagging everyone else to eat and drink properly, while totally neglecting himself.

Twenty minutes later, the sandwich was ready, and she carried it outside with a bowl of the fruit compote she'd brought.

"Come and get it," she called.

They sat at the table under the broad pergola that shaded them from the midafternoon sun.

Lord, Tessa wished the heat would break. Guests who'd expected more moderate weather for this time of year seemed to think it was Poppy Gold's fault.

"Aren't you eating?" Pop asked.

Tessa opened a bottle of mineral water. "Nope, I ate out. With Gabe McKinley."

Liam's eyes widened. "Gabe?"

Obviously he hadn't heard any rumors yet.

"We're just getting acquainted," she said carelessly. "Mostly I'm trying to convince him to be more approachable with guests."

Her father swallowed a bite of sandwich. "Don't you like him?"

"I'm not sure. He's good-looking, though to be honest, we're not finding much in common."

"Gabe is a good person. I know you didn't hit it off in the beginning, but I've been hoping you'd see his better points."

"Pop, this is just casual. *Don't* start hearing wedding bells," she said bluntly. "If nothing else, you know how much I want kids, and he's dead set against them."

"You might be able to change his mind."

Tessa groaned to herself. She did *not* need her father to see Gabe McKinley as a potential son-in-law. "It doesn't matter, because I'm not ready for anything serious. By the way, he suggested meeting us this afternoon at the Veterans Memorial Hall. If you're interested in going."

A mix of emotions crossed her father's face.

"You don't have to go, but the family wants to see you," she said gently. "You haven't been to any of the Sunday dinners or other family get-togethers."

"A lot of them work for us, and I see them here."

"It isn't the same."

Liam stirred the remainder of the compote with his fork, and Tessa was glad he'd eaten most of the food already, because he'd probably lost his appetite. She knew how hard it was for him to do the things he'd done with her mother, but she also didn't know any other way for him to move forward.

"So, Gabe is going," he said finally.

"Yeah."

"I guess...well, it'll be all right."

Tessa nodded and drank the rest of her mineral water, trying to keep her reaction low-key. Chances were that her father would still decide not to attend, but at least he was considering it.

The family *did* miss him. He'd stopped attending church, rarely went to community events and often seemed to be in a fog. The last time she'd taken him to the clinic for a checkup, Dr. Romano had suggested treating him for depression, but Pop wouldn't consider it, declaring grief wasn't depression. That was true, but clinical depression could be triggered by grief.

When it was clear her father wouldn't eat any more, Tessa cleaned up and suggested they work on the rooftop garden together.

She didn't want to give him a lot of time to sit alone and change his mind.

JAMIE WAS ANXIOUS as she watched her parents and Lance greet each other. They'd arrived at the ice-cream social early, and he'd met them on the street.

"I've never gone to something like this," Lance told them awkwardly.

"You're in for a treat," her father assured him. He was more comfortable with Lance than her mother. "Don't get fooled by all the different ice-cream flavors—homemade vanilla is the best."

"Yes, sir."

Her mom and dad went ahead of them, and Jamie leaned closer to Lance. "Where is your motorcycle?" she whispered.

"I parked it a couple of blocks away. I know people don't like it that much."

"Oh. Okay."

She was glad. Her mom had finally confessed she was worried about the motorcycle and had asked her not to ride it again. Jamie just wasn't sure how to tell him.

It was cool inside Veterans Memorial Hall, with the air-conditioning running full blast. People were bustling back and forth, setting out baked desserts along with containers of ice cream, some homemade and some bought from the store. Homemade was the yummiest, but not everybody had time or the equipment to make it from scratch.

Lance stopped and stared at the dessert tables; they were covered with cakes, pies and cookies of every kind.

"Is this for real?" he asked.

"Yup." Jamie leaned close again. "Be sure to get one of the brownies on the last table. The ones in the middle. They're Mrs. Tomlinson's and the absolute best, with chocolate chips, caramel and chocolate-fudge frosting."

"Okay. Uh, isn't that your grandfather over there? The boss preacher, or whatever he's called?"

"He's the senior pastor." She waved at Grandpa George, and he walked toward them.

Lance jumped, looking uneasy. "Maybe I'd better go."

He didn't wait for her to say anything, just bolted for the door. She caught up with him on the sidewalk outside. "Lance, what's wrong?"

"He's wearing a priest's collar."

"It's just a clergy collar. He wears it when they've asked him to do a prayer."

"Yeah, but your dad is a preacher, too. You're like, *holy*, or something," Lance muttered.

Consternation filled Jamie. People had always said that kind of thing to her, but she didn't want her *boyfriend* thinking it. "No, I'm not, and I don't want to be treated different because of my dad or grandpa. They're people, the same as everybody else."

"Whatever."

At Lance's stubborn expression, she began to understand why her two brothers had gotten rebellious for a while. Was that what preachers' kids had to do, act wild to get people to stop expecting them to be saints?

Jamie sighed. Love was much more complicated than she'd thought it would be. She was trying to think of the best way to convince him when her mouth dropped open.

"Lance, it's Uncle Liam and Tessa," she whispered urgently. "Uncle Liam hasn't come to anything since Aunt Meredith's funeral."

"Don't stare—you'll creep him out."

Jamie hastily looked down. Lance was right. It was rude to stare.

"Gabe came, too," Lance muttered.

It *was* Gabe McKinley walking inside the Veterans Memorial Hall next to her cousin and Uncle Liam. "Maybe things will go back to the way they used to be now," she said wistfully.

"They won't." Lance shrugged when she looked at him in dismay. "Nothing goes back to the way it was."

She sighed. "I suppose, but come inside with me again. If we don't get some soon, Mom's vanilla ice cream will be gone, and you won't get to taste Mrs. Tomlinson's brownies."

LANCE HESITATED.

Since he and Jamie had started dating, they'd mostly done stuff by themselves, walking by the creek or hiking, or just wandering around Poppy Gold while she told him stories about the people who used to live there.

It was nice that Jamie didn't understand the bad things outside her hometown. As for her being a preacher's kid? That really wasn't the issue, though admittedly it had made him a *little* uncomfortable in the beginning.

What Jamie didn't understand was that he had to be extra careful. He wasn't like her. He was a foster kid with a police record who didn't even *know* what his parents had done for a living... except that his dad was in prison and his mom had been in jail a lot, too, before she died. Maybe the social workers had done their best, but living in foster homes sucked. Even the nicer ones. He didn't really belong to anybody, and they'd just kept him because of the monthly checks from the state.

"What is it, Lance?" Jamie asked, squeezing his hand. "Don't you want to go back inside?"

"Sure, it's just..."

How could he explain that he didn't know how regular people with regular families acted? And if he tried, he'd have to tell her about growing up in one foster home after another. Jamie had asked about his family when they'd started dating, so he'd shrugged and told her it was like everyone else's. He'd even talked about one of his foster sisters, Maggie, as if she was a regular sister.

He'd hated lying, but it had seemed easier than the truth.

If only he could be like Gabe McKinley. Nobody would ever think Gabe wasn't good enough. Maybe it would be that way for him if *he* joined the military and got training. But it got back to the same old question—would they take him after what happened in Sacramento? An arrest wasn't the same as being convicted, but it was still on his record, and some people figured being accused was the same as being guilty.

Lance just didn't know how he could have done things differently. Maggie had called, crying, saying the old man was hitting her again, so he'd gone to help, only to have the asshole accuse him of breaking into the house. The cops had arrested him, though he was released when Stanton didn't press charges. Luckily Maggie was moved to another foster home right afterward, and he'd left town.

"Ohmigosh, are you diabetic and don't want to tell me?" Jamie asked. "Almost all the treats are sugary, and Mom says we shouldn't push someone to eat in case they have a medical condition."

"It's nothing like that," Lance denied quickly. "It's just that we, uh, didn't go to church when

I was a kid. I don't want to look stupid." It was true, though not the whole reason.

She hooked her arm around his. "Then let's go eat ice cream. We'd look pretty stupid not having any when everybody else is having fun."

He grinned and let her tug him back inside.

Tessa shopped for groceries on Sunday afternoon, taking several sacks to her father's apartment to stock his refrigerator and cupboards.

"I keep telling you not to do this. You're too busy," Pop protested as she folded the last paper bag and put it under the sink.

She hugged him. "It isn't a big deal. I have to get groceries for myself, too. Oh, I also picked up a new garden hose."

"Thank you, darling." Yet Liam seemed perplexed as he examined her purchase. Tessa didn't blame him; it was an expandable hose that the lawn and garden store had convinced her to try. It looked quite peculiar.

"According to the garden center, it expands when the water is turned on," she explained. "Up to fifty feet. Then when you turn the water off, it pulls itself back into a little pile."

As she'd hoped, her father was so intrigued that he immediately had to try it out. The hose was long enough to reach every corner of the rooftop garden, but it did indeed withdraw into a heap by the spigot when the water pressure dropped.

"It wouldn't work for slow watering," Liam said thoughtfully, "because the water pressure has to be high or else it shrinks back, but it should be excellent up here."

Tessa was pleased and left him to play with the new toy while she finished his laundry. She yawned and shook her head to wake herself up. Following the ice-cream social, she and Pop had talked well into the early morning hours at her apartment. He'd seemed to enjoy the event, only to become depressed afterward.

She didn't know what to do. In some ways he'd gotten better over the past few months; in other ways she wasn't sure.

Discouraged, she sorted out his clothes needing repair and put them in a bag before starting dinner.

At least Pop usually ate something when he was at work. She'd hired Uncle Kurt to stock the refrigerator and freezer in the maintenance kitchenette. That way Pop had supplies to make his smoothies and fuss over everyone on his crew with sports drinks and other food.

"Ready to eat?" she asked an hour later, pulling a baking dish from the oven. She would have preferred a main-dish salad in such warm weather, but lemon barbecue loaf was her father's favorite.

"It smells wonderful, dear, but you should have invited Gabe. There's plenty for three."

Tessa pressed her lips together. She'd already warned her father that she wasn't interested in anything serious with Gabe, but these days, Pop tended to be single-minded. He liked Gabe McKinley and had automatically thought about inviting him to dinner.

"I wanted you to have enough for sandwiches," she said finally. "I got horseradish sauce and that organic bread you like."

"Oh, that sounds good." He ate quietly for a few minutes and then looked at her. "You know, when I met your mother, I felt strongly about not having children. She's the one who changed my mind."

Tessa groaned to herself. "That doesn't always happen."

"No, but it's possible. You can't completely dismiss Gabe because of how he feels about kids."

"It's not the same at all. But when you met Mom it was a lightning bolt, while Gabe and I aren't even sure we like each other. There's attraction, of course," she added hastily, "but that only goes so far."

Her father nodded, looking unconvinced, and Tessa wanted to bang her head on the table. He didn't say anything else about it the rest of the meal, but she still couldn't relax.

In reality, she was uneasy about how *much* she liked Gabe. It turned out he had a sense of humor, was smart and had a caring heart, whether he'd admit to it or not.

Her mom had been confident that she could pull her husband away from the darkness he'd seen in the army, but Tessa wasn't so sure she could do the same for Gabe.

IN HIS STUDIO COTTAGE, Gabe pored over the list of Poppy Gold employees he'd compiled, including all the information he had found out about them. As he'd said to Tessa, it was remarkable how much you could learn about people's lives these days. She might dislike the loss of privacy, but it was reality.

Even if the police chief proved to be helpful, Gabe had every intention of pursuing the investigation himself, using his own resources. Because of that, he'd ordered background checks through KJ's security firm, providing as much identifying information as possible. It wasn't entirely a case of being the Lone Ranger; both Milt's and Tessa's judgment could be clouded by being too close to the situation.

What about you? challenged a voice in his head...a voice that sounded remarkably like Tessa's. *Aren't* you *too close?* It would have been a fair question for her to ask based on his connection to TIP.

Pushing the thought away, he called Rob.

"Did you talk to that FBI agent?" he asked when his brother answered.

"I'm fine, thank you for inquiring," Rob said ironically. "And yes, I've given the letters to the agent. He'll add them to the file, which is still tiny since we still don't actually *know* anything. Milt Fullerton also called about the copies of the letters that Tessa gave him."

"When did you give Tessa copies?"

"After I got home. I faxed them to her Friday afternoon. It's okay, she was there waiting by the machine."

Gabe tensed. Tessa hadn't said anything about getting the letters, and he wondered if she was trying to give him a taste of his own medicine. He couldn't completely blame her, but it could be risky.

"I've been thinking that I shouldn't have bothered you with any of this in the first place," Rob said slowly.

"I'm your brother. Who else would you call— the auto club?"

Rob chuckled. "Okay, but once we figured out the thefts must be happening at Poppy Gold, I could have simply switched to a different conference center or stopped having executive conferences altogether."

"It's better to catch the culprit. For all we know, this person would have found another way to target you. Surely the FBI sees that everything taken together is suspicious?"

"Come on, Gabe, they've got their plates full with bank robberies, kidnappings and terrorist threats. They'll analyze the letters when they get a chance. It's all we can expect for now."

"Fine. Have you compared my list of people connected to Poppy Gold with *your* list of disgruntled current and former employees?"

Early on Gabe had asked his brother to compile a list of anyone who might be upset with TIP, perhaps because they'd been fired or reprimanded. They seemed likely candidates since they might hold a grudge and possess enough inside information to use.

"Yes, but I don't see any links. I've sent the information to Mr. Fullerton, though, just in case."

"Well, stay cautious. Did Tessa mention she wants to know which visits you think the information leaks happened on? I didn't bring the list with me."

"Yeah, I sent it when I faxed the letters."

After they got off, Gabe stared moodily at his computer screen. He knew he had to be patient. Besides, he'd been in Glimmer Creek for only a couple of weeks. Sting operations could take months.

Curious, he did a search on Meredith Connor. The local newspaper barely had an online presence, but both the library and historical society had sites where he found numerous articles mentioning her name. Tessa hadn't exaggerated—her mother had *indeed* been involved in everything. Meredith must have been a great deal like her daughter, with boundless energy and determination. The shock of losing her to pneumonia must have been terrible for both father and daughter.

Gabe gritted his teeth and returned to more helpful research. It would be easier if he had an official employee list, including the names and details of the businesses Tessa had outsourced Poppy Gold services to, such as Sarah's Sweet Treats.

The catering staff delivered breakfast to every single guesthouse, every single day. Their familiar presence throughout Poppy Gold raised questions for Gabe, though he could imagine what Tessa or Milt would say if he mentioned the issue.

After all, Sarah Fullerton was family.

Tessa was devoted to her relatives, but there was a good chance they would discover that someone she'd trusted had betrayed her.

Gabe shut down the computer with a frown. He hadn't expected to regret how uncovering the truth would affect the innocent people in Glimmer Creek, but he did.

It also bothered him that he was mostly concerned about how Tessa would feel.

CHAPTER FOURTEEN

JAMIE WAS PLEASED when Lance drove down with her to Stockton for her next two classes; he even suggested they visit the library together to research the term papers she needed to write.

"Do you think something is wrong at Poppy Gold?" Jamie asked Lance as they ate burgers together in the old park square after work on Thursday.

"Why?"

"I don't know. Ever since Tessa fell, I keep thinking something isn't right, and it's gotten worse the last few days. Yesterday I asked her if something was wrong, but she said I shouldn't worry."

"I bet it's nothing."

But Jamie wasn't entirely convinced, especially since Tessa had only said not to worry. That wasn't the same as being fine, and it reminded Jamie of the time Grandpa George had needed a biopsy and was waiting for the results. Nobody had told her, but she'd known something wasn't right.

But she was eighteen now. How long would it take for people to realize she wasn't a kid?

Lance sipped his chocolate milk shake, and Jamie tried not to be envious. With all the hard work he did in the orchard, he could eat anything and stay skinny. *She'd* gotten skim milk. It didn't compare to one of the Burger Saloon's double-thick milk shakes.

He wiped his mouth. "Why do you think something's wrong?"

"I don't know how to explain. Mostly it's a feeling I keep getting. And Tessa is distracted, though I suppose it could be from dating Mr. McKinley. How does *he* seem?" Now that she thought about it, it was the most likely explanation. Gabe was rather grim and solemn, not at all the kind of man she'd expect her cousin to like.

"The same, I guess." Lance shook the bag from the Burger Saloon, making something rustle. "Hey, some of your French fries must have fallen out."

He handed it to her, and Jamie looked inside; it wasn't French fries—it was something silver. She tipped it out on her hand and saw an adorable heart locket on a chain.

"Oh, *Lance*…how beautiful."

He grinned, and she practically melted.

"I love it, but honestly, you shouldn't spend so much money on me," she protested.

"I like having someone to give things to," he said gruffly, and Jamie blinked back tears.

WHILE ON HER usual afternoon circuit through Poppy Gold that Friday, Tessa heard laughter coming from the carpentry building. It sounded like her father, and she smiled. Pop hadn't done any of his usual jobs since her mother's death, so it was wonderful to think he was working on a new project.

She peeked through the open door. Like the other facility buildings constructed at Poppy Gold, it was a replica of an earlier style. In this case, it resembled an old-time blacksmith shop.

Pop wasn't alone. He was chatting with Gabe as they consulted a diagram. Lately she saw them together often, working on various projects, with Gabe handling the heavy work.

Tessa sighed, almost feeling jealous. Yet how could she resent something that helped her father? She even understood some of the reasons they got along so well. Gabe was ex-military. And like Pop, he'd seen terrible things, so they shared a common ground she couldn't understand.

A moment later, Gabe looked toward the door, and their gazes locked. One of his eyebrows rose inquiringly, but she just shook her head and continued toward Old City Hall.

Once there, she resisted the temptation to ask

questions at the reservation hub about incoming calls, simply greeting everyone before doing the same with the event planning staff.

The truth was, she *did* have trouble delegating. That didn't mean she'd become a micromanager, but it was possible she'd slipped into bad habits. Officially naming Aunt Polly assistant manager might help, and getting an activities director wasn't a bad idea, either. It would be best to wait, though, until after the business with TIP had been resolved.

In the meantime, she had asked the staff to hold rooms for the first week of June as cancellations came in. The sooner they caught the spy, the better she'd sleep.

In the reception area, an older couple was waiting to register, and she chatted with them, telling them about various local activities and places to see. After a while, she became aware of another man gazing at her across the room.

He came over when the couple stepped up to the registration desk. "KJ Bermann, at your service."

Tessa immediately recognized the name of Gabe's associate. One of his security "contacts." She came close to gaping. Instead of coming off as a bad-tempered loner like Gabe, KJ had a warm grin and practiced charm.

"Tessa Connor."

"Delighted to meet you, Tessa. I'm here for a

few days, checking out Poppy Gold for a possible class reunion."

"Oh. That's nice."

He gave her a warm appraisal, subtle enough that it wasn't insulting, and obvious enough to be flattering. The guy was good, and she wondered if it was just an act or his real self. Probably real, she decided after they'd talked for another few minutes.

The couple finished registering and said goodbye as they left.

"Say, is there any chance I could get lucky enough to take you to dinner one evening?" KJ asked, his voice dropping into a low, inviting purr.

"Sorry, I'm pretty busy."

"I'll give you my cell number in case you change your mind." KJ took one of Poppy Gold's business cards from the desk and scribbled across the top. "Will I see you at the swimming pool later?"

"Afraid not. I work here."

"What a shame. I was hoping to demonstrate my breaststroke. I've got *great* technique."

He sauntered out the door, the image of masculine confidence, and Christine at the reception desk giggled. "Don't tell me you're buying his line."

"Not a chance. Did he flirt with you?"

"He started to...then he saw my profile." Christine patted her rounded stomach; she was seven months pregnant. "But I have to admit that he's delicious. Of course, maybe your tastes run to tall, dark and silent." She winked.

It was an obvious reference to Gabe, and Tessa tried not to grind her teeth in frustration. Poppy Gold's rumor mill was alive and well, and his supposed interest in her hadn't escaped the staff's notice.

Fortunately another group arrived to register, saving Tessa from having to reply.

She went outside, and down the street she spotted KJ again; he was chatting with another young woman. He wasn't the least bit grim or distant, and she recalled what Gabe had said about his friend. *I don't think KJ will stand out, at least not in the way you think.*

He was right.

AFTER WORK, LANCE went to cool off by the creek before going back to the locker room. He splashed cold water in his face, washing off the dust and sweat. There were glints of gold on the creek bottom as usual, but he tried to ignore them, knowing they were just pyrite.

He yawned.

A glint that was bigger than usual caught his attention, and he told himself it was nothing. The creek was high because the heat had melted snow faster than normal up in the Sierras, so a bunch more pyrite had likely settled into a crevice. Still...he reached in and flicked the shimmering speck. It didn't swirl away.

More curious than hopeful, he scooped out a handful of sand and gravel and saw a gold lump in the middle. It seemed awfully heavy for pyrite and didn't look the same, either. He turned it over in his hand, certain it was the real thing. Maybe the lump wasn't the size of a cow patty, but it was still a lump.

Yet even as Lance wondered how much it would be worth, he realized it didn't belong to him. The creek was on Poppy Gold property, so this belonged to the Connors.

He stood up and trudged back to the maintenance building. The swing crew had arrived, but Mr. Connor was in his office, talking to Gabe.

"Something up, Lance?" Liam asked, waving him inside.

"I need to turn this in. It was in the creek, and I don't think it's pyrite," he said, putting the lump of gold on the desk.

Liam looked the lump over and handed it back to him. "Looks real to me, but it's yours, son. Probably worth around nine hundred or so. Nice find."

The excitement Lance had tried to contain surged through him. "Are you sure? I mean about keeping it."

"Of course. Nuggets sometimes wash down

from higher in the mountains, not often, but occasionally. If you're interested, a jewelry store or assayer's office could verify it."

Lance nodded and backed out, almost afraid he hadn't heard right. Nobody gave away stuff like that in the kind of places where he'd lived as a kid.

He raced home to clean up, anxious to show Jamie.

GABE WAITED UNTIL Lance had disappeared before cocking his head. "Nice kid. Not too many people would hand that over."

"He's a fine boy," Liam agreed. "Never lets up on the job. I've told my in-laws how hard he works, but they're still concerned about him dating Jamie. After they met she started ducking the college class she was taking, and that motorcycle really bothers Emma. But I think it may also be a case of not knowing much about him. Living in such a small town spoils us. I used to know everything about the boys Tessa dated in high school."

"Maybe they're also concerned about how serious Lance and Jamie are getting," Gabe suggested. "They aren't even twenty yet. Maybe the Fullertons would rather she waited until after college to make any kind of commitment."

Liam smiled gently. "Perhaps, but my wife was just a year older than Jamie when we got married, and I was only twenty-two, right out of the service."

Gabe recalled what he'd read about Meredith Connor. He was willing to concede that some marriages could succeed, but he still believed that a good many contained hidden misery.

"How did you end up in the army, anyway?" he asked to change the subject. "Didn't your father want you to work in the family business?"

"I enlisted at eighteen, same as you. I'd done a semester at Stanford and was getting into trouble. My father didn't object too loudly, saying he'd hoped I'd learn discipline. When I got out, he sent me up here to sell Connor's Folly. His idea was to give me a transition period back into college. He never imagined I'd stay. Or maybe he did. Tessa claims my father understands me better than I think."

"He *did* give you Connor's Folly as a wedding present," Gabe murmured.

"Mmm, yes. I don't know…maybe it's destiny that sons and fathers never quite see eye to eye."

Gabe made a noncommittal gesture. While Tessa knew about his connection to TIP, he had to be careful what he said to her father. It was unlikely that Liam would figure anything out—he was too preoccupied with his grief—but there was still a risk. Of course, it remained possible that some of Liam's vagueness might come from secret drinking to drown his sorrow. Gabe had

seen his hands shaking different times, and if
Liam was that distraught over his wife's death,
he might occasionally take refuge in a bottle.

Gabe wondered if Tessa was aware or if he
should mention it.

He shifted in his chair, uneasy about the way
he was getting swept into the Connors' lives. A
year ago, he hadn't worried about anything that
didn't affect his SEAL unit. It wasn't like him
to worry about a bereaved man's state of mind.

WHEN GABE LEFT the maintenance building, he
turned on his phone and saw a text from KJ saying he'd arrived and had already met the dynamo.
His mouth tightened. Even if KJ had hit on Tessa,
he wouldn't have gotten anywhere. She was too
intent on running Poppy Gold. She also wouldn't
spoil the illusion of being involved with Poppy
Gold's newest maintenance employee.

Back at his studio cottage, Gabe got on to the
computer to Skype with Rob. His brother didn't
have anything new to report except that Tessa
thought TIP could return to Poppy Gold in a
couple of weeks. In the meantime, she was shifting reservations around to clear the El Dorado
Mansion for their visit, which had already been
repaired and put back in service.

Tessa had told Rob, but not him? It was the
second time he'd been the *last* to hear important
information, and it was frustrating.

Irritated, Gabe said goodbye to his brother and worked for a while, annotating his electronic list of employees with new information, but it was more difficult to focus than usual. Finally, he closed his laptop and got up.

Tessa had successfully avoided him for the past few days, but nobody at Poppy Gold would believe they were interested in each other if they didn't spend time together. Even though it was a Friday night, she was probably working. Now that she'd more or less recovered from her fall at the El Dorado, she was putting in even more hours.

First he went to Old City Hall. "Is Tessa around?" he asked at Guest Registration. "I was hoping to have dinner with her."

"I saw her around five but not since then," said the young man tending the desk. "Try her office. There aren't any special events tonight."

"Okay, thanks."

Gabe strode out, satisfied that word would get around that he'd been looking for Tessa.

A few guests were still in the train depot, so Gabe went in through the back staircase. Tessa's office door was open, and he stepped inside.

"How about dinner?" he asked. "I could get something at the deli and meet you at the Victorian Cat. And don't tell me you have work to do. You always have work, but it's after seven."

"I... All right."

"Good. What would you like?"

"Turkey, Swiss cheese and avocado on sour-dough bread," she said promptly. "No onions or mustard and light on the mayo."

"Don't tell me, you've been wanting that sandwich all day long."

"That's right, I won't tell you."

Gabe grinned and headed for the downtown area of Glimmer Creek and the Gilbraith Delicatessen.

With luck, Tessa might be more cooperative with what he wanted if she got fed properly.

Forty-five minutes later, Tessa set her sandwich down on her coffee table and stared at Gabe. "You want *what*?"

"Access to your employee files and everything you have on your contractors, such as Sarah's Sweet Treats," he repeated matter-of-factly.

She made a derisive sound. Honestly, he didn't have a clue. "That isn't going to happen."

"I suspected you weren't going to be reasonable, but it's important."

"Oh, *puleeze*. You can't honestly believe I'd do that. I gave a list to Uncle Milt with the proper authorization, but I can't give it to you."

Gabe glared. "I've researched everybody I know who works at Poppy Gold, but you've shot down my best suspects."

"I didn't shoot anybody down," Tessa denied

in a dry tone. "I just told you which ones had reasonable explanations for the money they were spending. If anything, I saved you time from pursuing unlikely suspects. But as promised, I mentioned Celina Noble to Uncle Milt, and he's going to see what more he can learn about her."

"Whatever."

Honestly, Gabe was impossible. Tessa ate the last of her sandwich and pulled out the box of chocolate mint cookies he'd gotten for dessert. "Showing you employee records would violate their privacy, but we could go over what you've compiled together. It might duplicate everything Uncle Milt is doing, but a different perspective could be valuable."

"I suppose," he grumbled. He ate one of the cookies, looking like a little boy who was sulking because he hadn't gotten his way. Tessa tried not to find it endearing. "I expect to get the background checks tomorrow from KJ's company."

"What can they do without Social Security numbers?"

"You'd be amazed," Gabe murmured. "By the way, did you keep copies of the hate mail that Rob faxed you?"

"Yes." She got up and fetched a file folder from a bookcase.

Gabe read through the letters. "These are disturbing, though they stop short of actually threatening violence. It's mostly implied. Apparently the FBI hasn't determined what magazines or newspapers were used to create them."

Tessa pointed to the letter on top of the stack. "There's something nagging me about that one. I'm just not sure why."

"A familiar turn of phrase, maybe?"

"Not too many people who talk that way around me."

"I suppose. Has Milt been able to determine anything?"

Tessa gave him a lopsided smile. "Hey, Uncle Milt won't share information with me, either, other than to say he's working on some ideas."

"Then you know exactly how I feel. Or maybe not since you don't think anyone in town could do anything wrong. Especially your family."

"People have faults here the same as anywhere, but that doesn't mean Glimmer Creek isn't a good place. I know you have awful memories, but aren't you giving them too much power? They seem to shape how you see the world."

Gabe's expression stiffened. "You don't know anything about me *or* how I see the world."

"I know what you've told me, which is a whole lot more than you think. I wouldn't be surprised if you closed down emotionally before becoming a SEAL. You mentioned your mother has a drinking problem and that your father is a workaholic."

"And I bet you'll be just as work-obsessed when *you* have kids as you are now."

Tessa's heart ached. Deep down, Gabe was still the boy who'd been left to deal with an alcoholic mom, while his dad buried himself at his company. She'd bet anything that he'd been the first to give food to hungry kids when he was on a mission, grieved over those he couldn't save, and was still haunted by their lost voices.

"I'm going to be involved with my children's lives, the same way my parents were with mine," she said quietly. "But I'm curious, since Rob is now running TIP, what is your father doing?"

"He retired to the Bahamas with his second wife. He gave us each a percentage of TIP and kept the rest."

"He gave you part ownership? Rob told me he was angry that you'd enlisted, so he must have gotten over it."

An odd emotion flitted across Gabe's face. "Perhaps. It's my mother who still won't talk to me. She was livid when I enlisted."

"If she was already having trouble coping with life, the thought of losing her son must have really made her freak. Maybe your relationship will get better now that you're out."

"Maybe. But to be completely honest, there isn't much to fix between us. I remind her too much of my dad, and they hated each long before they got divorced. 'Coldhearted monster' was her favorite description of us both when she was drunk."

"I'm so sorry." Tessa hated seeing the bleakness in Gabe's eyes. "I don't think you're the least bit cold. And you're certainly not a monster."

"Check again. I'm not Mr. Warm-and-Fuzzy."

"You have a thick protective layer, but underneath that I think you care more about people than you let on."

He shook his head, but Tessa was sure she was right. A man who didn't care about other people didn't become a navy SEAL. It was too dangerous and required too many sacrifices. What had Rob said—that his brother was honorable and decent?

Tessa leaned forward. "To change the subject, I want to explain why I'm working so hard right now. Poppy Gold's conversion to a conference center is relatively recent and we can't afford to fail. The town depends on us."

"I'm sure Patrick Connor would bail you out."

"I don't want to be bailed out, I want to succeed. But as a return gesture of honesty, I'm willing to admit that while I hate micromanagers, I've been turning into one. So thank you for helping me to see that. I'm trying to…well…"

"Let people do their job instead of doing it for them or looking over their shoulder every minute?"

She tossed a wadded-up napkin at him. "Something like that."

He chuckled. It was a curious moment of closeness and understanding—even shared humor—that tugged at her heart. It was also unsettling, because she'd never experienced a moment like that with a man.

Gabe gathered the trash from their meal and stuffed it in the bag from the deli. "By the way, I understand you think TIP can return in a couple of weeks? Why didn't you tell me?"

"I just told Rob today."

"But Milt already knows, too."

"Of course. Uncle Milt agrees that a sting operation is needed since industrial espionage is so difficult to investigate. He's also talked to Rob about the letters, even though technically it's out of his jurisdiction."

"I can't see that stopping Milt."

"Nope."

Gabe stood up and stretched. "I'd better get going."

Tessa got up to open the door. The hum of several conversations drifted in from the garden and Gabe quickly put an arm around her.

At first his kiss was more mechanical than sensual, but his lips slowly gentled. The mingled scent and taste of mint and chocolate drifted through her, and she relaxed against him.

The men she'd dated in San Francisco had worked in an office, usually too busy to stay in shape. A few had exercised, but none of them had possessed Gabe's sheer muscled strength. It was exhilarating, and she struggled to keep from encouraging more than a kiss. She didn't think he'd refuse…his arousal pressed against her, hard and insistent. If they hadn't been in semipublic view, she might have satisfied her curiosity about how he'd respond to a bold exploration.

No, a voice whispered in her head.

She didn't want to fall for a man like Gabe. Yet her thoughts scattered as his fingers spanned her rib cage. She wriggled against him, pleased to hear him groan.

The sound of nearby laughter was a cold splash of reality, and they both froze.

"I'd better go," he muttered, his arms dropping so fast she nearly lost her balance. "I'll see you tomorrow."

He left before she could find her voice again, which was a good thing or she might have suggested he stay.

CHAPTER FIFTEEN

GABE WENT OUT for a run before dawn the next morning, furious with himself for nearly losing control with Tessa.

Several miles outside Glimmer Creek, he stopped and wiped his face. Keeping in shape was a long habit, and exercise was a good way to work off excess energy.

A wry smile twisted Gabe's mouth.

He had an abundance of excess energy with Tessa Connor in his life, however temporarily she might be there. She had a way of getting under his skin in more ways than one. While he might believe she was *too* open for her own good, there was something appealing about it, as well. No wonder people gravitated to her. She was like finding a spring of clear, fresh water in the middle of a desert.

Yet as soon as the thought came to Gabe, he snorted.

He wasn't a blasted poet. Recognizing that Tessa had special qualities didn't mean he was getting soft—it just meant he was being observant. And it was smart to see that she was some-one who could get hurt if he wasn't careful.

Gabe set out on the return route to town, try-ing to let the steady rhythm of his feet on the pavement block out everything else in his head. He arrived at Glimmer Cottages shortly before 6:00 a.m. and saw Lance Beckley locking his door, clad in the clothes he wore while digging the new orchard.

"Hey," Gabe said, keeping his voice low to avoid disturbing the other residents. "I thought you worked Monday through Friday."

Lance shrugged. "Jamie is switching to week-ends so she can do more living history, so I asked to change my schedule, too."

"Have you thought more about going into the navy?"

"I don't know. Jamie might not want to leave Glimmer Creek."

Conflicting emotions flickered in Lance's eyes, and Gabe figured there was something the boy wasn't saying.

"If you enlist you'll be given an aptitude test. Depending on how you score, it could mean a lot of opportunities," he urged. "More education, training, all sorts of things."

"Maybe. I'd better go. I don't want to be late."

Gabe went to his cottage. The kid had to make his own decision; it wouldn't help to push. Or-dinarily he would have kept his mouth shut, but he must have been infected by Tessa's do-gooder attitude. Or maybe it had nothing to do with her being a do-gooder; maybe it was an extension of small-town nosiness.

Despite having gone away to college and worked in San Francisco, Tessa knew plenty about her Glimmer Creek neighbors. Perhaps getting involved in their lives was a natural extension of that knowledge.

Gabe made a face as he scrubbed his hair in the shower, deciding the sooner he could leave Glimmer Creek, the better.

JAMIE WAS SITTING on a bench eating lunch when she saw her cousin leave Old City Hall and head across the park.

"Tessa," she called.

Tessa looked up and smiled. "Hi, Jamie," she said, walking up. "You look terrific. Is that a new costume? I especially love the hat."

"Isn't it great? Mom finished it last night. Did Uncle Liam tell you about the nugget that Lance found in the creek?"

"Yes, it must have been exciting. Has he decided what to do with it?"

Jamie shook her head. "Not yet, but he gave it to me for safekeeping. It's funny, I told him about that big lump of gold someone thought was a cow patty, and now he's found one, too."

Tessa sat next to her on the bench. "I think the

cow patty story happened before either of us was born, and it might be just a very tall tale."

"Naw, I bet it's true." Jamie held a bunch of grapes out to her cousin, but Tessa shook her head. "What do you think?"

"I suppose anything is possible."

Jamie fidgeted. "Tessa, do you think guys from the city are different from the ones from Glimmer Creek?" she asked finally.

"How do you mean?"

"I don't know exactly, but Lance doesn't talk much about growing up, and he can get weird sometimes." Jamie cast a sideways glance at her cousin, wondering how much she should say. "Like the day you fell—he was uncomfortable when I asked if Uncle Milt had talked to him."

"Uncle Milt talked to everyone. Lance was probably just remembering the day he arrived in Glimmer Creek. An officer gave him a ticket when he drove around Poppy Gold on his motorcycle. He said he didn't see the signs about private vehicles being prohibited."

Jamie frowned. "He didn't tell me about that, though he says the police don't like the bike. Maybe that's what he meant."

"I'm sure he didn't mean any harm," Tessa assured her. "He's been very respectful since then, and I doubt anyone is concerned now."

"Mom asked me not to ride with him," Jamie admitted. "I kind of agree with her, but I don't know how to tell Lance. He's really proud of his motorcycle. He got it at a junkyard in Sacramento and did all the repairs himself. Before that he had to take the bus to work and it took forever."

"The longer you wait, the harder it will be," Tessa advised. "There's no saying how he'll react, but he might wonder why you didn't tell him sooner."

"I suppose. Are all guys so hard to understand?"

"A few may be less difficult than others, but pretty much. And to answer your first question, I don't think where they're from makes much difference when it comes to men being stubborn." Tessa sounded as if she'd been thinking about it recently, which probably meant she was talking about Gabe McKinley instead of Lance.

Jamie laughed. "Oh."

She felt better knowing her cousin was having guy trouble, too. Everybody knew Tessa and Mr. McKinley were dating…well, *almost* dating. The family kept hoping she'd fall in love and get married, but they weren't sure about her choosing Gabe McKinley. He was awfully stiff and didn't smile very much. Even at the ice-cream social he'd mostly stayed quiet and watched everyone.

"Being in love is wonderful," Jamie said after a minute. "Lance is awfully sweet. He's always giving me stuff. He says it's because he never had anyone to spoil before, but I bet he's had a bunch of girlfriends."

"PRESENTS ARE NICE, but some of the things guys do can be more romantic," Tessa murmured.

"Like what?"

"I think it's different for every relationship. In high school, one of my boyfriends was a fanatic about skiing. He talked the church youth group into planning a ski trip, then two days before we left I sprained my ankle. I told him to go anyway, but he stayed home, saying it wouldn't be fun without me. We spent the entire day watching old movies, eating popcorn and drinking hot chocolate."

"That was nice."

"I thought so."

Jamie fidgeted with the sleeve of her costume. "The thing is, I thought being in love would be easier."

"I know. Love may conquer all, but it takes a while to get there." Tessa patted her arm and wondered how she'd gotten old enough that a teenager would ask her for advice. Not that thirty was old, but it probably *seemed* old to an eighteen-year-old girl in love.

She tried to think how her own mother might have felt if she had dated a boy like Lance Beckley. It would have caused concern. Lance wasn't a bad kid, but he was socially awkward, moody and never talked about his past, which suggested it must have been unhappy.

The thought led back to Gabe, and Tessa stifled a groan. She'd gotten far too personal with him, talking about *his* parents and childhood.

As for what her mother would have said about Gabe? She would have worried he was too closed off and emotionally distant. Pop, on the other hand, obviously appreciated the company of a man who'd gone through some of the same things he'd experienced in the military.

"Do you think Lance and I are too young to get married?" Jamie asked out of the blue.

Tessa scrambled for something to say that wouldn't sound preachy. Finally she chose complete honesty. "I have no idea, Jamie. The statistics are against you, but my parents married young and were extremely happy. Are you two considering marriage?"

"No, but he talks about making it big so he can take care of me. I wouldn't mind getting engaged, but I don't think we should get married until I'm out of college."

Gabe's comments about Lance spending so much money on Jamie flitted through Tessa's head, much to her frustration. She didn't think Lance was guilty of wrongdoing. He'd shown he was honest, and it wasn't unusual for a kid to dream of financial success.

Looking up, Tessa saw Gabe across the street

watching them and let out a resigned breath. He must have gotten his background checks, and Gabe being Gabe, he didn't want to wait to discuss them.

"I'd better get back to work," Jamie said, dusting her fingers and adjusting her hat. It was a frothy number with pink grosgrain ribbon and lace, but no feathers. Elsie Lyman on the historical society was also a member of every wildlife organization on the planet. She was always quick to mention that the style for having feathers on women's hats had destroyed millions of birds in the 1800s. Nobody would dare to even put a fake feather on a Poppy Gold costume for fear of getting "the lecture."

Jamie tucked a "reticule" over her arm, along with the small wicker basket she'd used to carry her lunch, and set off for the train depot. Tessa sighed, hoping her cousin could avoid some of the heartaches that life could bring. She'd feel the same when she was a parent someday, worrying about her children and wanting all good things for them. She didn't have time for sentiment, however. Gabe was descending on her like a heat-seeking missile.

"Hello," she said sweetly. "How are you today?"

"Fine. Do you have a computer at your apartment?" he asked. "I have the information on a flash drive."

She thought about the work she'd planned to

do, but the sooner the spy was caught, the better, and right now there was little else she could contribute to the investigation.

"Sure."

They walked to the Victorian Cat, and she unlocked the door, unable to keep from recalling their heated kiss the previous night. How much had been pretense and how much real? Men had a harder time than women concealing their arousal, and he'd definitely responded to her, but that didn't necessarily mean anything. An old cliché floated through her head—*a woman needs a reason to make love; a guy just needs a place.*

"My office is upstairs," Tessa said.

Her parents had started their renovations with the Victorian Cat, partially because it was close to the edge of Poppy Gold, and partly because it had been easiest to carve out a private apartment in the back of the house. The first floor had a kitchen and living room, and on the second floor was a bathroom and two tiny bedrooms opening off a small central parlor.

They climbed the steep, narrow stairs to the second level, and Gabe looked around with obvious curiosity.

"Something wrong?" she asked.

"I was just wondering if one or more cats are in residence."

"They're all in their suites. Do you have something against cats?"

He shrugged.

"I bet you prefer dogs…adoring, faithful and blindly obedient."

"I don't believe in blind obedience."

Tessa tried not to smile. "How about adoring and faithful?"

"How about checking those files?"

She gestured to her office. "Fine, but the room is small," she warned. "I hope you aren't claustrophobic."

"Not a problem."

THOUGH GABE HAD seen some of the apartment on his first day at Poppy Gold, he'd gotten only a few impressions; his focus had been on Tessa as a potential suspect. Now he was curious…particularly when he saw bold outlines of friendly dragons and other fantastical creatures on the yellow walls in Tessa's office.

"Interesting decor," he commented.

She flushed. "This used to be my nursery. I was too busy to paint it when I moved in last year."

"The apartment was sitting empty until then?"

"More or less. It isn't suitable as a rental since the staircase is too steep. Actually, my mother used to say we must have a ghost on the stairs."

Gabe frowned. From everything he'd read, Meredith Connor hadn't sounded the type to have outlandish ideas.

"Oh?"

"Uh-huh. She nearly fell one day, but something grabbed the back of her shirt and pulled her upright."

Tessa's expression was so challenging, he decided to take a safe route. "I see. Lucky for her."

"That's right."

She sat in the chair in front of her computer and turned it on.

Gabe didn't have a vivid imagination, but as he sat on the padded window seat next to the desk, he could easily envision a cheerful toddler in the room, bright-eyed and filled with expectation. His mental image was no doubt prompted by the picture hanging on Liam's office wall... Tessa as a little girl. *Tessajinks.* She'd probably had a sunny disposition and an iron will.

Tessa took the flash drive he held out and inserted it in the computer. "I still don't think the thief could be someone from Glimmer Creek," she said.

"I appreciate your loyalty to your family and neighbors, but even criminals have relatives."

"Except contrary to what you seem to believe, most people aren't budding criminals, looking for an opportunity to illegally profit at someone else's expense."

Tessa opened the only file on the flash drive and began looking at the background checks provided by KJ's security firm. Most were innocuous. In fact, with few exceptions they were downright boring, and looking at them gave him entirely too much time to think about Tessa. *Nothing* about Tessa Connor was boring.

He could see how a woman like her could tempt a man to consider marriage and family. The idea was seductive. But it would be a mistake for Tessa, if nothing else. He was too hard and had seen too much to ever be with a woman like her.

Yet it was difficult to think clearly. The warmth was building in the small office and her skin was releasing a faint, elusive fragrance. Gabe had noticed the refreshing scent before, mostly when they were kissing. The pressure behind his zipper began building, and he shifted uncomfortably.

"THAT'S UNEXPECTED," TESSA said after a while, frowning as she read the file on her cousin's boyfriend.

"What?"

"This business with Lance Beckley. Arrested for unlawful entry? That doesn't sound like him."

"I saw it early this morning and made calls to some people who made calls," Gabe explained. "My contacts tell me that Lance was caught in an impossible situation, attempting to protect his former foster sister from a beating. Denny Stanton, his ex-foster father, is a piece of filth who ought to be in jail."

Tessa shivered, suspecting she was going to hear something that wasn't pleasant. "I have a terrible feeling you're going to say that Lance was an abused foster kid."

"Looks like it. He was trying to do the right thing, but Stanton called the cops and demanded that Lance be arrested for breaking and entering."

"That's outrageous," she exclaimed. "Didn't Lance's foster sister defend him?"

"Apparently she was too scared to say anything at the time, but she got her courage up and called the police station a few days later. Lance had already been released since Stanton hadn't come in to press charges. I don't think the officers took the accusation seriously, anyway, since they didn't even put him in a holding cell after he was processed."

Tessa lifted an eyebrow. "Surely some of that isn't the sort of thing usually found in a police file."

"I told you, I have contacts. They have ways of getting information that isn't through regular channels."

"Right, contacts. Like KJ Bermann. He's interesting. I heard this morning that he'd charmed a fellow guest into spending the night with him. He works fast—he only got here yesterday afternoon."

"That sounds like KJ. Anyway, the police

notified the girl's social worker that something wasn't right in the home, even before she called with her version of the story. She was moved into another foster placement right afterward and seems to be doing well there."

Tessa regarded Gabe for a long moment.

It was endearing the way he'd checked on Lance's record, determined to confirm the youngster's innocence. Gabe probably didn't even realize how much he'd revealed about himself. His disgust and anger when explaining about the abuse and false charges against Lance had tugged at her heartstrings more effectively than anything else he could have done. He'd even checked on how Lance's foster sister was doing.

Gabe McKinley wanted everyone to believe he was tough and emotionless, but he had his soft spots, just as she'd suspected.

And she wanted him more than she'd ever wanted a man.

Tessa fanned herself with a sheet of paper, then leaned across to push aside the curtains and crack open a window.

"Sorry," she murmured when her breast grazed his arm.

THE PRESSURE IN Gabe's gut became excruciating.

Tessa unbuttoned the top four buttons on her shirt. "Sorry about how hot it is in here. I don't usually turn on the air-conditioning. Except in the bedroom. I can't sleep when it's too warm."

"The bedroom?" Gabe stroked a lock of hair away from her forehead. "Am I misinterpreting?"

"No." She kissed him.

For the life of him he couldn't think what had prompted Tessa's mood. Not that he was complaining.

She got up, dispatched the rest of her buttons, and dropped the shirt on his lap. Her lacy blue bra left little to the imagination.

Tessa might not have a generous bust, but what she possessed was first-rate…round and pretty, with rosy nipples that puckered as he watched.

"I hope you're prepared," she whispered. "But if you aren't, I have supplies in my bedroom. With any luck, they aren't out of date."

"I'm prepared." He got up and pulled her close. His questions would have to wait, along with the background checks.

Some things couldn't be postponed.

MUCH LATER, TESSA yawned as she lay next to Gabe. She was pleasantly tired, but not so much that she wanted to go back to sleep.

Making love with him had contained a fair number of fireworks, though she was sure it could get better. For a loner, he was an accomplished lover.

She eased away a few inches and looked at Gabe as he slept. He was so tall, he took up a lot of space. If they got together, they'd have to buy a much bigger bed.

A mental groan went through her at the thought. There wasn't going to be a need for a bigger bed, because Gabe was leaving as soon as they caught the spy.

She took in his long legs and trim hips, at first seeing only the physical power of his body. But slowly, awareness crept in that his skin bore a number of scars. The one on his left shoulder was still reddish and new-looking. The others... Tessa drew a quick breath. There were too many to comprehend, some small, some larger, and each a testament to his years in a very, *very* dangerous profession. She shivered, thinking that except for luck and skill on Gabe's part, any one of these dangerous encounters, mapped on his skin, could have ended with his death.

Ice seemed to hit the bottom of her stomach.

She firmly believed men became navy SEALs out of a strong sense of duty and a desire to serve their country, but that didn't mean Gabe wasn't also an adrenaline junkie.

The memory of her father's face at the hospital filled Tessa's head. Her mom had just died, and it was as if every bit of life had vanished from him, as well. That was when she'd understood the risks of falling in love so deeply. Still, between trying to help Pop and running Poppy Gold, she hadn't thought a great deal about it… maybe because she hadn't *wanted* to think about it.

Tessa agreed with Jamie; love *ought* to be easier. She was trying not to fall for Gabe, and looking at him was a reminder that giving her heart to him could be disastrous.

She reached out to touch one of the marks on his arm, only to let her hand drop.

"Not pretty, huh? Some women can't stand the sight. Others think scars are sexy."

Gabe's sleepy voice made her jump.

"You've gone through a lot."

"I survived."

"Tell me something," Tessa said slowly. "Is one of the reasons you became a navy SEAL because you enjoy the adrenaline rush of risking your life?"

"I never thought of it as risking my life, just as doing something that had to be done."

His reply was reassuring, and she extended her hand again to trace the parallel ridges of jagged scar tissue over his ribs. "These look like claw marks."

"They are. I encountered a mountain lion during survival training. She didn't take kindly to me accidentally getting between her and her babies and refused to accept an apology."

"How did you resolve the disagreement?"

"I climbed the nearest tree and swatted a branch in her face when she came after me. Fortunately her babies started squalling. She spat a last warning and departed."

"Lucky you." Tessa swallowed.

Cats could be extremely protective mothers, and cougars were notorious. She was sure the encounter had been more dramatic than he'd revealed.

"How old were you when it happened?" she asked.

"Old enough to know I shouldn't get between a mama and her children."

"No wonder you aren't crazy about cats."

"Not at all. I respect them, and I certainly respected her determination to keep her babies safe." Gabe closed his eyes and Tessa tried to decide if he wanted to sleep or just stop talking.

Stop talking, she decided, as his body responded to her gaze. Her abdomen tightened in anticipation.

Tessa opened the drawer on her bedside table and removed the unopened package of condoms she'd brought from San Francisco. Luckily the expiration date hadn't passed.

She took a packet out and put it on the sheet before leaning over Gabe. His eyes shot open again.

"That was nice, but I like a little more fore-play," she told him.

"I'm twice your size. I don't want to lose control."

Deliberately, she brushed her breasts over his chest, hard and smooth except for his scars and a thin wedge of dark hair. "I may be little, but I'm tough. I won't break."

"You must still be sore from your fall. Your tailbone, that is."

"That's okay—I enjoy being on top. Variety is the spice of life." Tessa straddled his hips and grinned at the glazed expression on his face. "Your mouth is saying no. Your body is less convinced."

Gabe cupped her breasts, kneading them, stroking his thumbs over her nipples, teasing her until she squirmed.

Obviously, he'd taken her seriously about fore-play, so she began exploring his body as well, getting creative with her feet, which stopped when he pulled her upward to draw one of her breasts into his mouth.

When he released her, they were both gasping. She'd reached behind her to stroke his arousal when he groaned. "Enough."

Tessa quite agreed.

She grabbed the condom and put it on him.

With extraordinary ease, Gabe lifted her over him, and she settled, taking him into her body, filled to bursting. She moaned and enjoyed the fullness for an instant before moving, rising up and down with him, her blood pumping faster and faster until the world spun away.

CHAPTER SIXTEEN

GABE WOKE TO a phone ringing, and he frowned. It didn't sound like his cell. A split second later he realized he was still in Tessa's apartment.

"Hey, Pop. What's up?" said Tessa. She had rolled onto her side, away from him, to answer the phone on the table next to her bed.

Gabe half listened to the conversation, hearing tension in her voice as she assured her father that nothing was wrong, that she hadn't returned to her office because she was taking the rest of the day off. The conversation morphed from there into a variety of topics.

He put his arm behind his head and gazed at the graceful sweep of Tessa's back and the curve of her hip. Sex was the last thing he'd expected when he'd gone to find her to review the background checks.

From the daylight coming through the windows, he put the time at around 5:00 p.m. He never slept in the middle of the day and didn't sleep that much at night. Yet he'd fallen asleep in her bed, not once, but twice. As a rule it was something he avoided; in his experience, some women seemed to see it as grounds for a longer-term relationship.

He released a heavy breath. The previous night had been charged with emotion, with things being said that had dug deeply into places he didn't like exploring.

There were vast differences between him and Tessa. At Poppy Gold, she was surrounded by family. The bed-and-breakfast complex represented happy memories with her parents, and she was unquestionably devoted to her father. In contrast, Gabe had rarely seen his parents over the past twenty years.

Still, she'd given him something to think about. His dad *must* have gotten over being angry at his eldest son for going into the navy. A small percentage of TIP had been given to Gabe as a baby, but nothing compared to the share signed over once his father retired. Perhaps David McKinley's awkward "I'm proud of you, son," the last time they'd spoken meant more than Gabe had been willing to believe.

"I know, Pop," Tessa said softly, following a long period of silence. "We'll go out of town or whatever you think might help…No, Mom wouldn't mind. She'd hate having you hurt so much."

It was silent again, but Tessa wiped her cheeks. Gabe swore silently.

He suspected she had been so focused on running Poppy Gold and getting Liam through the loss of his beloved wife, she hadn't dealt with her own feelings about her mother's death. How could she have? She had one parent left and was intent on helping him in any way possible.

Gabe didn't know what it would be like to lose his mother or father, but Tessa's devotion was a reminder of what his relationship with his own parents might have been.

After another few minutes, Tessa said goodbye and turned to look at him. "Sorry. My mom and dad's wedding anniversary…" She drew a shaky breath. "What *would* have been their thirty-second wedding anniversary is coming up. Pop gets depressed thinking about it."

The memory of Liam's shaking hands and inability to concentrate filled Gabe's mind. "Are you sure it isn't more? Could he be drinking to forget?"

Instead of getting angry, Tessa shook her head. "I understand why you'd wonder about that, but alcohol makes Pop sick to his stomach. One drink and he gets ill."

"Maybe he should try talking to someone besides his daughter," Gabe said carefully. "You're hurting, too, and somehow you need to deal with it, the same as your father. He could get counseling, maybe from his pastor. A few of my men used to go to a priest before heading out on a mission. I didn't see the need, but they claimed it helped get their heads straight."

Tessa swung her legs over the side of the bed and began getting dressed. "That wouldn't work... Pop's pastor is also his father-in-law. I would have introduced you at the ice-cream social, but Grandpa George left early to be with the family of a parishioner having emergency surgery."

"Oh."

It was another reminder of how tangled the relationships were in a small town. Glimmer Creek might be worse than some, but all of them seemed complicated.

"I'm hungry," Tessa said with false brightness. "Want a pizza?"

"Food deliveries are allowed in Poppy Gold?"

"The delivery person goes to Guest Registration, and they're driven to the guest's room in an electric cart. It's a pain, but it's the only way we can keep the number of motor vehicles down and make guests happy. What are your favorite toppings?"

"Everything except anchovies. I'll get my wallet."

Tessa shook her head. "No need." She dialed a number on her smartphone. "Hey, Carlo, it's Tessa. I need an extreme meal, half a regular combination, the other half vegetarian...Right, baked...Thirty minutes?...Great, put it on my account…No, I'm at home. I also need an order of eggplant parmigiana, salad and bread sticks to be delivered to my father…Yeah, above central maintenance. Thanks."

Gabe sat up. "Are you and your dad becoming vegetarians?"

"I just like veggie pizza the best and got lasagna for Pop the last time. I'm going to look some more at those background checks while we wait."

She left the bedroom, and Gabe collected his clothes. The sex had been spectacular, but it presented problems, including the question of what Tessa might now expect.

Frustrated, he zipped up his jeans and disposed of the condom wrappers. Curious, he looked at the box Tessa had left on her bedside table—the expiration date was close, but it was nearly full, missing only the ones they'd used earlier. Obviously she didn't have sex that often.

Pushing the thought away, he crossed the small parlor into the office. The fanciful creatures painted on the wall seemed disapproving as he reseated himself by the window. He tried not to be uncomfortable. She wasn't a sweet-faced toddler any longer; she was a sexy armful who'd made the first move.

Though only by minutes.

Gabe wasn't sure how long he could have sat next to her in that stuffy little room without a serious meltdown.

Nonetheless, he shouldn't have succumbed to temptation. Tessa wasn't like the women he'd known before and it seemed a cheat to get involved with her. Perhaps she wasn't a complete innocent, but she was still filled with ideals and optimism, and he couldn't recall ever feeling that way himself.

Yet her ideals were part of what drew him to her. She was sweet, stubbornly idealistic, and seemed particularly full of life. To someone who'd seen so much death, it was nearly irresistible.

"Who are you looking at now?" he asked, trying to put the thought out of his mind.

"Wanda Donovan." Tessa scrunched her nose. "It isn't right for me to know she got a speeding ticket in Nevada. That's her business, not mine."

He leaned closer and looked into the computer screen. "The ticket was written in Reno, the land of casinos and slot machines. Any chance Ms. Donovan has a gambling problem?"

"Unlikely," Tessa said firmly. "Wanda was my Sunday school teacher when I was ten. She has a married daughter in Sparks, which is next door to Reno."

"That doesn't mean Ms. Donovan isn't gambling."

"It doesn't mean she *is*, either. I'll bet she got this ticket when Melissa had her baby. Wanda was probably speeding to see her at the hospital."

Gabe sat back. He didn't want to get in a fight with Tessa, but he wasn't going to ignore a lead. "Fine, but Milt should check it out. Debts can make people desperate. I still think the most likely scenario is that someone already working at Poppy Gold was recruited to steal data from TIP."

"Even if I agreed with you, which I *don't*, it's a gigantic step to move from information theft to attempted murder."

"The guilty employee could have been paid to let an unauthorized person into the El Dorado Mansion."

"You're reaching."

Okay, he was reaching. *A little.* But at least he was open to other explanations.

"Anyway," Tessa continued, "I meant to tell you before... Remember the no-show group that was supposed to stay at the El Dorado the night before TIP was scheduled?"

"Yeah."

"We were notified a few days later that the credit card they used was stolen. The name on the card doesn't match any of our guests over the past three years, which is good news for Poppy Gold, but also a dead end as a clue."

Gabe swore.

"I also compared the dates Rob thinks information was stolen from his suite, and I still can't see a pattern."

The doorbell rang and Tessa got up to head downstairs. After a moment, Gabe headed for the steps himself. In the middle of the staircase he looked up and down, tempted to dare any ghosts to show themselves. It was a foolish thought, probably brought on by a haze of sexual satisfaction.

Death was death. He didn't have metaphysical or religious beliefs about it. Perhaps it would be marginally easier if he *did* have those beliefs—then he might also have faith that villains would receive their just rewards and their victims would find comfort.

Jaw set, he continued down and saw Tessa talking to the pizza deliveryman, dressed in the vibrant colors of the Italian national flag.

"Is that the new uniform, Wayne?" Tessa asked.

"Yeah, it's cool. I couldn't talk Carlo into shorts, though. Let's see, I have a half combination, half veggie dinner special for you." Wayne handed her an enormous pizza box and two bags. He cast a less-than-subtle look at Gabe. "See you next time. I'll take the order over to Mr. Connor now."

"Thanks, Wayne."

Gabe took the food and put it on the sofa table while Tessa locked the door. She unpacked the bags; one contained soft drinks and salad, the other a large carton of chicken.

"I hope you like baked chicken." She pushed the carton toward him, along with a paper plate.

"The seasonings they use at Little Italy are terrific."

"It's fine. I thought you were just getting pizza. This is enough to feed a navy convoy."

"Leftovers are convenient. I've eaten many a slice of pizza for breakfast."

"Same here. My mom rarely cooked, so Rob and I usually ordered pizza from a restaurant where Dad had an account."

"It doesn't bring up bad memories for you?"

He looked at her incredulously. "Bad memories about *pizza*? Get serious. The last time I was injured in the service and they wouldn't let me eat, I told them to give me a pizza by IV."

TESSA CHUCKLED AND forked a serving of Greek salad onto her plate.

She was trying to decide if she regretted having sex with Gabe. Essentially, she was staying in Glimmer Creek, and he'd made it clear that he was taking the fastest route out of town once his investigation was finished. He'd been equally clear that he didn't intend to have children. She might have put romance temporarily on hold and have qualms about loving too deeply, but she still wanted it all, including a family.

They ate steadily and put the leftovers in the refrigerator before returning to her office.

It was cooler now, and she continued reading the background reports, occasionally making comments. She was careful not to say anything she'd learned exclusively as manager of Poppy Gold, sticking to what she knew as a member of the community.

"You have boring neighbors," Gabe said finally.

"Quiet, not boring."

"You mean Poppy Gold tourists are as blameless as the rest of Glimmer Creek?"

"*No*, but I think most people are basically good. By the way, you don't have to keep sniping at small towns," she advised wryly. "I get the message. And if you're trying to warn me off because we had sex, don't bother. The sex was okay, but I know we aren't compatible in any other way."

She wasn't sure, but she thought she detected annoyance in Gabe's eyes. Honestly, men thought *women* overanalyzed and picked things apart, but they were often the worst offenders.

Still, it *was* true that she wouldn't have had sex with Gabe if she hadn't liked him quite a lot—physical attraction wasn't enough for her. Maybe he'd sensed that and was trying to protect her in his own way.

They were looking at the next file when Tessa's phone rang. "It's my great-uncle," she said, looking at the display before answering. "Hey, Uncle Milt."

"Hello, Tessa. I got the report back from the state crime lab."

"Oh. Gabe McKinley is here—let me put you on speaker." She pressed the icon on the smartphone. "Go ahead."

"As I was saying, I got the report back on that wood from the El Dorado staircase. There are a lot of details in the report, but basically it's the considered opinion of the crime lab that both the step and railing were deliberately rigged to collapse."

"Hell," Gabe exclaimed.

"Exactly. It doesn't prove that your brother was the intended victim, but he's the most likely target, given the letters and that he was the next person expected to be on those stairs. It would be a good idea to contact the Los Angeles police and get him under protection."

"He's already under protection. Rob doesn't know it, but I've got two ex-SEALs tailing him," Gabe explained.

"Why doesn't he know?" Tessa asked.

"Because he's a stubborn jackass who refuses to have personal security. He'd refuse police protection, too. I know him."

Great-Uncle Milt's laugh sounded over the phone. "Sounds like brotherly love to me. What about this sting operation?"

"I want to create a stack of fake documents to tempt the spy," Gabe said. "I'm not a businessman, so I've been thinking that Tessa and I could work on it together and come up with the details. We'll run it past you, of course, and develop a plan of action for the week Rob is here."

Tessa's jaw dropped. They hadn't discussed the sting yet, and she'd expected to need to fight tooth and nail to be included.

"All right," Uncle Milt agreed. "My office isn't soundproofed, so I don't want to take any chance of being innocently overheard, but we can talk on the phone when I'm at home."

"Sure thing. Thanks for calling, Uncle Milt."

"Just a minute," Gabe interrupted. "I want to ask about Wanda Donovan. I've gotten some background checks of my own and apparently she's often near Reno. I understand her daughter is there, but it would be easy for her to gamble when she's visiting. Having money problems could tempt her to do something she shouldn't."

Tessa glared at him.

"That's a leap if you're going for guilt by association," Great-Uncle Milt said. "I'll look into it, but I probably would have heard something by now if Wanda had a gambling problem."

"That's how I feel," Tessa affirmed. "We'll talk to you later, Uncle Milt."

"Take care, darling."

Outside the sun had dropped low in the sky, and Tessa stood up. "Let's take this up again tomorrow. I'm going over to check on my father."

"I'll go with you."

She shook her head. "Pop has already suggested I could do worse than to get together with a man like you. The less he sees us together, the better."

Gabe stared. "You're joking."

"Not at all, though I've reminded him there wouldn't be any grandchildren if we got serious."

"Was he convinced?"

Tessa thought about her father's comment that she could change Gabe's mind, but she didn't want to discuss it. "Grandchildren are important to Pop, partly because he knows kids are important to me. As long as I keep reminding him of that, he won't push. He doesn't want to see me lose out on something I've always wanted."

"I'd still better go with you. It could be dark by the time you leave."

She gave him a tight smile, refusing to get into another debate about small towns versus cities. As far as Poppy Gold went, it was a world unto itself, with staff on duty around the clock, including security.

"Fine." Tessa turned off the computer and stood up.

They were both quiet as they walked to the central maintenance building.

"I didn't realize there was living space up here," Gabe commented as they climbed the rear exterior steps.

"The apartment has been mostly empty until the last year or so. Hi, Pop," she called, seeing him at the table under the pergola. The food containers from Little Italy still sat there, and she quickly assessed how much he'd eaten—not as much as she would have preferred, but more than half.

"Thank you for dinner, dear."

"No trouble. I was ordering food for myself and just added something for you."

For the first time, her father seemed to notice her companion. "Hello, Gabe. I see you've been more successful than the rest of us in getting my daughter to take time off. Thank you."

Tessa squirmed, recalling what she and Gabe had done with that time off, and was pleased to see he looked a little uncomfortable himself.

Gabe cleared his throat. "Uh, sure."

"Have a seat." Liam gestured vaguely. "There's probably soda or juice to drink if you're thirsty."

"I'm going to get soda water," Tessa said. "Do you want lemonade, Pop, or something else?"

"Lemonade is fine."

"Sounds good to me," Gabe added.

Tessa was grateful to get away, even for a few minutes. Spending so much time with Gabe was exhausting; she always had to be on her guard around him, and her instincts were totally screwed up by hormones and a growing understanding of the complicated, wounded man beneath the hard shell.

Tessa's throat was tight and she tried to suppress the melancholy going through her. Despite his professed lack of faith in human nature, Gabe was a protector—a soldier who'd risked his life to make the world safer. It was equally clear he was haunted by the people he hadn't been able to help, especially the children. His deepest wounds weren't the ones on his body.

But it wasn't up to her to heal him; he'd probably laugh at the idea that he even needed it. But he did. He *really* did. And a part of her already wanted to be the source of that healing.

As LANCE WAITED in the car for Jamie to finish her class on Wednesday, he looked through the printouts he'd found on his doorstep. They were from the US Navy website, and he figured Gabe McKinley must have left them there.

He just wished he could ask Gabe how being arrested in Sacramento might affect his chances. What if Gabe or the navy thought he'd actually broken into somebody's house and had gotten off lucky? That would be horrid.

Before coming to Glimmer Creek, Lance hadn't cared much about what people thought, but it wasn't the same now. Jamie was a sweetheart, and even if her parents still weren't sure about him, they were nice people. Liam and Tessa had given him a shot and the pay wasn't bad; it would get even better once he started training to take care of Poppy Gold's antique vehicles. But the navy could be a real chance to do something.

The driver's door opened suddenly and Lance jumped. It was Jamie.

"What's that?" she asked.

"Nothing." He hastily shoved everything into his backpack. "Did your professor say anything about the term paper you gave him on Monday?"

She smiled ecstatically. "I got an A. He said it was great and he's looking forward to reading my other one."

Lance kissed her, so proud he could burst. "I knew you could do it." He pulled out a small box from his pocket. "So I got you this to celebrate."

Inside was a little silver *A* for her charm bracelet.

Jamie looked at the charm for a long time without saying anything.

"Don't you like it?" he asked anxiously.

"Oh, yes, but I need to talk to you about something, and a gift makes me feel funny."

He'd never liked it when people said they had to talk. Usually it wasn't anything good. "What about?"

"The thing is, my mom asked me not to ride the motorcycle any longer. It isn't because she doesn't like you—it's because she worries about safety." Jamie drew a deep breath. "But this isn't just about Mom. I get sick to my stomach on the bike and riding it scares me, too."

Lance frowned.

"Please don't be hurt," Jamie begged him. "I didn't want to tell you because I know you love your bike. Only Tessa said the longer I waited, the harder it would be, and she was right. Please say something."

"I don't care about the bike," he said slowly, relieved it wasn't something worse. "I already figured your folks didn't like it, and I should have noticed riding it made you sick."

Her face relaxed. "I'm really proud that you fixed it up. Not too many people could have done such a great job. I bet that's why Uncle Liam wants you to work on Poppy Gold's vehicles."

Lance hadn't thought about being proud. He'd wanted something to drive, and the only way was to fix up a bike that somebody else had thrown away. Getting it to work had pleased him, of course. Buying a motorcycle, even a used one, would have been impossible.

"I guess." He was thinking about what she'd said, that putting something off only made it harder. She was right. It seemed almost impossible now to tell her the truth about his childhood.

"Do you want a milk shake before we drive home?" Jamie asked.

"Uh, okay."

She started the car—it was a Volvo that belonged to her dad—and drove toward a hamburger stand they'd eaten at before. Lance knew her father had wanted her to take the Volvo because of its safety record. Motorcycles were great, but her parents had a point—they weren't as safe as a car.

Only Volvos cost a lot. You sure couldn't buy one at the salvage yard and fix it up the way you could a motorcycle. It was scary to think about everything needed to take care of a family. And since Jamie wanted kids someday…his head started spinning.

They ordered their milk shakes and drank them at a park, but as they started back to Glimmer Creek, Lance thought about the papers in his backpack.

While he hated anyone knowing about the problems in Sacramento, maybe he'd better talk to Gabe. There wasn't any point in going to a recruiter if they wouldn't take him, anyway.

CHAPTER SEVENTEEN

GABE WAS STOWING equipment in the maintenance building on Friday afternoon when Lance came in, but instead of marking his time sheet and leaving, the kid hung around.

"Something up?" Gabe asked after a few minutes.

"Uh, yeah. Did you give me those papers about the navy?"

"Yes. I thought they might help."

"Thanks." Lance shifted his feet and glanced around.

Realizing he didn't want to talk where anybody else could hear, Gabe wiped his hands. "I'm off myself now, and I've been curious about this orchard you're digging. Any chance you have time to show it to me?"

The kid nodded eagerly. "We can go now."

As they headed toward the site, Lance explained how he'd first cut the brush, then dug out the roots and rocks and prepared the soil for the first orchard, and was now doing the same for another one.

"That's heavy work," Gabe commented.

"It isn't too bad. At first I didn't get why the Connors wanted to grow their own apples, but it's cool watching the trees grow."

"You wouldn't plant orchards in the navy, but you'd be able to get an education or other training."

Lance cleared his throat. "But, uh, I don't know if they'll take me," he said in a rush. "See, this thing happened a few months ago. It…well… I grew up in foster homes, and my last foster father would get drunk and smack us around, all sorts of crap."

Though he already knew about the abuse, Gabe felt a flash of anger.

"After I got my own place, my old foster sister would call me," Lance continued. "One night, Maggie was scared he was going to kill her, so I went over to help."

Gabe wished he could stop Lance and say that he understood, but it would require revealing too much.

Slowly, painfully, Lance finished the story, and Gabe wished the youngster had come to him earlier.

"You were just trying to protect her—she was lucky you were there. Does Maggie ever call now?"

"Sometimes. Her new place is pretty nice. They're even talking about adopting her."

"That's great. About the arrest, the recruiter will find out about it and ask what happened, so it's best to explain up front. They'll want copies of the police report and do some checking on your story. If they believe you're innocent, which I'm sure they will, you shouldn't have a problem enlisting. I'd be happy to write a letter of recommendation, and that should help."

Lance's face contorted, as if he was struggling with emotions he didn't know how to handle. "Thanks. I was never in any other trouble, but I didn't think anyone would believe me. It was my word against his."

"I believe you, and I'm sure other people will, too, if you decide to tell them."

Lance kicked a small rock and watched it bounce across the land he'd been clearing. "Nobody here knows about me growing up in foster homes and stuff. Jamie's parents probably won't like it. Especially if they…"

"Yes?" Gabe prompted.

"Well, I never met my father, but I know he's in prison for killing someone. And my mother died when I was born. She used to be in all kinds of trouble, too."

"You aren't responsible for your parents, and don't pay attention to anyone who judges you because of them."

Lance's expression reminded Gabe of the old men he'd met in his travels, worn down by a life-

time of violence and poverty. "That's easy to say
when you've got a proper family. When I was
growing up, none of the nice people wanted me
to be friends with their kids. I should have told
Jamie before, but I've been scared I'll lose her."

"Lance, you've grown up to be a decent person. You can't let anyone take that away. I'm sure
Jamie will understand."

Lance nodded jerkily. "I hope so. I better go
now. She's expecting me. But thanks."

"You're welcome."

Lance trudged away and a thread of sadness
went through Gabe. He didn't know if enlisting
was right for the kid; he just knew there were
opportunities in military service that he might
not get otherwise.

LATER THAT EVENING, Tessa was glaring at Gabe
when her cell phone rang. She grabbed it from
the sofa table and answered. "Hello?"

"Tessa, it's Bill Blaylock in Guest Registration. Some visitors are here who want to speak
with you."

"Sure. I'll be right over."

"We have more to discuss," Gabe warned as
she got up from her chair.

"And we can take it up again later. But we've
been over this time and again. I'm not releasing
information that I have solely as Poppy Gold's
manager. Period. End of argument."

They'd just finished going over the background checks, and aside from Wanda Donovan's speeding ticket in Nevada, there had been little to raise questions...even for someone as suspicious as Gabe. Now he was trying to talk her into giving him the names of everyone employed by her cousin's catering business, as well as the laundry service.

"Tessa, I know you have a full list of all the contractors' employees."

"Duh. But you don't need to worry. Uncle Milt already has it."

"Then you—"

"No," she stopped him. "Have you ever considered that you spent twenty years in the navy defending people's rights, and now you're asking me to violate them?"

Gabe jerked, and a dull flush crept up under his collar. He was so intent on finding whoever was threatening his brother, he couldn't have thought things through. He must have been one heck of a navy SEAL—dedicated, single-minded and target oriented. Maybe if his brother wasn't involved, he'd be able to see the bigger picture, but right now it was up to her and Great-Uncle Milt to make sure nobody crossed the line.

"You can stay here if you want," she murmured. "I need to go to Guest Registration."

"You're off duty—it's after seven."

"And someone wants to see me," she said patiently. "Registration wouldn't have called if it wasn't important."

Without a word, Gabe followed her down the steep, narrow stairs.

"Granddad," Tessa exclaimed as she walked into Old City Hall a few minutes later. She threw her arms around Patrick Connor and hugged him. "Why didn't you tell me you were coming?"

"I wanted to surprise my favorite granddaughter."

She tweaked his tie. "Lucky I'm your only granddaughter. Where's Grams?"

"Right behind you," said Sandra Connor.

Tessa gave her a kiss and hug, as well. "You look wonderful. Just give me a minute and I'll find you a room."

"I've already taken care of that," Bill interjected. "I've put them next door to the Victorian Cat in the Sutter House, and their bags have been taken over to their suite."

"Thanks, Bill."

Gabe stepped forward. "Mr. and Mrs. Connor, Gabe McKinley, at your service."

Her grandmother smiled, but Patrick's gaze narrowed. "Ah, yes, you're the young man taking so much of my granddaughter's attention these days."

"Guilty as charged." Gabe put an arm around Tessa's shoulders, and she wanted to kick him. At least her grandparents knew about the cover story and wouldn't get the wrong idea. "You have a very talented granddaughter, sir."

"As we well know," Granddad returned in a dry tone.

GABE MEASURED PATRICK CONNOR'S face and knew he might be old, but he was still tough as nails. Yet his expression softened whenever he looked at Tessa or his wife.

"You must miss her executive ability in San Francisco."

"I miss my granddaughter more." There was a steely edge in Patrick's tone. "But this is the place for her. I always knew she'd return to Connor's Folly, sooner or later."

"Connor's Folly?" Tessa chuckled. "You never change, Granddad."

Sandra Connor laughed. "Don't you believe any Connor's Folly nonsense your grandfather spouts. He's proud of what Liam and your mother accomplished here."

"Now, now, my dear, I'm willing to admit when I was wrong," Patrick acknowledged. "My father spent a fortune buying and maintaining the old part of this town, and everyone thought he was crazy. But when I look around today, I see it was a good thing. Have you eaten, Tessa? We'd like to take you out to dinner. Naturally, Mr. McKinley is invited, as well."

"I don't know about Gabe, but I'd love to go."

"Same here," Gabe accepted quickly. He was sure Tessa would prefer to get rid of him for a while, but he wanted to observe Patrick Connor. Tessa might be convinced her grandfather wouldn't take advantage of the situation, but Gabe wasn't as sure. The old guy had inherited a fortune, which he'd reputedly multiplied many times since. He hadn't done it by being a saint.

"Excellent. Tessa, how does the GC Steakhouse sound?"

"It would be great. Does Pop know you're here?"

"We spoke earlier. He said to let him know where we're eating and he could meet us."

After a call to Liam, Patrick and his wife declined the courtesy shuttle and walked briskly toward the parking area, belying their seventy-odd years.

Gabe watched the proceedings with a faint sense of disbelief. They drove to the restaurant on the edge of town and found Liam already there.

Patrick Connor and Gabe's father had to be cut from the same cloth, yet it was a pleasant evening, with no mention of industrial espionage or empire building. Liam mostly spoke with his mother, while Tessa and her grandfather debated California history. Gabe stayed out of the conversation, preferring to observe.

Back in front of the Sutter House, the Connors kissed Tessa. "Come over in the morning. I'll fix breakfast," she urged.

"No need to cook, dear," said Sandra. "Poppy Gold serves an excellent breakfast. But we'll see you afterward and make plans for the day. Is nine o'clock good?"

"That'll be fine, Grams. Sleep well."

Gabe stuck next to Tessa as she crossed the garden to the Victorian Cat. If the evening had accomplished nothing else, it had further solidified their image as a couple. Eating out with the grandparents? Everybody would be anticipating a wedding by the end of the weekend.

"It's late," Tessa said, turning at her door and putting a hand on his chest.

Gabe's body instantly hardened. She'd kept a careful distance between them over the past few days, but it hadn't kept him from wanting her again.

"We still need to talk," he murmured.

"All right, *talk*," Tessa emphasized. "That's all."

Inside her apartment she switched on the light, and he saw a huge black-and-white cat ensconced on the couch. "What's this one called?" he asked.

"Tiny Tim."

Gabe had to laugh; there was nothing tiny about the feline. "I didn't see him earlier."

"He was probably sitting in the kitchen window. That's where he spends most of his time when visiting, at least during daylight hours. He's the most dedicated bird-watcher of all the permanent VC residents."

"Why was Tiny Tim evicted from his own room?"

"One of our regular guests miscalculated. He'd planned a romantic weekend but hadn't realized his latest girlfriend is terrified of cats. When it came down to sex or having Tiny Tim remain in the suite, sex won."

It made sense to Gabe. He'd been thinking a good deal about sex himself, including something Tessa had said.

The sex was okay.

Okay?

His ego was reasonably robust, but no man enjoyed hearing his performance in bed was simply "okay." At the same time, he was irritated with himself for letting the comment bother him; it was hard enough getting her out of his head.

He'd gotten a real shock when he found himself reassuring Lance that Jamie would understand about his troubled background. It had been totally out of character, yet curiously, Gabe also believed it was true.

Tiny Tim was regarding him with curiosity, so he walked over and let the cat sniff his fingers... Anything to stop thinking about the ways Tessa had been affecting him.

"Give me your hand," Tessa said.

He extended his arm and she shook something that looked like herbs onto his palm.

"That's catnip. Let him lick it off."

Gabe was doubtful until Tiny Tim ecstatically licked it up with his raspy tongue. A rough purr sounded, and the cat gave him an approving, benevolent look. To test whether it was a ruse, Gabe scratched under his chin and the purr surged louder.

Then Tessa sank onto the couch and Tiny Tim abandoned Gabe to leap onto her lap, arching against her chest. Cats seemed to gravitate to her, taking all sorts of enviable liberties.

"I've been thinking about the sabotaged staircase," she said. "If the perpetrator is someone targeting the McKinley family or business, you need to be careful, too. You could be next if they realize you're related to Rob."

The chance of coming under fire *had* occurred to Gabe, but he was highly trained. His biggest worry was keeping Tessa safe—if this was someone with a personal vendetta, they might be completely wacko.

"Worried about me?"

"Of course I'm worried about you. I'd like to think we've become friends, or at least allies."

"Is that all?"

"You don't want it to be more, remember?"

"Yeah, except I know you don't sleep with just anyone. It's important to me that I don't hurt you, Tessa. You're really special, and I've seen too many special things destroyed in this world. I've been thinking a lot about the marriages that ended so badly with the men in my command. And the truth is, men like me are hard on women like you. We've seen too much."

"You can't...that is, don't worry about me," Tessa said softly. "I can take care of myself."

Gabe frowned, noticing she hadn't denied having feelings for him. Of course, she hadn't admitted to any, either. Nor was she likely to.

He sat down on the couch. Surprisingly, Tiny Tim left Tessa and draped himself over Gabe's legs.

Idly, Tessa picked up the sheaf of letters Rob had received and flipped through them. "I wish the FBI was taking these more seriously."

"As Rob says, they've got a lot on their plates. You're still bothered by that one note?"

"Yes. I've spent hours looking at it, going over old copies of the *Glimmer Creek Gazette* and magazines carried by the library and medical clinic. Anything that might tie the notes to our town. Uncle Milt is doing the same thing, but nothing matches up. Whoever created them is clever—Rob says they sent a photocopy of the original note, so it's even harder to trace where the cutout words and letters came from."

Her forefinger traced the *P* in TIP.

"I think it's the *P* in this letter that keeps striking a chord. I just don't know why."

Gabe had looked at the *P* as well, but he couldn't see anything there to identify. He rubbed behind Tiny Tim's ears and another loud purr roared from the cat's chest.

Tessa cleared her throat. "What sort of enemies does Robert have? He's always seemed like a straight arrow."

"Rob has a list of disgruntled former employees that he's compared with the list I've made of people here. But there are no connections he can see. He's also sent it to your great-uncle, just in case."

She frowned. "Doesn't Rob have any personal enemies?"

"How? My brother works as many hours as you do, and he's not the type to sleep with someone else's wife or anything like that."

"People with vendettas aren't always logical about *why* they have them. For that matter, we're still working on a lot of assumptions. It could still be someone who'd steal information from any convenient source. I don't know what I'm going to do if we don't catch the culprit before the next business conference at Poppy Gold."

Gabe looked at Tessa, wanting to comfort her as much as he wanted to take her to bed again. Seeing her as special was understandable, but it didn't make sense that he'd begun to care about her so much.

They had sharply conflicting ways of seeing the world. She was devoted to her extended family, while he was only close to Rob. Tessa was idealistic, while he'd seen horrors beyond imagining. He no longer believed in anything...well, except for protecting people's rights, as she'd pointed out earlier.

It had been a shock to be confronted like that.

He'd become a victim of tunnel vision, seeing only his brother's safety and his desire to protect TIP. The irony was that he didn't give a hoot for Thomas International Products except that the company mattered to Rob.

Still, in every other way, he stood in stark contrast to Tessa. They were as dissimilar as two people could be.

Maybe being opposites explained Jamie Fullerton's appeal to Lance—to a kid who'd seen nothing but trouble in his life, Jamie probably seemed like a fairy princess.

After a moment, Gabe realized Tessa was looking at him questioningly, and he cleared his throat. "Did you say something? I was distracted for a moment."

"Would you like a cup of coffee?"

"Sure."

Gabe went into the kitchen and watched as Tessa made a pot of decaf. "We shouldn't mention knowing Lance grew up as a foster kid. I don't think he's told anyone."

She wrinkled her nose. "I don't intend to say *anything* about what I've seen in those background checks."

"Most of it is boring and innocuous."

"Not boring," she corrected him. "Just a far cry from the excitement of life as a navy SEAL. When are we going to start working on the fake documents for the sting operation?"

"As soon as your grandparents leave. When Rob comes he'll set up the video cams again to catch anyone going through the papers in his suite."

"Unless someone takes out a camera and blatantly shoots pictures or goes through a briefcase, there won't be any real proof," Tessa said, pouring two cups of the coffee and handing him one. "Besides, aren't some cameras so small these days you might never realize one was in use?"

"It's possible." Gabe had seen highly sophisticated surveillance equipment during his career. If someone was willing to invest, they could take a picture with no one being the wiser. Since the thief had been exceptionally careful to date, they might well have purchased the best tools for their illicit activities.

Tessa took a sip from her cup, but it wasn't coffee she really wanted. The boyish pleasure in

Gabe's face while petting Tiny Tim had completely sunk her resolution to keep her distance. Then when the cat had taken up residence on his lap? She'd practically melted. The big, tough ex-SEAL, cuddling a purring feline...she would love having a video of *that*.

"The, uh, documents we create should try to trick the guilty person into revealing themselves immediately," she said, distractedly wondering what Gabe would do if she did a 180-degree turn and invited him to bed.

"How do we do that?"

"Put a time limit on how long the information is valuable." Tessa set her cup on the counter. She was a modern woman; she didn't need to be coy. "In the meantime, remember what I said about us just talking?"

Gabe looked confused. "Yeah."

"Forget I said it."

Gabe stared for a second. "Has anyone ever accused you of being unpredictable?" he asked hoarsely.

She stepped closer. "Are you objecting?"

"Not a chance."

Gabe drew her to him for a kiss, visibly aroused. She smiled, planning to make sure it was a very good night.

BEFORE DAWN THE next morning, Tessa was aware of Gabe getting out of the bed and collecting his jeans and shirt. She yawned and scratched Tiny Tim's neck. The cat had found a space between the pillows to sleep.

It was nice; for once she hadn't had one of her nightmares where she fell and fell.

"Are you leaving?" she murmured.

"Sorry, I didn't mean to disturb you."

She didn't doubt it. Gabe McKinley was probably a master at slipping away quietly.

"That's okay. See you Monday." Tessa was determined to make him think she was treating the night casually.

"Monday? Not a chance," he scoffed. "I'll be back before nine when your grandparents come. I just want fresh clothes so they don't guess where I spent the night."

She yawned and stretched. "This isn't the 1880s. Granddad isn't going to take out a shotgun and force us to the altar."

"You're still his granddaughter, and it's courteous to respect his feelings."

She closed her eyes as he walked out the bedroom door, reminding herself she'd known all along that sex was the only type of closeness he'd allow.

AN HOUR LATER, Tessa had just drifted back into an uneasy sleep when a cold nose nudged her forehead.

She opened her eyes and saw Tiny Tim's furry face.

"I hope you don't do that to guests," she grumbled. "Most of them don't want to wake up so early."

He sat back on his haunches and licked a paw.

Tessa looked around. Every sign of Gabe's presence had been erased, but she hadn't expected anything else. She was surprised he'd stayed even a few hours.

She pushed the thought from her head and got up to take care of a few chores. She flew around, getting the apartment in order and trying not to think about Gabe McKinley.

There was another wedding at Poppy Gold that evening, but with her grandparents visiting, she decided to call the weekend event staff to let them know she wouldn't be on hand to help.

"We love you, Tessa, but you don't *have* to be there," Colleen Ryan told her with a hint of exasperation. "We've got everything covered."

Tessa winced. "I know. It's a bad habit."

"I wouldn't say that, but you need to stop over-extending yourself. Enjoy your grandparents' visit and leave the worrying to me. That's what I'm paid to do."

"The mother of this particular bride is even more stressed out than most," Tessa warned.

"I know, but we'll get through it."

Tessa said goodbye, glad that Gabe hadn't

overheard the conversation with Colleen. Working at Poppy Gold wasn't the same as going to an office and being there eighteen hours a day. Here she was surrounded by family. The whole place was home, and most of the time it didn't even *feel* like work.

She sat down to eat breakfast, but she mostly crumbled her toast and let the coffee grow cold. Truthfully, she felt guilty when she wasn't doing something for Poppy Gold. Everything was *so* connected to her parents, and with Mom gone...

The familiar grief rose through her, but she forced it away. As she'd told Gabe, she was trying to back off a little, if only to let the staff know she trusted them. If there was a problem they could always call.

Tiny Tim wandered into the kitchen and meowed, as if asking a question.

She smiled at him. "Yes, you're staying for the rest of the weekend."

Seeming to understand, he jumped onto the windowsill and settled down for serious bird-watching. She was still petting him there when she saw Gabe walk into the garden with her grandparents shortly before 9:00 a.m.

She'd never gone weak-kneed at the sight of a man, but she came close with Gabe.

Frustrated, she called them inside. She was thrilled to have her grandparents at Poppy Gold and hoped she'd be able to ditch Gabe during part of their visit. He might not believe it, but family had more to talk about than finding industrial spies.

CHAPTER EIGHTEEN

DESPITE GABE'S BROODING PRESENCE, Tessa enjoyed the morning with her grandparents, probably more than her father. Though time and distance had softened his relationship with Patrick Connor, they still had little in common.

Pop had shown up before they could talk about the industrial thefts, so they'd visited until lunchtime, when she ordered a picnic from the general store. They ate in the park, entertained by a local barbershop quartet, who often performed in the bandstand. A large crowd had gathered by the time the singing had concluded.

"What a treat," Grams declared after the applause had died away. "I had no idea there was a barbershop quartet in Glimmer Creek."

"One of my second cousins started the group twenty years ago," said Tessa as she selected a peach custard tart for dessert. "They call themselves the Forty-Niners."

After the meal, Tessa escorted her grandparents around Poppy Gold to show them the most recent changes. Her father stuck close, making it impossible to discuss anything about industrial espionage.

"Red astrachans, eh?" Granddad murmured when he viewed the small orchard that had been planted, a nostalgic smile on his face. "My mother claimed red and white astrachan apples made the best pies."

"That's what Pop said, so we decided to plant them here. So far we haven't been able to get the white variety, but we're still trying. When the apples start coming in, you'll be sure to get part of the crop every year."

"Wonderful," said Grams with obvious delight. "My mother-in-law told me about cooking with astrachans. I'm looking forward to trying her recipes with the 'right' kind of apple."

Granddad gazed at the little trees. He was likely the only person alive who remembered the small apple farm where his mother had grown up. Tessa squeezed his hand, knowing he was pleased, even if he couldn't say so.

It was difficult knowing the two most important men in her life had so much trouble communicating. If her mother's death had taught her nothing else, it was that you couldn't count on having time to say the things that needed to be said.

GABE WAS UNCOMFORTABLE participating in the family outing, but he wanted to be there in case Patrick said anything to Tessa about the thefts.

It was also difficult seeing the tension between Liam and his father. In a way, it didn't make sense. According to Tessa, her grandfather had never made her feel guilty about leaving Connor Enterprises. Patrick had also deeded Connor's Folly to his son and daughter-in-law as a wedding gift. Surely that implied approval.

Perhaps it was simply because Liam and Patrick had such different focuses. Liam liked working with his hands, while Patrick was devoted to business.

"There's Lance," Tessa said. She waved to Lance and he came over. "This is the young man preparing our orchard land," she explained. "Lance, these are my grandparents, Patrick and Sandra from San Francisco."

LANCE EXTENDED HIS arm before realizing how dirty he was from digging up weeds and rocks. "Sorry," he muttered, frantically wiping his fingers on his jeans.

"Nonsense," said the old guy. "I'm delighted to meet the person responsible for those apple trees. My mother loved astrachan apples."

Lance blinked. These must be Liam Connor's parents and not related to Jamie. Jamie had tried to tell him the ways everybody was connected in Glimmer Creek, but she had so many relatives, he couldn't keep them straight yet.

Mr. and Mrs. Connor shook hands with him

as if they didn't care about the dirt he couldn't wipe off.

"Mr. Co...that is, Liam told me about his grandma growing up on an apple farm," he stuttered. Even after several months he had trouble saying Liam, but first names *were* easier when there were two Mr. Connors. "He's teaching me about growing apples."

Sandra Connor smiled warmly at him. "You've obviously done a huge amount of work out here."

"He's doing a terrific job," Liam said. "And when he's done, I'll teach him how to maintain Poppy Gold's antique vehicles."

Lance's face heated and he tried not to look at Gabe, feeling guilty that he wanted to enlist in the navy when the Connors were willing to give him a better job. He shuffled his feet. "Uh, I better go back to work."

He sped off and didn't catch his breath until everyone had walked out of sight. Was it dishonest not to tell them? But he hadn't *actually* made up his mind. Besides, he ought to talk to Jamie about it before he did anything else.

TESSA FELT BAD that she'd put Lance on the spot. He was awkward with people, which wasn't any wonder in light of his childhood.

The afternoon was turning warmer and Grams fanned herself. "If you don't mind, Tessa, I'd like to go sit by the pool while you continue the tour with your grandfather. I don't get many opportunities for sunbathing in San Francisco."

"I'll sit with you," Pop volunteered instantly.

Tessa held back a smile. Grams had known her son would prefer staying with her and that it would give her husband and granddaughter some privacy to talk with Gabe about the investigation.

With Gabe and her grandfather, Tessa returned to the Victorian Cat to discuss the thefts from TIP.

"My security team tells me that nobody has approached Connor Enterprises with an offer to sell insider information," Granddad explained as they sat at the kitchen table.

Tessa frowned. "That's odd."

"We aren't the only company who could benefit, my dear."

"That isn't what I meant. Surely by staging the thefts here at Poppy Gold, someone was hoping to throw suspicion onto Pop or me or Connor Enterprises. So why wouldn't they try to take it further?"

GABE WAS DISCONCERTED that the same thing hadn't occurred to him. Why *hadn't* the culprit tried to solidify the case against the Connors, if only by passing on the information that had been stolen?

"Maybe they still hope to follow through on their plan," Patrick suggested.

"Or else they think the connection alone is enough," Gabe said.

Tessa tilted her head challengingly. "Yeah, initially Gabe thought Pop and I might be involved."

Patrick's gaze turned coolly angry. "You suspected my son and granddaughter?" It was plain that whatever disputes Patrick might have with Liam, he wouldn't tolerate an insult to his family's honor.

"Not for long," Tessa interjected as she stood up, "and I already gave him a hard time about it, so he recognizes the error of his ways. Right, Gabe?"

"Absolutely," Gabe agreed, trying to keep a straight face. There was a difference between physical security and the wrath of a protective grandfather, but the idea that he needed Tessa to defend him was amusing. One of the reasons he'd opposed her getting involved in the investigation was concern for *her* safety.

"What are the chances an anonymous letter was sent to a company employee?" Gabe asked. "Say, something that could have been taken as a prank or inappropriate disclosure, but not an offer to sell data?"

Patrick shook his head. "Anything like that should still be forwarded to my security chief, who would notify the Securities Exchange Commission. TIP and Connor Enterprises may not be stockholder companies, but illicit dealings affect the market and stockholders from other companies."

Gabe nodded.

"What now?" Patrick asked.

"TIP is coming back a week from Monday." Tessa opened her refrigerator and took out a pitcher filled with iced tea. "We're setting up a sting operation with Uncle Milt."

Tessa put tall glasses on the table and filled them.

"I could have the head of my security team come up here with some of his crew to support Milt," Patrick offered.

Tessa sipped from her glass. "Thanks, but it isn't necessary. Gabe has 'contacts.'" She drew air quotes around *contacts* with her fingers, and Patrick lifted an eyebrow.

"Contacts?"

"I'm a retired navy SEAL," Gabe interjected, giving Tessa a stern look. She was enjoying herself too much at his expense. "So I know a number of ex-SEALs who are now in the private security business or doing similar work."

Tessa plucked a leaf from a spearmint plant on the table and crushed it into her tea. The cool, crisp fragrance filled the air. "Don't be offended, Granddad. I doubt that Gabe trusts anyone who hasn't successfully finished SEAL training and gone on a few missions. The rest of us are just defenseless rabbits who don't have enough sense to come in from the rain."

To Gabe's surprise, her grandfather smiled at him. "She's a handful, isn't she? Sharp as they come and loves to tease."

"I'm not sure she's teasing," Gabe objected, reminded of the way Liam would say things about his daughter. They both seemed to have the same indulgent view of Tessa.

Tessa rolled her eyes. "Granddad, we're devising a strategy to trick the thief into revealing their identity immediately—to put a time limit on the value of the information. Whoever it is has managed to avoid suspicion until now, which means they're smart and exceptionally careful."

"Perhaps you can use me as a form of bait—try to convince the thief that I'd be particularly interested in buying the information. A phone tap could be put on all my office lines."

She nodded. "It's a thought."

"Just let me know what I can do to help."

TESSA CAUGHT AN incredulous glance from Gabe that seemed to ask, *Is he for real?*

She almost snickered.

Her grandfather was genuine. Though Patrick Connor had his faults, including the hot temper she'd inherited, he ascribed to Benjamin Franklin's philosophy of being able to do well by doing right. He was a tough competitor, but he wouldn't do anything illegal or underhanded.

A short time later, she saw her father and grandmother pass by the kitchen window.

"I think this meeting is over," she announced. "Grams must be tired of sunning herself by the pool."

She opened the front door before they could ring. "Did you have a nice time?" she asked.

"Yes, but it got too frantic for quiet conversation," her grandmother said with a laugh. "Quite a few children must be staying at Poppy Gold this weekend, and they all descended on the pool at once."

"It'll be even worse when more schools are out for the summer."

"How nice to have so many families."

Tessa felt the same way. Christmastime was particularly special when kids were staying. Poppy Gold went all out for the holidays and she was looking forward to sharing it with her own children one day.

She glanced at Gabe, only to kick herself. No woman in her right mind should think about family and Gabe McKinley together...even if it was what she wanted more than anything else in the world.

"Jamie, why do people call this a Carnegie library?" Lance whispered on Thursday evening as Jamie sat at a table in the library, typing notes on her computer. "I thought it was the Glimmer Creek Library."

"A rich guy gave money to the town to build it, like, a zillion years ago," she whispered back. "My mom says the town was upset about the architecture he wanted, but it was nice having him pay for most of it. Mr. Carnegie built libraries all over the place."

"I wonder how he got rich enough to give that much money away."

She shrugged and tucked her notebook computer into her backpack. "Do you want to go now?"

Lance nodded, and they returned the books she'd been using to the shelves. Outside, he looked up at the building. "It sure doesn't look like Poppy Gold."

"Nah. Mom calls it classic revival style…whatever that means. I like the buildings in Poppy Gold better."

He grinned. "You like everything in Poppy Gold better." Then his smile faded. He needed to talk to her and didn't want to wait any longer. "I've been thinking. You know, about the future."

"Yes?"

"Well, uh…" He swallowed. "I've been thinking about enlisting in the navy."

Jamie looked so startled he wished he'd thought of a better way to tell her.

"I thought you were happy in Glimmer Creek."

"I *am* happy, but Gabe says I can get training in the service. I want to do right by you, and how can I do that if I don't do something like enlist? I thought if I got to be a navy flier, I could work for an airline after I got out. Pilots make a ton of money."

"Money isn't everything."

Lance stuck up his chin. "It is when you don't have any."

"But it could be dangerous. I couldn't stand anything happening to you, Lance."

He hadn't thought about getting hurt, and it meant a lot that Jamie was worried. But it was the only way he knew how to do what he wanted. "At least will you think about it? The navy might even send me to college, and I know that's important to your family."

"Okay."

She was quiet as he walked her home and he wished he was better at saying the right things. More than anything, he wanted to tell her about his childhood, but now didn't seem the right time, either.

He just hoped that Gabe was right...that Jamie would understand.

JAMIE WENT TO bed early, but she couldn't sleep. She kept remembering when her uncle Tate went down flying a navy plane and how Aunt Jessica had come home with her two little boys, all quiet and different, the way Uncle Liam was now.

Finally Jamie turned over and looked at the charm bracelet on her bedside table, barely visible in the moonlight coming through curtains. She couldn't wear it to work, but she kept all his gifts there so she could look at them at night. Now she wondered if she should have tried harder to make him stop buying her presents. Maybe he wouldn't be so worried about money if she'd made him understand that just *being* with her was enough.

Even though it was warm in her bedroom, her toes were cold, so she got up and filled a hot water bottle. She sat on the padded window seat, clutching it to her stomach.

I've been thinking about enlisting in the navy.

Jamie closed her eyes. Was it selfish to object? The only reason he wanted to enlist was because he thought it was best for their future. As much as she adored Glimmer Creek, it wasn't a place where people got rich.

But what if he got hurt or died, just because he thought enlisting was the only way for them to be together?

Jamie traced an infinity symbol on the cushion, wondering how to sort it out. The truth was, even though they'd known each other for a couple of months, they'd never talked about anything really important.

She'd guessed things, of course, and had pieced together bits of information from the little stuff he did say. There'd been some sort of trouble in Sacramento, and she thought he might have been in a foster home. He hadn't realized it, but he'd once called a girl named Maggie his foster sister, not his sister.

None of that mattered, except that Jamie didn't think it had been very nice. What *mattered* was that Lance was good and decent and would never hurt her. But why didn't he trust her enough to explain?

All at once a terrible thought occurred to her… Had he bought her all those presents because he thought it was the only way she'd love him?

It was a horrible idea.

Hours crept by, with one question after another popping into her head, but Jamie couldn't come up with any answers except that there was clearly more wrong between her and Lance than him wanting to enlist.

"So FAR I haven't found anything suspicious on anybody I've checked out," Great-Uncle Milt reported over the speakerphone.

Tessa and Gabe had called him every evening since her grandparents' visit, discussing various scenarios for TIP's upcoming trip to Poppy Gold.

"What about Celina Noble?" Gabe asked.

"I can't tell you specifics about anybody, just that I haven't seen anything questionable."

Great-Uncle Milt's tone was measured and Tessa tried not to laugh at Gabe's frustrated expression. He'd been fairly good about accepting the limits of what they could provide…at least lately.

"I've also requested a tap on your grandfather's private phone line through the authorities in San Francisco," her great-uncle explained. "It was a good idea to use him as bait, though there are no guarantees the thief will contact Connor Enterprises."

"I know, Uncle Milt. All we can do is try."

After they got off the phone, Tessa brought up the latest fake document they'd created to use in catching the industrial spy.

"I've told Rob to write notes in the margins," Gabe said, "about keeping things confidential and mentioning Patrick Connor as the chief rival for the data."

"Nothing overdone," Tessa warned.

"Of course not, but I've seen some of the papers Rob prepares for speaking at meetings. He already writes 'confidential' on certain sections, which the thief must have seen. Actually, it probably highlighted what pieces of information were the most valuable."

"So with all the recent problems," she said slowly, "it wouldn't seem unusual to increase the warnings, as if Rob wants to urgently get the message across."

"That's right."

"Then he could write a note that the contract needs to be signed and faxed before leaving Poppy Gold. *That* should prompt the thief into immediate action."

"Sounds good," Gabe agreed.

Tessa shot a look at him as she typed. For the past few days, they'd been excruciatingly polite, with no repeats of an afternoon or night in bed together.

In the heat of the moment, it was easy to convince herself that sex didn't have to be meaningful. But it wasn't true; she was crazy about Gabe.

"Could somebody working at Poppy Gold be using a false identity?" Gabe asked.

Tessa wrinkled her nose. "I suppose it's possible. But we check IDs and verify Social Security numbers when we hire anybody, and there's even more checking to get employees bonded."

"It's too bad you don't run background checks on your guests."

She narrowed her eyes, torn between annoyance and appreciation. A few days ago, two of their visitors had tried to depart in the early morning hours with a pair of antique side tables. An alert had gone out on the radio, but Gabe had gotten to the thieves, even before the security staff.

"How did you know what was happening?" she asked.

Gabe unhooked the facility radio he carried on his belt and held it up. "I take this home and keep it on. I couldn't let someone get away with theft."

Tessa typed another sentence into the computer, thinking about something she'd told Jamie—that men could *do* things that were far more romantic than a gift. While Gabe wasn't trying to woo her, he was still tugging at her heart, in the same unceasing way the moon pulled the ocean tides back and forth.

"Well, thanks," she said, keeping her head down in case her face revealed too much.

"YOU'RE WELCOME," GABE MURMURED.

He watched Tessa, churning with emotions he didn't want to examine too closely. While she wasn't as naive as he'd thought, he couldn't share her belief that most people were basically good. After all, she was helping him track down a thief and an attempted murderer, someone who'd violated her home and business.

It didn't help that he wanted to take her back to bed so badly, he was in a permanent state of arousal.

"When do you want to send these to Rob?" Tessa asked without looking up.

"By Saturday morning. He isn't going to talk about the fake plans with his executives—that would cause its own problems—but he needs time to review the documents and write the notes in the margins. Also to make any changes he thinks are needed."

"Okay."

Gabe rose and paced restlessly around the living room. The apartment was small, but it retained the charm of Victorian architecture.

"You're making me dizzy," Tessa complained finally.

"I'm used to action, not sitting back and waiting for something to happen."

"We aren't just waiting, we're setting a trap. Surely there were extensive planning stages when you were a SEAL."

"It's different with Rob involved."

She rolled her eyes. "Everything is different when family is involved. My family is just bigger than yours."

The statement took Gabe aback. He hadn't thought about it that much, seeing only Tessa's blind faith in her relatives and neighbors. But he might be just as blind when it came to his brother.

Tessa got up and stretched. "Do you want to go for a walk?" she asked. "I'm ready for an activity that doesn't involve composing fake business scenarios."

Gabe extended his hand and ran his thumb over her mouth, hating himself for giving in to temptation, yet unable to resist. "There's another activity I'd prefer."

Her eyes darkened. "Aren't you worried I'll get ideas about us?"

"I'm worried about hurting you, that's all."

"Because we aren't compatible."

"We *aren't* compatible...except in bed. Or do you want to characterize our last encounter as simply 'okay'?"

She grinned. "Did that bother you?"

He drew her closer. "You know it did. What I haven't decided is whether it was a deliberate knock on my ego."

"Maybe subconsciously. Your gift for aggravating people is unparalleled."

Gabe kissed Tessa, trying to quell the voices clamoring in his head. She reached inside him and shook all the certainties he'd lived with so long...the certainties that had helped him survive.

There were a thousand reasons to keep his distance, but only one to take her to bed...and that was the reason that won.

CHAPTER NINETEEN

FOR THE FIRST TIME, Tessa was having trouble focusing on Poppy Gold. Part of it was the sense of being in limbo until Rob and his executives returned. But it was mostly Gabe.

She'd been determined not to sleep with him again, only to give in with barely a murmur.

Tessa swallowed at the memory and pushed her grocery cart down the supermarket aisle in Stockton. She'd actually left Poppy Gold on a Friday afternoon, just to go shopping. It had felt as if she was escaping.

Working fewer hours gave Tessa a faint sense of panic, as if things were spinning out of control. Yet in many ways it was better. But it was Gabe who was giving her the biggest headache.

His protectiveness would be endearing if it wasn't so frustrating. Did he *really* believe that seeing terrible things should close him off from love and warmth? Her father had witnessed his share of horrors and had still been able to fall in love and believe in people again.

Not fair, Tessa's conscience screamed. She'd

never experienced any of the things Gabe had. How could she criticize the way he dealt with his memories if it helped him survive?

Of course, there was one thing she knew for certain—it didn't matter how wary you were of falling for the wrong man. When you fell, you fell. The heart made decisions the brain knew were insane.

Depressed, she stared at a display of barbecue supplies. Fun in the Sun declared the cheerful banner hanging from the ceiling. There were beach balls and elaborate barbecue tools, myriad bottles of sunscreen lotions, more kinds of charcoal briquettes than she'd ever thought existed, along with grills, skewers, sauces and seasonings of every type.

And right in the middle was a book titled *Barbecuing for Beginners*.

A gremlin in Tessa made her put it into the cart.

She could imagine what Gabe would say if he saw the extravagant display. Despite growing up with wealth, he was a no-frills guy. If he'd ever barbecued, it was probably to survive in some distant part of the world. But for her, barbecues meant family gatherings and community fundraisers, teenage trips to the beach with the church youth group and picnics along the meandering creek that the town had been named after.

"Which one do you think is best?" asked a voice, startling Tessa from her reverie.

"Excuse me?"

"My husband told me to get charcoal, and I don't know what kind he uses." It was a mother with a toddler belted into her cart, a small boy holding her hand and a significant bulge in her midsection.

Tessa picked up the book she'd put in her own cart and displayed the title. "I have no idea."

The woman laughed and the little boy next to her laughed, too, though he probably didn't know what was amusing.

"That's the one my dad used to get." Tessa gestured to the brand her father had bought before getting a gas grill.

"Looks good to me." The young mother reached for the bag, but Tessa insisted on loading it for her. "Gosh, thanks."

"You're welcome."

Tessa watched the three make their way down the grocery aisle, her throat tightening painfully.

Did Gabe's warnings mean he was starting to care about her? Her own heart was committed, but she didn't expect him to change his mind about having children. He truly believed it was wrong to bring kids into a society with so many problems, unable to see that every child offered the chance to solve those problems.

And just as important...could she spend a

lifetime with someone who had such a different outlook on the world, no matter how much she loved him?

Tessa finished her shopping and loaded everything into her car, unable to get Gabe out of her head. They *were* different, but her mom had also fallen for a former soldier, the son of a business mogul. Her parents' marriage hadn't been perfect, but it had been extraordinarily happy for the time they'd shared.

If only...

The familiar grief rose through Tessa at the memory of losing her mother. She was on the little highway that led toward Glimmer Creek, and when her eyes began watering too much to be safe, she pulled off the road.

Stop, she ordered.

Yet the waves of pain didn't stop, and she finally turned off the engine. With the need to put up a brave front with Pop, it seemed harder than ever to stop thinking about her mother and how unfair her death had been.

She'd wanted to be strong for her father, but Gabe was right. She was hurting, too. Finally Tessa closed her eyes, letting memories and tears flood through her in a way she hadn't allowed since the week of the funeral.

LANCE DECIDED TO work on the rock wall for a few minutes after his shift. He'd gotten more of the quick-setting concrete and was trying to make it as nice-looking as possible.

He hadn't said anything more to Jamie about the navy, but he knew she was thinking about it. She got a faraway look in her eyes and was even quieter than him most of the time.

Finally he gave the apple trees extra water and trudged back to Maintenance.

Gabe was still in the locker room when he got there. "Hey, Lance."

"Hey." Lance put away his gloves and started to leave, then turned around. "Uh, Gabe…?"

"Yes?"

Lance shuffled his feet. "Jamie is worried I could get killed in the navy. I'm not scared, but what happens if you have a family and you die?"

Gabe closed his locker. "A recruiter can tell you more about family benefits than I can." He seemed to hesitate. "But somehow I don't think that's what bothers Jamie. She doesn't want to lose you, any more than you want to lose her."

Lance nodded and walked home to shower before meeting Jamie. He rounded the corner and sucked in a breath. She was waiting in front of his cottage.

"Hey."

"Hey. May I come in?"

"Uh, sure." Lance fumbled as he stuck the key in the lock and opened the door. "It isn't like your place," he said uncomfortably. Even though the studio was nicer than anywhere he'd lived before, it couldn't compare to the Fullertons' big house.

"Is that why you haven't wanted me to come here?"

He shrugged. "Partly. It also didn't seem right, you know, because you're a preacher's daughter."

"I *told* you, being a PK doesn't make me any different from other girls."

"Don't get mad. You *are* different."

She crossed her arms and looked mad anyhow. "Oh, yeah?"

"Yeah. But it's mostly…well, because I haven't cared that much about any other girl."

He must have said the right thing because Jamie smiled. "That's how I feel about you. I mean, that I haven't cared about any other boys the way I love you. But we have to talk about real things, Lance, not just something that *might* happen someday. No secrets. I'm going to love you no matter what, but if we don't trust each other, then I don't know how we can make anything work."

Lance sighed. Maybe he *hadn't* trusted her enough to love him if she knew the truth.

"I'll go first," she said, her cheeks turning pink. "My mom says women don't have to wait to be asked out, but deep down I felt funny about it—as if I'd broken a rule or forced you to go out with me because you were too nice to say no."

"But I liked it," he said, astonished. "Only the popular guys in school got asked out by girls."

"Maybe, but Glimmer Creek is old-fashioned. Anyhow, I think it made me feel better when you gave me presents or talked about taking care of me because it seemed to prove it wasn't important that I'd made the first move. It was dumb and selfish, and I'm sorry."

Though Jamie's confession was small in comparison, Lance could see that she'd hated admitting it.

He let out a breath. "Okay, my turn. That stuff I told you about my family wasn't true. My father went to prison for killing someone when my mom was pregnant, and she died when I was born, so I never even met them. But I heard she was in trouble before that. I grew up in foster homes. Most of them were okay, but the last two were lousy and I got knocked around a bunch," he continued hurriedly.

"Oh, Lance, I'm sorry." Jamie started to reach for him, but he held up a hand to stop her. He needed to get through the rest of his confession.

"Anyhow, I left the Stantons' a year ago when I turned eighteen. But my old foster sister was still there, and I talked to her sometimes. In December, she called and said she was hiding in the basement because Stanton was drunk and looking for her."

"So you went over to help."

"Well, *yeah*. Maggie is just a little squirt, and she was crying, sure he'd kill her this time. But when I got there Stanton called the cops and claimed I'd broken in."

"What a jerk."

Lance had called Denny Stanton much nastier things. "Anyhow, the cops arrested me, but they let me go when Stanton didn't come in to sign a complaint. I didn't hear more about it, and Maggie got moved to a new home right away, so I left Sacramento and ended up in Glimmer Creek."

"Why did you keep it a secret, Lance? You didn't do anything wrong."

"Nobody believes a foster kid, especially when their dad is in prison. My old boss even fired me when he found out, so I didn't think the navy would want me with that on my record."

"*I* believe you. And I bet Gabe did, too."

Lance was startled. "How do you know I told him?"

"Isn't that why you talked to him first about enlisting?"

A huge weight seemed to roll from Lance's chest, and he hugged her. "I'm sorry," he whispered. "I should have told you, but I was afraid it would ruin everything."

JAMIE TRIED NOT to cry.

"Lance, you don't have to go in the navy for me. Is it something you really want to do?"

"I don't know," he admitted. "It seems like a good way to take care of you, and getting to be a flier would mean I could make a bunch of money after I got out."

Jamie hesitated. "I'm not trying to change your mind, but…uh, Aunt Jessica's first husband died flying a navy jet in a stupid training flight. So it re…really scares me to think about you doing that."

"Jeez, Jamie. I forgot about that."

She looked at him, feeling more grown-up than she'd ever felt before. "If you enlist, it has to be what you want, not because you think it's best for us."

"But I promised to take care—"

"I know," she interrupted quietly. "But isn't it all right if we take care of each other?"

LANCE BLINKED, REALIZING Jamie was right. He *could* count on her; it didn't have to be all up to him. It sounded stupid, but it was like a door had opened, and all he had to do was step inside.

"Okay."

Jamie's smile was brighter than he'd ever seen it, and he hugged her close. He still didn't know how her parents would react; he just knew she'd feel the same way about him, no matter what.

AS TESSA DROVE back into Glimmer Creek, she hesitated about going home immediately. The town's private animal rescue group had called that morning to say they had a cat newly available for adoption. They kept an eye out for potential VC residents, and Poppy Gold reciprocated by referring guests who wanted to adopt.

She decided to stop at the shelter. Inside she was introduced to Rocky, a long-haired brown tabby who'd been found abandoned on the highway near Glimmer Creek.

"Whoa, he's enormous," she exclaimed. "Part Maine coon?" she asked the attendant.

"The veterinarian wrote Maine coon crossbreed on his chart, but that's just a guess based on his size."

Rocky settled in her arms, purring madly and looking up with apparent adoration. While his fur had the faintly sticky, dull texture that came from living in a kennel, it was long and thick.

The volunteer looked at the file again. "Rocky has been in the medical section for the usual shots and tests, et cetera. This says he's around two years old and quite mellow."

Tessa scratched behind the feline's ears, his purr doubling in volume as he arched against her chest. "I'll take him," she said, already in love.

"Shall I put the adoption fee on Poppy Gold's account?"

"No, I may keep him for myself." She shifted Rocky to one arm and pulled a handful of twenties from her purse. "Keep the rest as a donation."

The attendant filled out the adoption request and she signed it. He brought out a cardboard carrier, which Rocky regarded dubiously.

"Come on, buddy. I know it's small, but you only have to stay in there a little while."

Rocky barely fit in the carrier and meowed until she got into the car with him. At the parking area closest to the VC, she decided to take him to her apartment before dealing with the groceries.

Though it was late afternoon, Pop wasn't home when she went over to his apartment, so she unpacked the supplies she bought for him and returned with her own bags to the Victorian Cat. Inside Tessa found Rocky had already discovered the broad windowsill in the kitchen. He sat, his plush tail waving gently, as she put everything away, but the instant she'd folded the last sack, he leaped down and demanded affection.

It seemed selfish to keep him, but none of the VC cats were ready for retirement, and he'd be company when Gabe left. Her stomach went hollow at the thought. Almost as a distraction, she opened the file of ominous notes Rob McKinley had been sent. He'd received only one since her accident on the staircase. It was mostly the same as the others, though much longer.

Whoever had authored the letter was meticulous. It would have taken hours to cut out enough letters to create several paragraphs of vitriolic hate. Nevertheless, like the others, it stopped short of threatening physical harm.

Her knowledge was vague on the legalities of anonymous mail, but apparently the FBI had pointed out to Rob that while the tone was menacing, no *actual* threat had been made.

"Tessa?"

It was Gabe's voice from outside the door.

"Come in," she called.

He was frowning as he stepped inside. "You should always lock. Oh, I see you have another furry visitor."

"This is Rocky. I just got him from the animal shelter."

"I didn't realize the VC needed another cat."

"It doesn't. He's mine."

NATURALLY, GABE THOUGHT WRYLY.

There were shadows under Tessa's eyes, and he frowned. "Are you okay?"

"I'm fine. What's up?"

"I thought we should go over everything again before sending the file to Rob tonight," he explained.

"All right."

They worked steadily, coming up with a few last-minute ideas to incorporate into their trap. Tessa sat cross-legged on the floor in front of the sofa table, leaving the couch to Rocky, who lay there, stretched out on his back as if he'd lived with her for years. Every now and then, Gabe reached over and petted him, impressed with the animal's mellow temperament.

He could almost see himself becoming a cat person, but when he offered Rocky some of the catnip, the feline turned up his nose at it.

"I don't understand. Tiny Tim loves this stuff."

"Cats require a specific gene to respond to catnip, which apparently Rocky doesn't have. Try the tuna cat treats."

Sure enough, Rocky ecstatically gobbled down a handful. Gabe wiped his hand, feeling slightly ridiculous, but Tessa wasn't watching. She was looking again at the collection of letters.

"Still can't let it go?" he asked.

"I just…" She frowned suddenly. "I'll be right back."

Tessa went up the stairs and returned a few minutes later with a thick accordion file. She sorted through the contents and pulled out a brochure, then began comparing it with one of the photocopied notes under a magnifying glass.

"Look at the edges of the darker areas around the *P*," she said. "They match up to the California poppy logo on the brochure."

Gabe took the magnifying glass and compared the letters. She was right. "How in *hell* did you spot that?"

"Because this is the original brochure I designed to promote Poppy Gold Inns as a conference center. The words *Poppy Gold* were overlaid on the logo, but I redesigned the whole thing a year ago."

"That means that at least *some* of the letters used are from your original brochure."

"Yes, and possibly other promotional material for Gold Country attractions. They'd be easy enough to collect and probably wouldn't be as easily tracked as something from a magazine or newspaper."

"We have to get this evidence to Milt," Gabe said. "It's the first reasonable proof that the author is linked to Glimmer Creek. He can contact the FBI and do whatever else is needed."

Tessa immediately picked up her phone and dialed her great-uncle. She quickly explained her discovery, and Milt whistled.

"Great eyes, Tessa. Email me the file and I'll contact the FBI. Is there anything else?"

Tessa glanced at Gabe, but he shook his head.

"No, that's all for now."

While Tessa went upstairs to email the information to Milt, Gabe ran out to pick up food from the Hong Kong Palace. When he got back, he discovered she'd changed into a pair of her skimpy shorts and a T-shirt, sending his blood pressure soaring.

"Uh, is your grandfather on board for next week?" he asked hoarsely.

"He'll stay in his office and wait for any calls. I noticed KJ arrived yesterday."

"He has another guy coming on Sunday, too. It's fortunate you had enough cancellations."

Tessa forked a serving of lo mein onto her plate and took two more cartons from the bag. "He called me when they couldn't get reservations, so I released a couple of the rooms we keep available for emergencies. Oh, good, you got orange chicken."

Gabe let out a frustrated breath.

He didn't know if she was being deliberately provocative, but his body didn't care. It was as if he was addicted to her, and not just physically. Her bright smiles and energy were as much a part of the attraction as her figure.

He was in serious trouble. His head knew the right thing to do, but his gut wanted something different entirely. Except it wasn't just his gut. He wanted everything with Tessa. Even a family.

"Aren't you going to eat?" she asked, raising an eyebrow.

Food was a poor substitute, but he sat down. "Have you found the wontons?"

She handed him a container. "Obviously Uncle Milt will be on alert next week. But Pop is going to be extra distracted, so I doubt he'll notice anything we're doing."

"Because of his wedding anniversary? I know it's a week from Sunday."

"Yeah." Her mouth wobbled. "I suggested going to San Francisco or up to Tahoe for the weekend, but he wants to stay here."

"He'd be better off getting away."

"Maybe, but you can't escape memories." Tessa drew a deep breath and cocked her head. "I wouldn't even want to. My mother was an amazing woman."

Gabe wished he knew what to say, but he was the last person to offer comfort, so he dipped a wonton in sweet-and-sour sauce and tossed it in his mouth.

"Are you going to eat all of those?" Tessa asked, breaking into his thoughts.

"Nope." He handed back the container.

They ate the rest of the meal in companionable silence and returned to looking at their documents. Tessa made a few adjustments and saved them on the computer.

"I don't know what else we can do," she said, standing up to stretch and yawn.

Gabe's mouth went dry. His tastes had always run to tall, generously built women, but Tessa had changed that. After all, a man didn't need more than a handful, and she certainly provided a very *nice* handful.

He was crazy about Tessa and wanted her to be crazy about him, but it would be like entrusting a bulldog with a priceless piece of art.

How could he take the chance of damaging the very thing that had made him feel truly alive for the first time?

CHAPTER TWENTY

TESSA WAS STRESSED as the TIP executives began arriving Monday afternoon. It was hard to keep from second-guessing all the things she normally did, but she still greeted Rob and made sure to put a courtesy basket in the Joaquin Murrieta suite for him.

Though the housekeeping staff assigned to the El Dorado Mansion was of particular interest, she simply kept an eye on the schedule. It was difficult not to inquire whether anyone had specifically requested the assignment, yet even a request wouldn't necessarily be suspicious. While some of the housekeepers had a favorite work location, others liked to rotate between the houses.

Around seven that evening, she was still working in her office when Gabe showed up.

"Time for dinner," he announced, holding up bags from the Gilbraith Delicatessen. "Let's eat at your place."

She nodded and shut down her computer. They rarely took a chance of anyone overhearing them at her office, whatever the hour.

"Have you been on edge all day?" Gabe asked when the door of her apartment had closed behind them.

"That's an understatement. It's like waiting for a volcano to erupt. I swear I could hear a pin drop on the other side of Poppy Gold."

"Operational readiness," he murmured. "Awareness heightens, adrenaline revs in the bloodstream, and focus narrows to the essentials. Not that it's a big leap for you—Poppy Gold is always your focus."

Tessa sank onto the couch and petted Rocky, who was taking up most of the space. "Are you *trying* to start a fight?"

"No." Gabe handed her one of the bags from the deli. "I just want the whole thing resolved. Rob is my kid brother. I'll keep security on him for as long as it takes, but there's always a chance of someone getting lucky."

Tessa unwrapped the end of her sandwich and took a bite. She wasn't surprised to discover it was her favorite, turkey and avocado; Gabe never seemed to forget anything. Rocky watched with an interested gleam in his eyes, but she didn't want to start giving him table scraps.

Gabe swallowed a mouthful. "KJ has sent me a couple of texts. Believe it or not, he's sleeping with one of Rob's executives tonight."

She choked. "At the El Dorado?"

"What can I say? KJ enjoys women and it's the best way to keep an eye on the situation."

Tessa hoped the woman knew it was just casual sex. Most likely, she decided. While KJ was charming, he was obviously a player. It was difficult to imagine him being friends with Gabe, but the comrade-in-arms thing was probably the explanation. On the other hand, maybe Gabe didn't have friends; he just had contacts.

"Is KJ a sex addict or something?"

"He just enjoys the game and doesn't see any reason not to enjoy himself."

Tessa ate her sandwich, trying to fight off renewed depression. Gabe was leaving Glimmer Creek as soon as the thefts were resolved. It seemed ridiculous to think about what she'd do if he asked her to go with him, yet the thought kept going through her head. No children, a cynical life partner, away from family...but with the man she loved.

What about Dad? said a nagging voice in Tessa's head.

Or Poppy Gold?

The bed-and-breakfast complex provided employment for half of Glimmer Creek in one way or another. Of course, somebody else could run it, and her father *had* improved a great deal over the past few months. He was just having more trouble right now because of his upcoming anniversary...

Tessa's head began to ache.

She didn't know why she was tearing herself up about it. Gabe wasn't asking her to leave with him, and he wasn't going to stay, so she didn't have any decisions to make.

Except that wasn't entirely true... She had to decide whether to have one or two more nights together with Gabe.

"Tell me, does operational readiness require celibacy?" she asked lightly.

He stroked the curve of her jaw with his finger. "I used to think it did. Don't get me wrong, I like sex as much as most men—"

"No argument here," she threw in with a grin.

"Brat. No wonder you used to be called Tessajinks. Anyhow, I thought it might make my guys less sharp, so I encouraged abstaining for a few days ahead of time. Now I wonder..." A faint expression of regret crossed his face.

"Wonder?" she prompted.

"Nothing. For the record, while it may be self-serving, I no longer advocate celibacy."

She leaned closer and kissed him. "In that case, how about retiring upstairs? Rocky has claimed the couch, anyway."

Gabe eyed the feline. In their brief acquaintance, Rocky had proved quite likable except for his habit of hogging the cushions. Rather than curling into a ball, the cat was stretched out on his back with legs extended an impossible distance. The pose suggested ultimate trust; he'd landed in a cushy life with Tessa, and he knew it.

"Doesn't he sleep with you?"

"Definitely. He's a lovebug. Jealous?"

Gabe put a hand out and pulled her to her feet. "I'll survive. But let's go upstairs before he wakes up and decides to join us immediately. That mattress is small enough without him."

Smothering chuckles, they raced up the narrow stairs to the second floor. The bed wasn't nearly long enough for a man his height, but it had one thing no other bed had ever offered.

Tessa.

GABE LAY AWAKE for a long time while Tessa slept. Rocky had waited until the commotion ended before jumping up and parking himself by her feet. The cat was purring so loudly it would have been difficult to sleep even without the thoughts circling in Gabe's brain...pointless thoughts, like memories of the men he'd lost, and whether his rigid approach to mission prep had stolen important moments from them.

Would those men agree that staying away from their wives and girlfriends had been worth the questionable benefits? Wouldn't they have been better off enjoying reminders of why they were about to risk their lives?

He hoped they'd ignored him.

He hoped they'd taken advantage of every minute, in whatever way that meant something to them, whenever possible, whether it was making love or riding a bike or reading stories to a child.

Children...

He swallowed a groan, thinking of the whimsical creatures outlined on the walls of Tessa's old nursery. The air must have rung with her happy childhood giggles back then. Sometimes he could almost hear the echoes of those giggles, however ridiculous that sounded.

Was it possible for emotion to be imprinted on a place? Sadness had seemed to shroud some of the beautiful, ancient lands Gabe had visited, lands torn by centuries of warfare or tragedy. Equally, happiness seemed to brighten the room where Tessa had spent her early years.

"What's up?" Tessa asked sleepily.

"What do you mean?"

"You got tense."

Without realizing it, his body *had* become rigid. And however fanciful it might be, Tessa's voice was like a lifeline in the darkness. In a few short weeks, she had turned him inside out, making him question the certainties he'd stood upon for so long.

"Sorry I disturbed you," he murmured. "Maybe I should go work out."

"Mmm, I can think of another way to relax." She kissed his neck and slid her knee across his groin.

He smiled.

She *did* have the best ideas.

GABE WAS GONE when Tessa woke in the morning. She was disappointed, though she knew he'd wanted to get to work early. He'd asked her father to assign him to the various gardens near the El Dorado Mansion for the next few days, so that was where he'd be spending most of his time. She just hoped the thief hadn't identified him as Rob's brother.

Whatever Gabe claimed about being able to take care of himself, it still worried her.

"Mrrrow," Rocky trilled, putting his paws on her arm.

"Hey there," she murmured, glad for his comforting presence. He couldn't replace the man she loved, but he'd be company when Gabe left Glimmer Creek for good.

With a sigh, Tessa finally got up and dressed. She'd carefully charged her cell phone the night before and put it in her pocket before heading out to the office. It was important to follow her usual morning pattern, which was to work a few hours at her desk and then do a walk-through of the facility.

But instead of making calls to her contacts on the East Coast, she mostly sat at her desk, thinking about Gabe.

He'd said little about his future plans. With his

connection to TIP, he couldn't lack for money, but he wasn't the kind of person to enjoy a life of leisure.

Tessa got up and gazed out the window. She still had her dreams for Poppy Gold; they'd have to be enough once Gabe left.

Of course, there were no guarantees the industrial thief would reveal him or herself right away, but since the fake plans mentioned a contract to be signed Wednesday morning, they hoped for immediate action. Rob had even brought a fax machine as a prop, though Poppy Gold provided a business center.

Restless, Tessa waited until her usual walk-through time and headed out.

TESSA HAD RETURNED to her office when a text message from her grandfather came in on her cell phone.

Am tlkng 2 thf cllr id shws p gold bllrm.

Gabe's warning to act normally flitted through her head as she jumped to her feet, but hang it all, this could be the only chance they got. Poppy Gold's phone lines each had a unique caller ID. She might be able to spot the thief red-handed, still on the phone.

Besides, she was probably the closest of anyone who knew what was going on. Gabe was staying near the El Dorado Mansion, and she could only presume KJ and his security guy expected to be near there, as well.

Tessa hurriedly sent a return text to her grandfather, Gabe and Great-Uncle Milt, then ran down the back staircase and headed for Old City Hall.

GABE WAS SWEEPING the walkway of the house next to the El Dorado Mansion when a text alert sounded on his cell. He pulled the phone out, and a chill went through him when he saw the message from Tessa.

He took off running for the old town center. The second floor of the historic town hall boasted an elegant ballroom, useful for large meetings, but nobody was scheduled in it that week. He silently ascended the back staircase, reassured to hear the low murmur of Tessa's voice, followed by another that was loud and shrill.

Cautiously peering around a corner, he saw Tessa with Judy Stokes, a member of the housekeeping staff he'd met only a couple of times. They were alarmingly close together. Tessa's gaze flickered briefly, acknowledging his presence, even as she remained focused on the other woman.

He stopped and saw Milt Fullerton on the other side of the ballroom, coming in through the front gallery.

"Robert McKinley is so high and mighty,"

Judy said with a sneer. "He deserves what he gets. Born rich. He doesn't know what it's like to scramble for a living."

"Is that why you've been selling information about TIP?"

"No. My father would be alive today if it wasn't for him." Judy's voice rose higher. "Dad made a little mistake five years ago. Just a single, tiny error in judgment, but McKinley couldn't overlook it. Instead he made sure Dad was indicted for smuggling."

"You must have been devastated."

"That isn't the half of it. My father killed himself before the trial. Just one little mistake," Judy repeated, edging toward hysteria. "He'd be alive today if that SOB had a heart."

"So you decided to get back at Rob by selling information from TIP to his competitors."

"What else could I do? I just wish McKinley had fallen on that staircase and broken his neck. Dad deserves justice."

"It was clever getting TIP to use Poppy Gold for their business retreats," Tessa said casually. As Gabe crept forward, he detected a hint of disgust in her eyes.

"Yeah. I was researching import-export companies that might buy information and found an article about Poppy Gold and its connection to Connor Enterprises. That's when I got the idea. Now get out of my way. I'm leaving."

"Surely you realize the police will be right behind you."

"There's no proof. I made sure of it." She strode forward, only to have Tessa kick a chair in her path.

While Gabe got to Judy first and restrained her, Milt was a fast second. He snapped handcuffs on her wrists so fast it was impressive.

"You can't prove anything," Judy screamed. "Hearsay isn't admissible in court."

"Actually, I recorded your confession on my phone," Tessa said. "And by the way, *you're fired.*"

Judy screamed again, struggling and kicking.

"What do you mean about recording her confession?" Milt asked.

"I activated the sound recorder on my phone before I came in. It was in my pocket, but she's pretty shrill, so it probably worked."

No wonder Tessa had gotten so close to the other woman. It had been smart, but additional proof wouldn't have been any comfort if she'd gotten hurt or killed. Gabe wanted to yell and kiss her at the same moment.

For the first time in his life, he'd been truly terrified. If Tessa died or got hurt...

With abrupt clarity, he understood Liam's anguish at losing his wife, the wound that could never truly heal.

When two other officers arrived and took charge of Judy Stokes, Milt turned his attention to Tessa and gave her a royal scolding. "Don't ever do anything like that again," he concluded, only to have her kiss him on the cheek.

"You're sweet to worry, Uncle Milt."

"I'm serious," he insisted, but his gruff expression had vanished. "Now give me your phone. It's evidence."

With the scene quieting down, Gabe immediately rang Patrick Connor.

"The suspect is in custody, and Tessa is all right," he said as soon as the call was answered, going on to explain what had happened.

"Thank God. We'll leave for Poppy Gold in the morning. My granddaughter is going to get a blistering lecture. I *never* would have cooperated if I'd thought she would confront the thief by herself."

"Do it over the phone before you arrive," Gabe advised, thinking how Milt had crumbled beneath his great-niece's charm. "I suspect she has you wrapped around her little finger along with everyone else in Glimmer Creek."

A bark of laughter came over the phone. "Excellent point. We'll see you tomorrow."

Gabe's next call was to his brother, who showed up at the ballroom within minutes. Judy Stokes promptly began shrieking profanities until the two officers took her away.

"Her father was guilty of a whole lot more than a single lapse in judgment," Rob explained, his face grim. "Norman began smuggling from China and other countries before I became president of TIP. Diamonds, art pieces, anything he could slip into a shipment. I worked with customs authorities for months to catch him."

Tessa looked sad. "She believed his story, but why didn't her name raise a flag for you? Stokes isn't that common."

"Because her father's last name was Chambers. I remember he had a married daughter, but not much more. It never occurred to me to add him to any of our lists since he's deceased. I'm sorry you got caught in the middle of this."

"Hey, it wasn't your fault."

Rob still looked guilty and Gabe understood how he felt. He might be furious with Tessa for taking chances with her safety, but she was still an innocent bystander. While Rob could repay the financial losses Poppy Gold had suffered, he couldn't make up for her fall on the staircase.

Tessa talked briefly to her father, giving him an explanation and reassuring him, while Milt finished processing the scene. Gabe silently apologized to the white-haired giant. Despite his age and lack of big-city law enforcement experience, the police chief was efficient and knowledgeable.

The formalities took a while, but finally they all agreed to come the next morning to sign their statements. Tessa left to call her grandfather with a more in-depth explanation.

"What now, big brother?" Rob asked when they were alone.

"What do you mean?"

"Where are you going from here?"

It was a good question; Gabe just didn't have an answer. What he wanted and what was best for Tessa were two different things.

TESSA HAD JUST gotten home when Gabe pounded on her door.

"How could you do such an insanely dangerous thing?" he demanded when she answered. "Confronting that woman alone was crazy."

"I couldn't take the chance of her getting away." The scolding didn't bother her; she was just glad they'd caught the guilty party. The call with her grandfather, on the other hand, had been slightly more upsetting. She'd reassured him over and over that she was all right, but he and Grams were still coming to Glimmer Creek to see for themselves.

"You're impossible," Gabe declared.

"I'm just me." Tessa had expected him to be angry, but he looked even more upset than she had anticipated. "Have you found out more about Judy Stokes?"

He glared. "She got divorced after her father's suicide but kept her married name. Apparently she was more interested in getting revenge than in discarding reminders of her ex."

A thought occurred to Tessa, and she cocked

her head. "Why aren't you giving me a hard time about blind loyalty? That's what Judy is guilty of…in addition to everything else."

"Because you aren't capable of plotting revenge for years and breaking the law to get it."

Gabe's reply was a curious compliment.

"Don't think I'm done," he added. "You weren't supposed to risk your life. What if she'd had a gun? Chairs won't protect you from a bullet. I thought you had brains, but that was the most idiotic stunt I've ever seen."

"Imagine, I didn't think you cared about me."

"Of course I care," Gabe snarled, without seeming to realize what he'd just said. He went on ranting and she sighed. There was probably just one way to stop him.

Tessa started unbuttoning her blouse and Gabe's gaze was suddenly riveted on her. She moved closer and put her arm around his neck.

"Don't think you can distract me," he said hoarsely.

"Wanna bet?" She rose on her tiptoes and kissed him.

He didn't say another word the rest of the evening.

TESSA WOKE ALONE the next morning.

It was what she'd expected, but a flash of anger went through her.

She was certain that Gabe loved her as much

as she loved him, and if she was willing to risk getting her heart broken, that was her decision. Anyway, her heart had already made the choice.

Tessa threw her clothes on and marched to Gabe's studio. She found him outside packing his SUV.

"I wasn't going to just go without saying good-bye," he said quietly.

"What difference does that make?" she demanded. "You're riding off like the Lone Ranger, but just like the Lone Ranger, you're your own best proof that people have good in them."

"Tessa, I'm older than you."

"Eight years," she scoffed. "You're being ridiculous. If I was eighteen that might mean something, but it doesn't at our ages, as you well know."

GABE SIGHED.

She was right, the years didn't matter, but the experience *did*. He'd seen more terrible things over those eight years than Tessa would see in a lifetime. But they weren't sights that had made him wiser or stronger…just older. He'd tried to convince himself that it would be all right, but how could he be with her and not destroy her spirit?

An inner voice jeered at him.

How could a force of nature be destroyed? If Tessa's mother had been anything like her, the two of them together must have been overwhelming.

"Tessa, it's best for you if I—"

She crossed her arms and stuck her chin up in challenge. "*Don't* try to decide for me. I'll decide for myself, thank you. Maybe if you stopped leaving, you'd discover something worth staying for, or something worth taking with you."

Gabe wished it was that simple.

Yet as he looked into Tessa's eyes, he wondered if it *was* that simple. The problem with being the one who rode to the rescue was that all the villainy became overwhelming. Tessa was a lifeline in the darkness, but was reaching for it worth the chance of hurting her? Because if there was one thing he was certain about, he'd cut off his arm before he would cause Tessa pain.

"I bought something the other day," she said unexpectedly. "Don't ask me why, but something told me to get it for you. Think of it as a going-away gift."

Gabe took the book she held out, and his mouth twitched as he read the title: *Barbecuing for Beginners*.

While people barbecued in the city, it seemed the quintessential small-town activity, signifying home and family and everyday life. Nothing had ever sounded more wonderful, though a life with Tessa wouldn't be calm; she was a one-woman tornado. Perhaps his choice was similar to the one Liam had made.

"What if I admitted that I love you and hope to stay in Glimmer Creek, but still don't want kids… What would you say?" he asked.

"Is that a test?"

Maybe it was, though the idea of Tessa pregnant with his child was seductive beyond belief. Then Gabe remembered what she'd told him once—that every child represented a shining light of hope. It was true, and Tessa was his own shining light.

"Forget I said that," Gabe whispered, pulling her close. "I've decided I want it all, too. Tell me you love me. I've never wanted anything more in my life."

TESSA KISSED GABE BACK.

"I'll love you forever," she promised.

An excited cry startled them both, and they looked around to see Jamie and Lance.

"Are you getting married?" Jamie asked.

"I haven't proposed yet, but I'm planning to," Gabe told her. "How about it, Tessa? I happen to know Poppy Gold puts on great weddings."

"Goody!" Jamie shrieked before Tessa could accept. "I can't wait to tell everyone."

"Hold on," Tessa ordered. "In the first place, yes, I'll marry you, Gabe. In the second, *I'm* going to tell the family, Jamie. You'll just have to wait."

"Can I at least get everybody to come to the old town square park for a potluck picnic?" Jamie begged. "There aren't any events tonight and you could tell them then."

The family was always having impromptu gatherings, but Tessa wondered if it would be too much for Gabe. She glanced at him and he nodded, seeming unconcerned.

"All right," she agreed.

Jamie and Lance left excitedly, but Tessa had little hope her cousin would resist hinting about the upcoming announcement, at the very least.

"We'd better tell Liam before he hears it another way," Gabe advised, apparently coming to the same conclusion.

Back at Poppy Gold, they finally found her father in Guest Registration. The elder Connors had arrived, and when they hadn't been able to reach Tessa, they'd called him.

Pop smiled the first real smile she'd seen from him in over eighteen months.

"That look in your eyes…it's just like your mother on our wedding day," he said simply.

"I hope you don't mind," Gabe interjected, "I proposed to your daughter without talking to you. We're getting married."

Delighted exclamations came from Tessa's grandparents and the other employees working in Guest Registration, and she soon found herself being hugged by everyone in the building. No doubt the family would know about her engagement hours before the impromptu party that night; good news traveled at the speed of light in Glimmer Creek.

Tessa finally ended up back in Gabe's arms, and the expression on his face was a priceless gift.

He gave her a long, slow kiss.

Of all her dreams that had come true, Gabe was the best one of all.

* * * * *

Look for the next book in the
POPPY GOLD STORIES *miniseries,*
CHRISTMAS WITH CARLIE,
available December 2016 wherever
Harlequin Superromance books are sold.

LARGER-PRINT BOOKS!

GET 2 FREE LARGER-PRINT NOVELS PLUS
2 FREE GIFTS!

HARLEQUIN®

Romance

From the Heart, For the Heart

YES! Please send me 2 FREE LARGER-PRINT Harlequin® Romance novels and my 2 FREE gifts (gifts are worth about $10). After receiving them, if I don't wish to receive any more books, I can return the shipping statement marked "cancel." If I don't cancel, I will receive 4 brand-new novels every month and be billed just $5.09 per book in the U.S. or $5.49 per book in Canada. That's a savings of at least 15% off the cover price! It's quite a bargain! Shipping and handling is just 50¢ per book in the U.S. and 75¢ per book in Canada.* I understand that accepting the 2 free books and gifts places me under no obligation to buy anything. I can always return a shipment and cancel at any time. Even if I never buy another book, the two free books and gifts are mine to keep forever.

119/319 HDN GHWC

Name _____ (PLEASE PRINT) _____

Address _____ Apt. # _____

City _____ State/Prov. _____ Zip/Postal Code _____

Signature (if under 18, a parent or guardian must sign) _____

Mail to the **Reader Service:**
IN U.S.A.: P.O. Box 1867, Buffalo, NY 14240-1867
IN CANADA: P.O. Box 609, Fort Erie, Ontario L2A 5X3

Want to try two free books from another line?
Call 1-800-873-8635 or visit www.ReaderService.com.

* Terms and prices subject to change without notice. Prices do not include applicable taxes. Sales tax applicable in N.Y. Canadian residents will be charged applicable taxes. Offer not valid in Quebec. This offer is limited to one order per household. Not valid for current subscribers to Harlequin Romance Larger-Print books. All orders subject to credit approval. Credit or debit balances in a customer's account(s) may be offset by any other outstanding balance owed by or to the customer. Please allow 4 to 6 weeks for delivery. Offer available while quantities last.

Your Privacy—The Reader Service is committed to protecting your privacy. Our Privacy Policy is available online at www.ReaderService.com or upon request from the Reader Service.

We make a portion of our mailing list available to reputable third parties that offer products we believe may interest you. If you prefer that we not exchange your name with third parties, or if you wish to clarify or modify your communication preferences, please visit us at www.ReaderService.com/consumerschoice or write to us at Reader Service Preference Service, P.O. Box 9062, Buffalo, NY 14240-9062. Include your complete name and address.

HRLP15

LARGER-PRINT BOOKS!

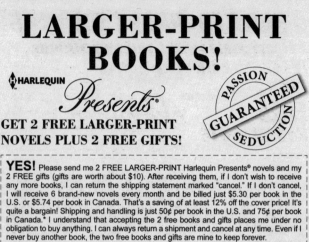

HARLEQUIN

Presents®

GUARANTEED
PASSION
SEDUCTION

GET 2 FREE LARGER-PRINT NOVELS PLUS 2 FREE GIFTS!

REQUEST YOUR FREE BOOKS!
2 FREE WHOLESOME ROMANCE NOVELS
IN LARGER PRINT
PLUS 2
FREE
MYSTERY GIFTS

⁂⁂⁂⁂⁂⁂⁂⁂⁂⁂⁂⁂⁂⁂⁂⁂⁂⁂⁂⁂⁂⁂⁂

HEARTWARMING™

⁂⁂⁂⁂⁂⁂⁂⁂⁂⁂⁂⁂⁂⁂⁂⁂⁂⁂⁂⁂⁂⁂⁂

Wholesome, tender romances

YES! Please send me 2 FREE Harlequin® Heartwarming Larger-Print novels and my 2 FREE mystery gifts (gifts worth about $10). After receiving them, if I don't wish to receive any more books, I can return the shipping statement marked "cancel." If I don't cancel, I will receive 4 brand-new larger-print novels every month and be billed just $5.24 per book in the U.S. or $5.99 per book in Canada. That's a savings of at least 19% off the cover price. It's quite a bargain! Shipping and handling is just 50¢ per book in the U.S. and 75¢ per book in Canada.* I understand that accepting the 2 free books and gifts places me under no obligation to buy anything. I can always return a shipment and cancel at any time. Even if I never buy another book, the two free books and gifts are mine to keep forever.

161/361 IDN GHX2

Name _____ (PLEASE PRINT)

Address _____ Apt. #

City _____ State/Prov. _____ Zip/Postal Code

Signature (if under 18, a parent or guardian must sign)

Mail to the **Reader Service:**
IN U.S.A.: P.O. Box 1867, Buffalo, NY 14240-1867
IN CANADA: P.O. Box 609, Fort Erie, Ontario L2A 5X3

* Terms and prices subject to change without notice. Prices do not include applicable taxes. Sales tax applicable in N.Y. Canadian residents will be charged applicable taxes. Offer not valid in Quebec. This offer is limited to one order per household. Not valid for current subscribers to Harlequin Heartwarming larger-print books. All orders subject to credit approval. Credit or debit balances in a customer's account(s) may be offset by any other outstanding balance owed by or to the customer. Please allow 4 to 6 weeks for delivery. Offer available while quantities last.

Your Privacy—The Reader Service is committed to protecting your privacy. Our Privacy Policy is available online at www.ReaderService.com or upon request from the Reader Service.

We make a portion of our mailing list available to reputable third parties that offer products we believe may interest you. If you prefer that we not exchange your name with third parties, or if you wish to clarify or modify your communication preferences, please visit us at www.ReaderService.com/consumerchoice or write to us at Reader Service Preference Service, P.O. Box 9062, Buffalo, NY 14240-9062. Include your complete name and address.

HW15

LARGER-PRINT BOOKS!
GET 2 FREE LARGER-PRINT NOVELS PLUS
2 FREE GIFTS!

H HARLEQUIN®

INTRIGUE
BREATHTAKING ROMANTIC SUSPENSE

YES! Please send me 2 FREE LARGER-PRINT Harlequin® Intrigue novels and my 2 FREE gifts (gifts are worth about $10). After receiving them, if I don't wish to receive any more books, I can return the shipping statement marked "cancel." If I don't cancel, I will receive 6 brand-new novels every month and be billed just $5.49 per book in the U.S. or $6.24 per book in Canada. That's a saving of at least 11% off the cover price! It's quite a bargain! Shipping and handling is just 50¢ per book in the U.S. and 75¢ per book in Canada.* I understand that accepting the 2 free books and gifts places me under no obligation to buy anything. I can always return a shipment and cancel at any time. Even if I never buy another book, the two free books and gifts are mine to keep forever.

199/399 HDN GHWN

Name	(PLEASE PRINT)

Address	Apt. #

City	State/Prov.	Zip/Postal Code

Signature (if under 18, a parent or guardian must sign)

Mail to the **Reader Service:**
IN U.S.A.: P.O. Box 1867, Buffalo, NY 14240-1867
IN CANADA: P.O. Box 609, Fort Erie, Ontario L2A 5X3

Are you a subscriber to Harlequin® Intrigue books
and want to receive the larger-print edition?
Call 1-800-873-8635 today or visit www.ReaderService.com.

* Terms and prices subject to change without notice. Prices do not include applicable taxes. Sales tax applicable in N.Y. Canadian residents will be charged applicable taxes. Offer not valid in Quebec. This offer is limited to one order per household. Not valid for current subscribers to Harlequin Intrigue Larger-Print books. All orders subject to credit approval. Credit or debit balances in a customer's account(s) may be offset by any other outstanding balance owed by or to the customer. Please allow 4 to 6 weeks for delivery. Offer available while quantities last.

Your Privacy—The Reader Service is committed to protecting your privacy. Our Privacy Policy is available online at www.ReaderService.com or upon request from the Reader Service.

We make a portion of our mailing list available to reputable third parties that offer products we believe may interest you. If you prefer that we not exchange your name with third parties, or if you wish to clarify or modify your communication preferences, please visit us at www.ReaderService.com/consumerchoice or write to us at Reader Service Preference Service, P.O. Box 9062, Buffalo, NY 14240-9062. Include your complete name and address.

HILP15